THE
HORSE ROAD

THE
HORSE ROAD

TROON HARRISON

BLOOMSBURY

NEW YORK LONDON NEW DELHI SYDNEY

Originally published in Germany as *Kallisto: Reiterin der Wüste* in March 2011 by
Bloomsbury Verlag
First published in the United States of America in August 2012
by Bloomsbury Books for Young Readers
www.bloomsburyteens.com

For information about permission to reproduce selections from this book, write to
Permissions, Bloomsbury BFYR, 175 Fifth Avenue, New York, New York 10010

Library of Congress Cataloging-in-Publication Data
Harrison, Troon.
The horse road / by Troon Harrison. — 1st U.S. ed.
p.   cm.
Summary: In ancient central Asia, thirteen-year-old Kallisto, a superb equestrian, and her
friend must warn their families and protect the Ferghana horses from invading Chinese
armies.
ISBN 978-1-59990-846-5
[1. Horsemanship—Fiction. 2. Horses—Fiction. 3. Fergana Valley—History—Fiction.
4. Central Asia—History—Fiction.] I. Title.
PZ7.H25616Ho 2012   [Fic]—dc23   2012014010

Typeset by Hewer Text UK Ltd, Edinburgh
Printed in the U.S.A. by Quad/Graphics, Fairfield, Pennsylvania
2 4 6 8 10 9 7 5 3 1

*For my dear friends, Shelley, Patty,
Jane and Henry.
You have deeply enriched my
life for many years!*

Chapter 1

The golden stallion danced beneath me, his coat flaring like flame as the morning sun tipped its brightness over the Alay Mountains.

'Everyone ready?' Batu cried, fighting his snorting mount to a standstill.

'Ready! Ready!' we all cried in reply, our horses bouncing along an invisible ragged line at the crest of the hill. In our imaginations this line marked the beginning of our race, and we had ridden out from the nomad camp at dawn to reach it.

The Hsiung-nu boys and girls gripped their legs around horse blankets, for no one except me owned a saddle, and hauled on reins. Their faces were tense with excitement, focused with determination. Back in the camp, there would be prizes of harness and ribbons for winning this race, but more glorious than that was the honour of riding the winner.

Gryphon and I had to win; my mother's horses were much sought after. If we won this race, the nomads would barter for the right to have their mares bred by Gryphon; every year, my mother and I would bring him out here into the mountains, into the summer pastures. In return, the nomads would give my mother felt rugs to sell in the city, and hard cheese they'd dried on the roofs of their yurts; they would come to my Greek merchant father when they needed new iron daggers, or coral necklaces for their wives and daughters. It was our horses that helped to support us, that helped to pay for my brothers' schooling, and for the beautiful objects from all over the world that filled our city home. It was our horses that helped to make us so rich that my father could betroth me, his only daughter, to the son of the king's Falconer.

I must win this race! Then everyone in the camp would crowd around Gryphon, the winner! They would admire his glorious golden coat with its hard metallic shine, its pale dapples. They would run their hands down his long, clean legs with black stockings; his elegant face with its fine veins; his black tail tied in a knot behind his hindquarters. 'He's the best one!' they would cry, their wind-reddened faces alight with respect.

'Steady now, steady,' I muttered as Gryphon shied, his hooves sending small stones clattering downhill. Patting his neck, I felt the tension in his muscles. I couldn't hold him much longer, my beautiful Persian horse.

'Come on, Batu!' I yelled to my friend, crouched on a bay mare to my right. He grinned mischievously, his long black hair lifting in a breath of chilly air. He liked making us all wait. We were like arrows, held against quivering bowstrings before the moment of release.

'Kalli!' Batu called to me, teasing as usual. 'You ready to lose? You ready to run in dust?'

'You'll be running in Gryphon's dust!' I cried back.

Beneath us, the valley plunged downwards through the mountains. It seemed impossibly steep, strewn with stones and low-growing shrubs. Beyond the valley the foothills lay like dropped fabric, in soft folds of lush summer grass and wild flowers: the bright splash of poppies, the tall stems of blue iris. Further away still, two days' ride in the distance, lay my city home of Ershi, in the wide Golden Valley of Ferghana where vines and wheat and apricot trees grew beside irrigation canals.

My stallion bounced sideways, dragging at the thin leather reins bunched in my hands. He mouthed at his bronze bit, and his curb chain rattled. My mother insisted that I ride him with a curb instead of with a snaffle bit and she was right; I would never have been able to control him in a snaffle. She had learned about curbs from the Celtic tribes, long ago when she lived in the sea of grass far to the north, before she was taken as a slave. On the side shanks of Gryphon's bit, little bronze eagles became covered in foam as he dragged at his reins and grew more excited.

I gripped tighter, felt his muscles straining beneath me as he longed to run down that shadowy valley. The sunlight gleamed on the snowy peaks that hung over us like a wave, white with foam, in a spring river.

'Run!' Batu yelled suddenly, taking us by surprise. His dark face broke into excited laughter. 'Run!' he yelled, flinging one fist high into the air.

Gryphon soared forward and for one moment we seemed to hang suspended over the world as the blue sky dipped to meet us. Wind whistled in my ears. On either side of us, along the line of riders, people whooped and yelled. The horses poured forward over the crest, hooves thundering. Then the valley rose under us. Gryphon's front hoof hit the ground. We were earth-bound again. I dug my booted heels into his golden flanks. My legs tightened around his ribs, beneath the bright blanket that my father had brought back from a trading trip to Samarkand. Its woven hems, embroidered with flowers and stars, flapped against my ankles.

Down, down!

We plunged through the valley. Now we were arrows let loose, a volley of rushing speed. Wind poured into my open mouth. I was laughing, yelling, feeling the summer morning fill me with joy. 'Run, Gryphon!' I cried, and my stallion burst past the horse ahead, its tail whipping across my arm. In the corners of my eyes, I saw the other horses, their riders crouched over their necks. Shoulder to shoulder we streaked down that narrow valley as it tipped us, like a torrent of stones in a riverbed, towards the foothills. Gryphon dodged a boulder; we swerved past it like one creature, like the centaurs in the Greek stories that my father liked to tell as we sat around a fire on snowy winter evenings. Gryphon and I were moulded together by sheer determination, and by the pleasure of our speed. I was only half a girl; the other half of me was all running horse: long sinews, big heart, pride.

Just ahead, a grey horse filled my squinting eyes. Gryphon's nose was almost against its flank as we pulled closer. The heavy breathing of horses surged in the air. We were flying, soaring, we were shoulder to shoulder with the grey horse. 'Run, run!' I yelled and Gryphon's hooves pounded the ground faster and harder. We pitched down a final steep fall of valley into a swell of foothill. The grass rose around us like the pile of a huge wool carpet. We rushed through it. The shadows of the mountains were behind us now, and sunshine gleamed on Gryphon's black mane. The nomads trimmed their horses' manes short, but I liked to let Gryphon's mane grow long. I liked the tickle of it against my cheek as he galloped, and I liked tying small red tassels into it for decoration.

I glanced back over my shoulder and saw that

most of the horses were behind us now. Only Batu still galloped beside us, away to the right. Perhaps he felt my glance for his head turned and I saw his wide, bright grin. Then he crouched lower on the bay mare, and dug in his heels.

'Come on, Gryphon!' I shouted. Neck and neck our horses streamed downhill, then up a rise. For a few minutes we were the only two people running along the crest of a foothill, angling back towards the shadow of the mountains. The other horses crested the slope behind, and rushed after us in pursuit of victory. Branches flicked against my arms as we galloped through a thicket of pistachio nut trees. We clattered down a rocky bank beneath willows with their long leaves licking our backs like dogs' tongues. Gryphon leaped into the rush of the mountain stream at the bottom of the bank. The roar of water filled my ears and I felt its cold bite on my legs. It sprayed around Gryphon's slender black legs. With a final heave, he pulled himself up the far bank, and I heard Batu's mare breathing just behind. Then we climbed uphill again, following the whisper of track that snaked into the folds of the mountains. Shadow threw itself over us like a cloak.

I burst through a thicket of wild apple trees covered with late blossoms; they floated in the valley like clouds resting. Suddenly I realised that the only hoof beats I could hear were Gryphon's pounding along the narrow trail. We were winning! Now we would hold the lead all the way eastwards, galloping finally through one last narrow valley and coming to the white felt yurts of the nomad camp. Gryphon would win!

'Good boy, good horse!' I yelled, my heart leaping high in my throat.

We dodged around a walnut tree, flew across a patch of grass filled with hollyhocks and wild onions. I smelled their tang as Gryphon's hooves crushed the tender stems.

But where was Batu? How had we managed to leave him so far behind? His bay mare was a cross between a Persian horse and a nomad pony; although stockier than Gryphon and shorter in the leg, she was brave and determined, and she often won races. I glanced back once more but there was no sign of Batu and the bay. Now other riders galloped into my line of vision: the girl on the grey gelding that we had overtaken high up the valley, a boy on a sturdy sorrel with a white star. I fought Gryphon, trying to slow his headlong rush, trying to see Batu. The sound of hoof beats coming up behind Gryphon filled his narrow golden ears; he laid them back, then tightened his jaw against the curb chain and plunged onwards. We hurled down a dip, pounded up the other side with snowy peaks filling our eyes.

Perhaps something has happened to Batu, I thought. *Perhaps I should turn back and find him.*

But then I might lose the race, and no one would

rush laughing and exclaiming from the nomad camp to meet us; no one would run their hands along Gryphon's arched neck and speak admiringly of his speed. Gryphon deserved to win! I wanted the glory of it for him. Anyway, why would anything have happened to Batu? He had been racing this track since he was a sturdy little boy of six years old, competing in the festival of the First Moon of Summer. He knew every rock, the swell of every slope. He knew where the wild boar rooted with their hard tusks, where the wolves gathered to howl their mournful songs, where the brown bears denned. Yesterday, in the midst of a wild mounted game of buzkashi, as men and horses fought for control of a goat's carcass, someone had blackened Batu's eye. Surely this injury could not be causing him problems now. Or did he have other injuries that I didn't know of?

Gryphon and I pounded on, still in the lead but with the grey mare gaining while I tugged on the reins and tried to decide what to do. Gryphon's eyes rolled as the mare's hoof beats grew louder.

Batu would turn back to find you, whispered a voice in my head. *Batu is a loyal friend.*

I kicked Gryphon hard in the ribs, taking him by surprise. Hauling on one rein, I wrestled him off-balance and off the thread of track, and the grey mare shot past. A shower of pebbles bounced against us, and then the sorrel horse went by. Gryphon bucked in protest, his hard hooves hammering the grass. His arched back tossed me upwards so that colours whirled in my vision: golden light, flaming green grass, blue sky. I clung on with my legs tight as a wrapping of rawhide. The two pads of my saddle, stuffed with horsehair, bounced on either side of Gryphon's spine. Their loose framework of leather strips and carved wood strained against each other.

'Whoa, whoa, steady, easy, Gryphon!' I soothed him, fighting his head around until we were facing back in the direction from which we'd come. The reins cut into my palms. The curb chain dug into Gryphon's lower jaw, the little carved eagles on the shank of the bit pulled back beneath his bent head. If anything broke now, I would lose control of this ball of fierce energy that my horse had become. Fighting Gryphon was like fighting a sandstorm or an avalanche. I pummelled him with my boots, driving him back as other horses streamed by us and were lost from view over the next hill.

Silence filled my ears, and the song of a finch in a birch grove danced inside the silence. The thin mist of dust, kicked up by the horses on the stony path, sifted down to coat the summer grass. Gryphon's breath heaved. He tossed his neck angrily against the pull of my tight reins, and snorted impatiently as we trotted along.

'Batu!' I yelled. 'Batu, where are you?'

If only he would answer, I could turn Gryphon's

head again and kick him into a gallop; I knew already how he would leap away, determined and eager to catch up to the other horses, to pass them by, to win. We thought alike, Gryphon and I. At home on our horse farm in the Valley of Ferghana, Gryphon would stand sleepily in his pasture with his eyes half closed, his belly stretched tight with lush alfalfa. And I, in my father's two-storey brick house, bent over my bride-wealth embroidery, was a shy, plump girl who couldn't speak to dinner guests. But out here, in the mountains, when we visited the nomad camp every year, Gryphon and I transformed into wild things, free and fierce and alive. For a short time, I became the daughter that my mother probably wished for. And for a short time, I could forget about the life that waited for me in the city of Ershi, the life where I would be trapped indoors, separated from the horses, doomed to be married to a boy I had met only a few times and was too shy to speak to. My unthinkable future.

Tears prickled in my eyes. Perhaps I was over-excited, or overtired, or simply overcome with the great looming silence of the mountains. I rubbed the tears away impatiently, holding the reins in one hand. Crying was for a city girl, not for a girl whose mother had survived losing her own people, and being sold at auction. *Forget about your city life*, I scolded myself. *Just find Batu!*

'Batu!' I yelled again but only my echo answered,

ringing off the rocky cliffs in the mountains. *Annoying boy*, I thought. *He's probably just playing a trick on me, as usual.*

A crow flapped across the treetops, cawing harshly. Gryphon trotted angrily on down the trail, tossing his head and snorting, threatening at any moment to tear around in a circle and run downhill without my permission. I held him straight onwards with my legs, and ignored the agitated swishing of his knotted tail.

'Batu!' I yelled again. A marmot gave a shrill whistle, peering at me from a rock pile, and holding grass between its front paws. It looked like a little man, sitting up on its furry brown haunches. Then it dived suddenly into the dark mouth of its burrow.

A trickle of apprehension ran down my spine. For the first time, I began to truly believe that something had happened to Batu.

I felt very alone. The silence seemed larger, crouching somewhere near me, ready to pounce. A cold eddy wafted off the mountains and fanned my flushed cheeks, blowing my long black curls. I patted Gryphon's shoulder for comfort, and my hand came away damp with pink sweat. No one knew why the Persian horses sweated blood; it was simply one more thing that made them different from other horses.

The murmur of running water filled the air as we approached the place where the path crossed the mountain stream. Suddenly Gryphon's ears pricked, straining towards some sound that I hadn't heard. He stopped in the path, snorting, and I laid my hand upon the hilt of my dagger fastened at my waist. Then I heard it too: a thread of sound, a boy whistling. Out from the shadows of the willow trees came Batu, brilliant in an orange tunic held at the waist with a turquoise sash, and trudging steadily beside his limping brown horse.

'What's happened?' I cried, urging Gryphon into a trot. Reaching Batu, I slid from Gryphon to stand beside him.

'My poor mare,' he said gloomily. 'That boy on the sorrel gelding? He knocked into us going down the bank into the water, and my mare stumbled and fell. She's hurt her leg. See?'

I squatted beside him and ran my hand down the mare's left hind leg, feeling the heat and the swelling in the flesh above the fetlock joint.

'So now we're both riding in dust,' Batu said with a rueful grin. 'I'm sorry, Kalli. I should have ridden Rain instead.'

'It doesn't matter,' I replied, trying to feel my friend's worry and even the pain that perhaps throbbed in the mare's leg; trying to ignore the heavy lump of disappointment that filled my stomach. I straightened, stared at the mare's hanging head, and at Gryphon's neck where the sweat was drying and leaving his coat stiff and salty. It wasn't fair! Now Gryphon had lost his chance to win, even though he was the fastest horse I knew! This might be the last year that I raced. Perhaps at this moon next summer, I would be behind walls in Ershi, smelling mountains far off in the wind like a horse that tries to smell its way to water across a desert.

I kicked at a stone in the track, and fought against the fresh sting in my eyes.

'Kalli,' Batu said kindly. I glanced up into his dark, angled eyes; the bruise a blue stain like spilled water. His wide brown face, framed by his mane of long hair, was as familiar as my own for I had known him all my life. Now his forehead was wrinkled in a worried frown.

I was suddenly ashamed of being such a child. 'It's fine,' I reassured him, mustering a smile. 'I wanted a summer walk. I love dust!'

Batu's face broke into his flashing grin, then suddenly his gaze sharpened on something above me. I swivelled to look upwards. High against the light, a golden eagle soared on the mountain wind. The shadow of its wide wings slid across us and passed on; I glimpsed the cruel curve of its yellow beak, the glint of its eye. It wheeled in against the face of the mountain, and swooped around a pinnacle of grey rock to disappear from view. Batu breathed in sharply, like an excited horse.

'Maybe there's a nest there!' he cried, the race forgotten. His father was a white bone chief, a fearless hunter who rode a dark horse and carried an eagle on a leather gauntlet upon one arm. Together, man and eagle hunted for rabbits to cook, or for the foxes that attacked the nomads' herds of sheep. Batu had told me that a trained eagle might even fight the great grey wolves that roamed like vengeful ghosts. The eagle, he said, flew right at their eyes.

'I must climb up and see if there's a nest!' Batu said. 'Then I can return here another day and capture an eaglet! It is time, Kalli, for me to train an eagle of my own! Do you want to climb with me?'

I looked where Batu gestured and saw that a narrow ravine led up the side of the mountain to a ridgeline that lay between two peaks. Where the ravine and the ridgeline merged, there was a dip like the curve in a horse's back, the place where you lay a saddle.

'From there, we might be able to see around the rock outcropping into the nest!' Batu said. 'Also from that ridge, you can see down into a large valley, where the track from Osh runs out of the mountains into the Ferghana Valley. The merchant caravans travel eastwards on that track towards the great Taklamakan Desert where nothing lives. Come on, Kalli!'

'We will be late returning to camp!' I protested. 'My mother might worry.'

'She is drinking *koumiss* with the other women, and forgetting her troubles,' Batu said, flashing another grin. He caught me by the arm and tugged. 'Come on! Help me find my eagle!'

Batu's excitement was contagious; suddenly I wanted to see if the eagle had landed on a pile of sticks larger across than a chariot wheel, and to peer down into a valley where traders passed by with their long strings of donkeys, yaks, horses and two-humped camels.

And if my mother was drinking *koumiss*, the fermented mare's milk, she would be smiling the rare, gracious smile that wiped the queenly sternness from her face.

We unbridled, then hobbled the horses and left them wrenching greedily at tall grasses. Gryphon ate so fast that half-chewed grass fell out of one side of his dark, wrinkled mouth. He was always an eager, impatient animal. I smiled and followed Batu's shoulders up the ravine. Stones clattered beneath my second-best pair of riding boots. Their feet were of red leather, while the tops, rising to my knees, were of yellow leather decorated with appliqués of more red leather cut into the shapes of rams' horns. I admired them as I climbed, bent over, trying to ignore the throb in my leg muscles.

The sun rode higher as we struggled upwards. I thought of my father's Greek god of the sun, Helios, driving westwards in his chariot pulled by horses as golden as Gryphon. Sweat ran down inside the legs of my trousers with their embroidered stripes of brown and red. My embroidered tunic stuck to my back.

At last, we reached the ridgeline, and Batu edged along its sharpness, craning for a view of the eagle. I glanced downwards to where the horses grazed; they seemed contented in the grass and summer herbs, their backs gleaming. I straightened and looked to the south where the Pamir mountains rose in a vast wall, rumpled between us and the country called India. To the north, further away than I could see, lay the land from which my mother had come, a place of grass and tribes and the mighty Volga River. To the west lay deserts, and trading cities, and the bright Mediterranean Sea, and the land of Greece which my father had left when he was a young man filled with the spirit of adventure. And here I stood now, in the heart of all this world. I smiled to myself, and tipped my face towards the afternoon sun.

Then I inched forward to where the ridgeline fell away in a long drop into a deep valley. My head spun. I lay on my belly and peered over. For a moment, all I saw was miles of shimmering summer air, rocks, trees. Then movement caught my attention. I stared, knuckled my eyes, stared again.

No! It couldn't be!

I froze. Even my breathing became shallow with terror.

'Batu!' I whispered urgently. 'Batu, come here!'

Then I stared again, down into that valley where the track from the east trickled over the mountains towards Ferghana, my home and the heart of the world.

Batu dropped down beside me. 'Who is it?' he whispered harshly.

16

I scrutinised every detail: the foot soldiers marching doggedly along with light shining on the tips of their spears, the cavalry units on their small horses raising a pall of dust, the donkeys and black yaks and brown camels laden with boxes and bales of supplies, the loaded ox wagons lurching over stones. Above the army fluttered bright red banners made of the cloth called silk, the marvellous cloth that came from far away, in the east, and that my father longed to trade for. But to his frustration, our king in Ershi would not consent to trading agreements with the east; he was said to hate the emperor who ruled that foreign place.

'It's the Chinese,' I breathed. 'My father has described them to me. They are sending another army to attack Ershi.'

'For the horses?' Batu muttered.

'They want our Persian horses,' I agreed. 'Don't you remember? Years ago, they sent an ambassador over the roof of the world to ask the king of Ferghana for horses. But the king wouldn't give them any of our horses, and the ambassador and his men were attacked and beheaded.'

'Then what happened?' Batu asked, swivelling to look at me, his dark eyes serious.

'Then the Chinese emperor was very angry, and two years ago he sent an army over the mountains, a march of many starving months, but the army was defeated in the land of Osh, high above the valley of

Ferghana. Now, he is sending another army to take our horses!'

Batu let out a long breath. 'The Middle Kingdom has long been the enemy of my people,' he muttered. 'The Hsiung-nu tribes have been driven westwards like sheep by its armies. Now the kingdom is building a great stone wall to hold back the nomads.'

'I have heard this too in the city,' I agreed.

Batu glared at the troops marching far below, massed like ants, pouring out of the mountains, filling the valley, steadily moving westwards towards the safety of Ershi, and my family's farm where our horse herd grazed the alfalfa in the shade of poplar trees.

'I must ride for my mother!' I cried, and I sprang up and began leaping and sliding down the mountain with Batu at my heels. Gryphon flung up his head, startled, grass trailing from his mouth. My mother would know what to do, I thought; my strong brave mother who had once been a warrior in her own Sarmatian tribe, far to the north. My mother, trainer of horses. She would know how to save us, our mares and foals, our pastures and stables. Gryphon. Me. And most important of all, my white mare, Swan. My most precious white mare.

'Hurry!' I screamed, fear clawing at my heart. 'Hurry, Batu! We must save the horses!'

Chapter 2

'I cannot ride this mare hard!' Batu cried as we sprinted across the grass towards the grazing horses. 'You must ride to camp without me!'

I nodded, reaching into the tree where I had hung Gryphon's bridle. The blue clay beads, woven on to the cheek pieces, glinted as I swung the bridle free and slipped it on to my horse's head. Then I squatted and undid the hobbles of woollen rope from around his fetlocks, my fingers fumbling with haste. 'Batu,' I called over one shoulder, 'I hate leaving you alone! Promise you won't climb back up looking for eaglets. You might be attacked by the parent birds!'

'Forget about eagles! You must ride to warn the warriors!'

I nodded again. I knew that the fighting men of Batu's tribe had sworn allegiance to the king of

Ershi; in partial return for wheat and millet from Ferghana's fields, they were bound to come to the city's aid in time of attack. I straightened and scowled at Batu as he crossed his arms over the wiry strength of his chest and scowled in return.

'Please, no eagles!' I said, for I could be stubborn too; city neighbours thought I was a sweet girl only because I was too shy to speak. Batu and the horses knew better; they knew that my shyness was like the soft murmur of a stream that flows over a hard boulder beneath the surface.

'No eagles!' Batu agreed, still scowling. 'Now *go*, RIDE! I'll join you when I can!'

With one hand I caught hold of the rawhide loop that hung from my saddle's belly band, and then poked my left foot into it. An Indian trader had described these loops to my mother, and she had made one for me to try. Although the nomads could spring on to their short horses simply by grasping a handful of mane, our taller Persian horses were harder to mount. The foot loop, hanging down, usually made it easier to swing myself into the saddle.

Now, however, Gryphon had absorbed the fear that had sent me sliding down the ravine from the high ridge. He bounded sideways with rolling eyes, threatening to topple me off balance and drag me along by one booted foot caught in the loop. I pulled on my reins with my left hand, hopped on one leg, and then sprang into my saddle as it surged beneath me in constant movement. There was only time for a fleeting glance back at Batu, standing forlornly watching, before Gryphon burst into a gallop, heading across the hillside in the direction of the track. I knew that Batu would be longing to race after us, to see if his father would let him join the warriors, carrying his bow over one shoulder, and a quiver of arrows against his thigh. I also knew that he was too fine a horseman to endanger his mare's injured leg even for what he considered to be the thrill of riding to war. Instead, he would walk calmly back, making the best of the situation as he always did; it was one of the things I admired about him.

Gryphon dodged around the first pine tree in a grove that lay darkly dancing on the hillside. A cloud of sweet, resinous scent filled my nostrils. Suddenly Gryphon shied, his hooves skidding in fallen needles and scoring marks into the grey dirt beneath. I lurched over his bent neck, my legs gripping harder, my body swaying to maintain balance. Now my stallion was bunched beneath me, head flung up, listening. I laid one hand soothingly along his neck, watching his narrow ears strain forward, and ran my gaze admiringly over the profile of his turned head. His fine golden hair did not conceal the veins that lay like dropped threads beneath his thin skin.

For the second time today, I strained to discover what Gryphon could hear.

In a moment, I heard it too: someone singing

softly in a husky voice, and the thud of hoof beats. Gryphon gave a shrill neigh, his ribs vibrating against my legs, and was answered by a fainter cry. Over the slope of hills, beneath the sway and freckle of pine branches, came a woman, tall and regal as a mountain spirit, riding a sleek mare and leading a yearling filly at one shoulder by a rope.

Coins of afternoon light lay in the woman's braided crown of golden hair, sprinkled the high angle of her pale cheeks, and filled her blue eyes, clear as pools of mountain water.

I heaved a gulping sigh of relief. 'Mother!' I called, the heavy air beneath the pines muffling my cry.

But she had seen me before I spoke. Her gaze ran over me, noting that all was well, but registered no surprise. It was seldom that I saw surprise in my mother's eyes, or laughter, or fear; she surveyed the world with a calmness that was like the calmness of a wild animal, assessing every scent, alert to every clue; giving little away. Although I had inherited my father's black, springing curls and round Greek face, my eyes were as blue as my mother's – but not steady like hers. Even in this moment, my eyes were betraying my agitation, as was Gryphon who was side-stepping between the pines as though joining their summery dance.

'What is wrong, Kallisto?' my mother asked in her husky voice, halting her horses. 'The racers returned to camp without you, and Batu was missing also. I have ridden out to find you.'

As my mother spoke, Gryphon stepped forward to touch his nostrils against the dark muzzle of Grasshopper, my mother's mare, in greeting. She let out a squeal but my mother touched her on the withers with one hand, and she stilled instantly.

'The army is coming for our horses!' I cried. 'The army from the Middle Kingdom, with their banners of red silk! They are marching down the trading route from the mountains, high up towards Osh!'

'How do you know this?'

'Batu and I climbed a ridge and saw them ourselves! And Batu is following me back to camp, leading a mare with a swollen fetlock.'

'Yes, I see him coming now,' my mother replied, staring past me to the slope of hill where the late afternoon sun washed the grasses. She waved and I twisted in my saddle to see the distant bright dot of Batu's orange tunic.

For a moment, my mother pondered the situation, weaving her fingers through Grasshopper's mane while the filly fidgeted alongside.

'The army will not travel at night,' she stated. 'They will make camp in the foothills. Tomorrow they might journey on to the plain. Such an army does not arrive unseen; Ferghana scouts will have brought news to our king in Ershi already. To assemble a great army for battle is a lengthy matter; there are tents to pitch, fires and food to tend to, decisions to be made before the men go forth. Time is on our side still.

'We will wait for Batu, not leave him alone in the mountains. There is a stream at the bottom of this pine wood, and Batu can soak the mare's leg there. Then we will travel back to the Hsiung-nu camp together, and still have all night in which to begin riding for home; the moon is full. We will reach our horses well ahead of the army.'

'But, Mother, there were so many of them, marching so fast . . .' I muttered doubtfully, trailing off beneath her steady regard. Every time that I thought of the great army, massed beneath the tips of its spears, I felt panic welling in my belly like a spring of cold water. I had to reach Swan before the army did.

'The larger the army is, the more slowly it organises itself,' Mother responded calmly. 'And men cannot march on empty stomachs. They will halt to eat and sleep tonight.'

She reached into the cloth bag hanging from her saddle, and handed me a piece of sun-dried mutton to chew. I gnawed it gratefully, for Batu and I had not eaten since our breakfast of sheep yoghurt, in the smokiness of a dark yurt before sunrise.

Mother and I waited while Batu crossed the hill to reach us. Then my mother slid from Grasshopper and ran her long, strong hands, calloused from ropes and leather thongs and reins, down all four of the mare's legs. On almost every finger, my mother wore a silver ring inlaid with semi-precious stones: lapis lazuli, carnelian, coral, even pearl. She was like the nomad women of the Hsiung-nu who carried their wealth with them wherever they journeyed, threaded through their ears, hung around their necks, sliding on their arms. My father preferred to store his wealth at home, in the niches of our plastered walls, where he could display marble statuettes, and carvings lacquered in gold leaf, and drinking horns with silver rims.

The mare stood as still as a black horse painted on a red Greek vase; only her ears flickered as my mother spoke softly in her own tongue. At home, my mother and I spoke Greek to my father and brothers, and Persian in the neighbourhood and markets; in the nomad camp we both spoke Turkic. But to horses my mother always spoke a foreign tongue, the private language of her Sarmatian childhood in misty hills and lush river valleys, the land she had lost in a tribal raid, and that no other person spoke in the slave market of Tashkent. Here in Ferghana, only the horses had truly learned my mother's language; although I could recognise the phrases she used frequently, I could not understand the long monologues that sometimes she muttered to horses. And sometimes, when she gazed at them, I thought she was seeing things that I couldn't see: a ghost world of dreams and spirits. It was said amongst the nomads that my mother spoke the language of horses, but perhaps it was the other way around; perhaps my mother taught to horses the language of her lost days.

She straightened now, her dark green tunic falling to the top of her black boots, and gave Batu a glance that was brief but kind. 'You did well to spare her from the race,' she said. 'With rest, and poultices of herbs, her sinew will heal as though nothing has happened.'

At this praise, the faintest blush rose into Batu's high cheeks, although he was usually so independent and fierce. He ducked his head, and led the mare on down the track between the murmuring trees, heading for the valley's mountain water. My mother turned Grasshopper and followed with the filly, Tulip, walking alongside whilst I brought up the rear. How could my mother be so unconcerned, while the Chinese spilled from the mountains with horse greed burning in their hearts? If only she had seen their lumbering camels staggering beneath bags and bales of supplies! If only she had watched their tight-packed cavalry formations jogging steadily westwards! In my thoughts, the warriors' banners snapped and soared in the thin air of the high mountains, bright as wounds against the dark rocks.

'Hurry, hurry!' I wanted to shout at our horses as they went quietly downwards, tails flicking at flies. The filly had a reddish tail that flared in the late sloping light, for she was a red roan, and I had named her Tulip when she was born. My mother liked to lead the yearling when she rode, giving Tulip exercise, teaching her manners, making her listen to my mother's spoken commands, exposing her to city roads and mountain tracks so that by the time she was old enough to be ridden she would be wise beyond her years. In the markets of Ershi, Andijon and Kokand, my mother's horses were famous for their training as well as for their stamina and great beauty.

The valley into which we rode was deep and narrow, with rocky walls that the track trickled steeply down, washed out by spring rains. The horses skidded, set back on their pasterns, hocks bent under their bellies, as we descended into blue shadows and the roar of water. My saddle blanket slipped higher on to Gryphon's withers; only the crupper, decorated with bronze flowers and passing beneath his tail, prevented it from sliding on to his neck.

Near the base of the cliff, we dismounted on a ribbon of gravel and sat upon rocks licked smooth as melons. Batu backed the mare into a pool of water, eddying behind a boulder, and let it suck away the heat and pain of her swollen leg. She stood placidly, eyes drifting shut. The other horses were not as patient. They ambled up and down on the gravel, their reins knotted around their necks, their lips working across the cliff face in search of any plants or clumps of grass that clung there. Gryphon caught hold of the branches of a shrub growing from a crevice, and pulled them sideways through his mouth, tearing off the leaves. Grasshopper balanced on three legs and reached one hind leg forward to scratch delicately at her face, where flies had bitten it, using the edge of her hoof. Tulip backed into a boulder, careful as a dancer learning new steps, and began to rub her rump and tail on the hard surface.

'She's smiling,' I said, watching the filly's soft lips quiver and wrinkle.

The shadows grew deeper as we waited, drinking water from the stream in our cupped hands. The moon began to rise in the east, although the sky was still a veneer of brilliant blue. 'Selene, the moon goddess,' I said, pointing. 'Her white mares are eager to run.'

'This is one of your father's goddesses?' Batu asked.

I nodded. 'She drives her chariot all night, whilst Helios drives his golden horses all day across the sky.'

'I don't know how you city people keep track of all your deities,' Batu said, running his hand down the mare's neck. 'Here in the mountains, my people know every rock and river, every peak and valley. It is easy to speak to our spirits, and our ancestors. They are all around us every day.'

'In the city, there are many other gods,' I agreed. 'My mother's people were like yours, they listened to shamans and worshipped sacred places. My father has all his Greek gods and goddesses; he tells wonderful stories about them.'

'But does he truly believe in them, in their power?' Batu asked, his face serious and intent.

I shrugged. 'He's a trader, he must give respect to the beliefs of all the nations and peoples he trades

28

with. At home now, both my parents worship Ahura Mazda, the Supreme Being. He is always in a great struggle with Angra, the wicked evil one who opposes him. While Ahura Mazda creates fertile fields and peaceful work for men, Angra sows thistles and bitterness; he provokes men to deceit and dishonour.'

Batu rubbed his hand in swirls along the mare's back. 'It's all so complicated, so many of them,' he said. 'A trader in the market last year gave me the statue of a little plump man with a smiling face; he said he was the Buddha and could teach men the way to enlightenment through letting go of suffering. Ha! Maybe my mare is getting enlightened here in this pool!' He laughed, his strong teeth pale in the canyon's shadows.

Behind us, my mother stopped humming.

'War is suffering,' she said. 'War is coming into your lives. At this moment, the Chinese are planning victory around their evening fires. They are grinding their sword blades, cleaning their horse harness, filling their bellies with confidence by calling on their celestial gods.'

A chilly breeze drifted down the canyon and I shivered and tightened the sash holding my robe together. My eyes filled with all those faces, laughing, eating, talking about winning our horses and taking them far away, where they would never be seen again, past the great Taklamakan Desert where nothing lives, nothing flies. How would Swan survive such a migration? And how would I survive without her soaring gallop, her gentle eyes set in her pale, shimmering coat, and the curve of her neck, graceful as the throat of a bird?

I stifled a whimper. 'I think Batu's mare can walk now, I think we should –'

My mother held up her hand, and I fell silent as she began to speak again. 'Did I ever tell you, Batu, how your mother and I became sworn to help one another?'

'No,' Batu said, for my mother rarely spoke of herself. Now she sat cross-legged on a flat rock, and stared off into time.

'In the slave markets of Tashkent,' she began, 'I was a girl old enough to be wed but now I had lost my people, my fine young men, my fast horses. I had lost my mother-tongue, my bride-wealth chest, my spears, my bronze mirrors, my spinning distaff. I had lost my path, and my spirit wandered alone while my body was bargained for. I wished then that I had fallen upon my spear rather than been taken by the raiders that swooped upon my village on a night without moon. To have died swiftly would have been a mercy but now, in this slave market, I must die slowly every day for I had lost the two most important things in life.'

'What things?' I asked.

'I had lost my freedom, walking my own path, riding my own horse. And I had lost the opposite of freedom: the tie of loyalty and love that holds us like

30

a horse at a tethering post outside its master's yurt. A person must have one thing, or the other, to have a spirit in one's body. To find both things is richness, something to fight for.'

'How can you have them both, when they are opposite?' Batu asked.

'You can find that path,' my mother answered enigmatically. 'Now listen. In the slave market, a young man bought me, a tall broad man with a big laugh and a curling black beard. He had journeyed many miles alone looking for his own life. Like me, he had left much behind, much that could never be reclaimed. Like me, he had to learn new words for hunger, for loneliness, for home. He brought me to the city of Ershi in the beautiful valley, amongst the pomegranate trees. For two years I cooked in his kitchens, hauled water from the pools, searched the markets for sweet honey. Then the young man gave me my freedom; he told me to choose whether to return to the plains of my people, or whether to stay and marry him.'

Behind my mother's shoulders, our horses went on cropping the sparse vegetation along the cliff base.

'I said that I could not live without horses because they were my freedom,' continued my mother, 'and that without them, I would remain a slave. So the young merchant bought me a Persian stallion and mare, and gave me my freedom, and married me.

'When I was a young mother, with two boys born

and a daughter still curled in my belly – you, Kallisto – a nomad woman came begging at the gate of our outer courtyard. She was without any jewellery, her cloak was ragged, her boots worn flat from walking when she should have been mounted. A boy of about two pressed against her side and he was you, Batu. She begged for work, although to work in town is as bad as slavery for a nomad. Losing their freedom to roam is like losing their spirit; it was only her body begging at my gate. Her spirit was running with her lost herds; I knew this suffering well. Her husband, and her family's flocks and herds, had died in a bitter drought the previous year, and the people had come to Ershi searching for work.

'So I took her in to my household and she helped take care of my farm. And later, after my daughter was born, this nomad woman, Berta, and I began to teach each other everything we knew about horses. We lived in the pastures of my farm, and in the stables. We lived for the feel of rope, for the touch of a muzzle, for the moment when a horse trusts you and lets you fly with it. And that was how your father, Kallisto, and your mother, Batu, and I all found a way to cajole our souls back into our bodies despite the suffering. It was how we found both our freedom and the thongs binding us to each other's tethering posts.'

'Then what happened?' Batu asked; perhaps, like me, he enjoyed the sound of my mother's husky voice rising and falling against the river's murmur.

'Then your mother went to a festival and met a white bone chief, a nobleman nomad with huge herds of sheep and horses, and with fine brother warriors to ride beside him, and with an alliance with the king of Ershi. And that chief married your mother, and took her back to his yurt along with little Batu, whom he adopted as his own. But Berta and I, before she left, swore an oath that we would always be each other's companions in war or peace, in drought or richness. And in all those years since, she has always brought me her cheese, wool, gold and felt in exchange for horses. So we have helped to keep each other from the years of hunger, and we have raised children that speak the same tongue. This is a good thing to remember on the eve of war: how freedom and loyalty, though opposites, can keep your spirit in your body.'

Now my mother's keen gaze focused suddenly on Batu; I saw his shoulders straighten. I tilted my chin as her eyes swept my face; sometimes, I wondered what my mother saw when she looked at me. My father, when he was briefly at home between trading trips, merchant business, dinner parties, the gymnasium, or the bath house, called me his sweet peach, his plump dove. He stroked my springing black curls, hugged me to his great belly that often quivered with laughter; he told me horse stories that he'd collected from all over the world. He fed me sugared almonds, dates stuffed with apricots and honey; he brought me necklaces and Parthian gowns that I seldom wore, preferring to dress in riding tunic and trousers as my mother always did. Things were easy with my father, although I sometimes felt that he had no idea who I really was.

But with my mother, who could say? Did she wish I was taller like her, faster at jumping on to a moving horse, stronger in the leg when galloping bareback between poles stuck into the ground, more accurate when shooting arrows at targets, twisted backwards from the waist? Did she wish I had her regal bearing, the golden hair of her tribe, instead of being my father's plump Greek partridge? Did she wish I could speak clear, calm words suitable to any occasion, instead of being tongue-tied and blushing in market-places and by city pools?

I bit the inside of my lip and steeled myself to meet her level gaze without flinching. Her voice took me by surprise: soft, soothing, the voice she used for agitated horses. 'Kallisto, times are always uncertain, but there is nothing uncertain about the troubles of war. In war, choose your friends wisely, keep fast to your loyalties, find the ones who will support you through suffering. And freedom! It is more important than life and –'

She broke off, turned her head abruptly as Gryphon let out a blasting snort, warning of danger. He flung his head around, searching for its source. I narrowed my eyes, watching. Sometimes Gryphon liked to play games, getting himself into an excited lather or a tremble of fear just because he was young and had the energy to do so. I wasn't sure now whether he was playing, or whether danger truly threatened us.

The yearling, Tulip, grazed a tussock of grass beneath a ledge. Grasshopper stood still, further down the gravel bar, watching the stallion as he repeatedly tossed his head, snorting fiercely. My mother rose stealthily from her rock, pulling her dagger from her belt as Batu let go of his mare and waded from the water where he'd been standing on a rock.

One heartbeat. Two. Three.

Wind whispered, grass quivered.

The stallion snorted again, his black nostrils flaring so wide that I could see the redness inside them.

'Perhaps we should start for camp and –'

'Mother!' I screamed.

It was airborne. It was all drift, power, grey and white, blizzard. It had launched itself from the ledge above Tulip. It was all hard muscle, long sinew, raking claw; a snow leopard, silent and deadly, the great carnivore of the high mountains that could appear and disappear like a shaman into whirling snow or dappled rock.

It will kill her! my thoughts screamed although my mouth was silent.

My mother lunged with her dagger raised but at that moment – the leopard still dropping through air – Gryphon barged forward, knocking my mother on to her back on the stones. He drove Tulip away from the cliff with ears pinned back, head low and snaked out, eyes rolling and wild. The yearling, still oblivious to the leopard, squealed and shot across the gravel away from the stallion's wild rush.

'Gryphon, Gryphon – no!' I cried. The great dappled cat landed across Gryphon's hindquarters in the moment before he could whirl to face it. I saw blood spurt from my golden horse, streaking his flanks and haunches as the leopard clawed at him, half hanging from him, paring back layers of skin and flesh like the layers of a wild onion bulb.

Gryphon's high scream of rage and pain filled the canyon, ricocheting through our ears, almost masking the deep vibration of the leopard's snarl.

'Gryphon!' I yelled again and the horse lunged forward, simultaneously kicking backwards with all his strength into the leopard's dangling body. The cat twisted, and fell off on to the rocks where he left pawprints of blood. Gryphon whirled to face him, and the leopard crouched, ready to spring again. My mother flung herself between them, arms upraised, yelling wildly, her dagger glinting in her hand. Batu and I sprang to join her; for a moment we stood between the leopard and Gryphon in a ragged line, staring into the cat's burning golden eyes, its stiff whiskers drawn back over heavy teeth that could break an arm bone or pierce a skull.

My mother stepped forward, yelling, as the leopard crouched lower, its long tail brushing the gravel in a mesmerising arc.

Then it sprang again, right at my mother. I heard her dagger strike rock as it flew from her hand and bounced off into the river's rush. They were locked together, my mother and the great cat, rolling over the stones, in and out of pools. Blood and splashed water sprayed around them. Batu lunged beside them, his dagger darting in and out but not meeting its mark as he was too afraid of stabbing my mother. Her yells became fainter, buried in the cat's heavy coat, muffled by its deep snarling. I shot suddenly across the rocks and caught the cat by the tail; its thickness and weight filled my hands. I yanked on it hard, like yanking in a fighting horse; I twisted it, like twisting a lead rope around a tether post. I snatched up a rock and brought it down hard on that twitching, writhing tail. The leopard roared angrily, and my mother's hand struggled out from beneath its neck, so that Batu could slip his dagger into her hand. I saw her plunge the knife into the cat's shoulder as I tried to haul it backwards by its tail, away from her body.

With a rushing roll, the leopard untangled itself from my mother and crouched flat against the rocks, glaring at our ragged circle of raised daggers and stamping hooves. Then it turned, swift as a winter wind, and bounded towards the cliff. Gryphon plunged after it, rearing, striking at it with his flinty front hooves. The cat ignored him and leaped impossibly high from the ground on to a ledge of rock. It seemed to fly up the side of the cliff, and disappear amongst the shrubs. Only a smear of blood marked where it had passed.

'Mother!' I cried, wrapping my arms around her, pressing my face into the horsy smell of her tunic. I was shaking like a leaf, and for a moment I felt her shaking too. Then she drew herself erect and straightened her shoulders.

'Perhaps there is some warrior in your spirit, Kallisto,' she said, placing her palm upon my head as though bestowing a blessing. She stooped and kissed my cheek; not a soft, absent-minded kiss like those my father gave, but a firm, decisive kiss that felt like a brand. I was her daughter now, perhaps, at last.

Then she stepped away from me, and I saw how the entire left side of her tunic hung in shreds and how blood poured from the pale skin beneath, raked by leopard claws.

I yanked off my sash and dipped it into the river.

'Batu! See to Gryphon!' I yelled, but already he was ripping off his own tunic and leading the trembling, sweating stallion into the cool water. He dipped his tunic in and used it to wash the deep wounds on Gryphon's hindquarters while I washed my mother's shoulder and left arm and ribs, and bound my sash around her to staunch the frightening flow of blood.

Tulip and Grasshopper and Batu's mare paced restlessly in the shallow water, where they had plunged in panic and now breathed heavily, huffing warnings of danger.

'We must ride at once, before it gets any darker,' my mother said.

I led the horses from the river, and helped my mother mount Grasshopper who for once stood mercifully still, not giving her usual series of hops upon being mounted. My mother held the reins in her right hand; her wounded shoulder sagged and her face was pale as chalk.

'Mother, can you do this? I could –'

'Lead Tulip beside Gryphon,' she said. 'Batu, you can bring up the rear.'

I held Gryphon's face in my hands and kissed him beneath the eyes, and told him softly how sorry I was for his injuries, and how proud of him for saving Tulip. I tickled him behind the ears, and ran my palm down his neck beneath the silky mane. His skin quivered all over as though he were being swarmed by flies; I waited while he pressed his face against my ribs and became still. Then I mounted him carefully, keeping my leg and boot away from his torn quarter and flank, already rising in swollen ridges around the lips of ragged wounds.

We fell into step behind Grasshopper as her hooves slipped and scrabbled on that steep path. Shadows barred our way. Wind made grasses twitch and swing. Shrubs crouched menacingly. My skin crawled and chilled, my eyes darted from grass to shrub to dark line of rock crevasse snaking towards the path like a snare line. The horses swung their heads from side to side, flinched and snorted. Their skin shivered. As their hooves reached the top of the canyon wall, they all broke into a canter; we had to fight with them to make them walk with the lame mare across the moon-drenched hills.

All the way back to the yurts, I could feel the fierce eyes of the leopard glinting in the darkness over my turned shoulder, and the bright sparks of fires burning in the high mountains as the Chinese prepared to invade our peaceful valley.

Ahead of me, my mother swayed in the saddle, clutching her torn shoulder with blood seeping over her hand. *Father is away trading in the Levant*, I thought, *and my brothers, Petros and Jaison, are with him, and Mother is wounded, and how will we save the horses? Oh, how can we save them now?*

Chapter 3

I opened my eyes as dazzling light fell across my face; struggling on to one elbow, I saw that Berta's wooden door, painted blue as summer sky, stood open. Rolling hills, waving with grass, filled my line of vision. I swivelled my head, my glance flicking around the yurt's pale gloom. I must have slept in late for the cots were empty, and only the breeze eddied against the reed mats, woven with bright woollen patterns, that lined the walls. The hearth fire was banked so low that it barely smoked. I threw back my covering of fox fur, swung my feet on to the felt carpet, and stretched tall, reaching my arms towards that perfect sky arched over the high hills.

Then, memory jolted through me: the leopard's swift attack, Mother and Gryphon's injuries, the army. The army! Even now, as I had sprawled sleeping, it might be on the move, spilling out of the hills and swirling like a torrent of spring flood water across the plain towards the pastures. The boots and hooves of that army, its rolling wheels of chariot and wagon, would be crushing the tall grass flat, breaking the stems of lupins and leaving the purple flowers to wilt and die.

And Mother! Last night, when we had reached the yurts, riding into the throbbing heartbeat of the shaman's drum, the singing and feasting, and the fierce barking of guard dogs, Mother had slipped from Grasshopper outside Berta's yurt. Then her knees had buckled under her, like the legs of a newborn foal, and she had staggered and fallen. Berta and Batu had carried her inside and laid her on a cot, then Berta had poured water into the copper kettle standing over the fire, and thrown in handfuls of dried herbs, and finally roused my mother enough to sip the pungent brew.

Where was Mother now? I spun on my heel and saw that I had been mistaken, that I was not the only person still lying indoors, for on a cot behind me, beneath a rumpled woollen blanket, my mother lay looking somehow flattened and smaller. I tiptoed to her side and stared down at her pale face. Sweat beaded her forehead. Fright tickled the back of my neck for I had never seen Mother look like this; in all of my fourteen summers, she had been swift and strong, tall and straight as a favourite spear. I tiptoed to a cauldron of water and dipped a linen cloth into it, then gently wiped my mother's forehead, creased into lines beneath her crown of golden braids. Her eyelids fluttered and for a moment hope leaped in my throat, but her eyes didn't open.

'Let her sleep,' Berta said softly behind me, her shoulders silhouetted in the yurt doorway. 'The herbs will help her to rest. She lost much blood last night; I have burned her tunic and trousers, ripped and stained beyond recovery.'

'But how long will she sleep?' I cried. 'We must leave this morning, now! We must ride for home!'

'She will not waken before the sun reaches its highest point,' Berta said. 'Then you can talk to her about riding for home.'

Her wide brown face, burnished to a gleam by wind and sun and stinging snow, softened in her kind smile. Gold glinted in a tooth. Spiral earrings caught the light as she moved to me, gathering me against her tunic in a hug that smelled of smoke and horses, the sweetness of grass and flowers, the sour tang of cheese. I pressed my face into her for I had known her all my life and she, the mother of five sons, had always treated me like a daughter.

'Don't fret,' she soothed me. 'Your mother has survived more than this; she will not let any army take away her horses. You will soon be reunited with Swan. You know, don't you, that amongst the nomad peoples, a white horse is a divine protector? And the

43

goddess who protects birth may appear in the form of a white mare. I do not believe that you and Swan can be separated for she came to your valley in the summer when you were born.'

Berta smoothed my long curls behind my ears and stroked the curve of my cheek as though I were a young animal.

'Here, I have something for you.'

Releasing me, Berta stooped over a wooden chest, lifting its painted lid to search through its contents: bedding and clothing, a bronze mirror, a spindle, small pots of chalk and cinnabar body paint. 'Ah,' she said with satisfaction as her fingers found what they were searching for; she lifted a small pouch of yellow leather tied with a woven cord of scarlet threads. Turning, she picked something up from her bed: it was a tuft of dappled grey hair – leopard hair!

'It was caught in your mother's dagger sheath,' she said as she slipped the hair into the leather pouch. She placed the cord solemnly around my neck.

'Wear this from now on. It holds strong power that will protect you from evil spirits, from the strength of Erlik Khan, ruler of the underworld.'

Finally, she bent over her chest again and retrieved a woman's slender torc of pure gold; the neck band was twisted along its length and the two ends were shaped into the heads of leopards with snarling muzzles and tiny eyes inlaid with lapis lazuli. I knew at a glance, because my father dealt in jewellery, that it was very valuable; perfectly executed in every detail by a master goldsmith in some city alleyway where the nomads took their raw metal.

It was the rivers that brought gold to the nomads, for although the winged gryphons guarded the mountain flanks where the gold lay, the melting snow and spring torrents released it to wash downstream into the traps of sheep fleece that the nomads used. It was said that even an ordinary nomad was richer than the peasant farmers in the valley of Ferghana, though the nomads had only yurts and wagons to live in. And Berta was not an ordinary nomad; she was the wife of an aristocrat whose sleek horses and fat-tailed sheep fanned out over the rich pastures to which his clan owned the rights of grazing from generation to generation.

Berta laid the torc around my throat. She placed her hands on my shoulders and gazed at me, a look deep as a pool beneath a willow tree. 'Now you are protected,' she said. 'War is coming, but the power of the leopard walks with you. If you do not come again to the mountains, still all will be well with you and your horses.'

'But I will come again!' I cried, apprehension quivering through me. 'When the war is over, Mother and I will come for the festival of the First Moon of Summer, and bring Gryphon to cover your mares!'

'Let us pray to see this moon,' Berta said, but there was no laughter in her eyes, only the brooding of one who sees a wind lifting black sand over the horizon.

'I will come here again!' I muttered stubbornly.

'A war is like a door that can only be walked through once, in one direction,' Berta said. 'When you have walked through this war that the Middle Kingdom brings, you might find that it has closed upon your childhood years. You are a woman now, Kallisto.

'Your father has betrothed you to the son of the king's Falconer. You might not have the freedom that your father so generously allows your mother. She has it only because of the great love that he carries for her, even when he is far away, in strange cities and on foreign paths.'

I nodded; a great weight seemed to settle on to my shoulders. On the subject of my betrothal, my father was obdurate; he said it was a fine match, one for which I should be grateful. It would lift me into the aristocracy of Ershi, into the long arched hallways of the castle on top of the city's central hill, and secluded behind its battlemented walls of mud brick. He said that Arash, my intended husband, was a handsome, intelligent young man skilled in reciting Persian poetry, in hunting lions from horseback. 'I will not listen to you fretting about marriage,' my father had said, glowering over a wine bowl the last time that we spoke of Arash. 'You scarcely know the young man.'

And that much was true, for on the rare occasion that we attended the same celebration or dinner, I was too shy to speak and he kept his haughty, aquiline profile turned away from me.

'Can't you talk to my mother?' I asked Berta now as she closed the lid of her chest and stirred her fire of sheep dung into a flower of tiny flames. She shook her head.

'Your mother will not go against your father in this matter,' she said. 'To secure your future is important to them both; your mother knows too well the dangers of being a woman alone and without status or protection. It was only the mercy of Tabiti, goddess of hearth places, that brought her to your father's love. And you, even married in Ershi, will still have Swan.'

Swan! For a moment, her white head filled my eyes; I saw her drifting through the pasture like a feather dropped from high overhead; I saw her long legs sweeping aside the flowers as she trotted to me, to flutter her soft nostrils against my neck. For a moment, a smile quivered on my lips but then I glanced again at the cot where Mother lay, pale and sweating still, and my smile died.

'Mother must wake soon!' I said urgently to Berta. 'If she doesn't awake, how will I know she is healing? And how will I save Swan?'

Berta didn't reply, simply shooed me out through the open door into the sun's dazzle. 'Come back later,' she commanded, and I stood forlornly outside the yurt with my tunic flapping in the breeze. Tied to its perch with a leather thong, the eagle belonging to Batu's father regarded me with yellow eyes, cold as glass beads. Nervously, I moved away from the reach of its sleek wings, folded now, that were wider than a man is tall.

Around me, the hills rose in protective folds. Sedges and rushes grew along the banks of the river that sparkled downhill over small stones. Sheep and horses grazed peacefully, guarded by shaggy dogs and mounted herdsmen carrying lasso poles. Close to the yurts, a woman on a stool milked a mare whilst a boy struggled to hold her feisty foal. The woman's baby, tightly swaddled on a cradle board, watched from a patch of shade.

Gryphon! I thought. My heart clenched when I remembered his courage in saving Tulip from harm, his cry of pain and terror ringing from the rocky walls when the great cat landed upon his smooth hind-quarters. Oh, Gryphon! How could I have lingered in the yurt so late into the morning, worrying about Mother and Swan and my betrothal and war, talking to Berta? There seemed to be suddenly so many things to fear; my hand flew to the yellow pouch of leopard's fur and closed around its promise of strength as I scanned the hillsides for Gryphon. Where was he? Was he lamed or weakened by his injuries; had he been bleeding? Batu had been tending the herd last night whilst the stars moved around the sky's great circle, each one a horse wheeling about the tether post of the pole star. Batu had promised that he would tend to Gryphon in the darkness, poulticing the raking claw wounds.

My heart beat hard, as though I had been running, and the amulet became damp in my sweaty clasp. Finally I glimpsed Gryphon's flash of gold. He was corralled deep in a patch of flowering wild carrot, in a makeshift pen of poles. I broke into a run, calling his name. He lifted his head and watched me approach, slowing down to wend my way between the other horses grazing nearby. Some reached out with questing noses, inhaling my unfamiliar scent, but others stamped a back hoof warningly and flattened their ears.

When I climbed in the corral, Gryphon rested his muzzle momentarily against my shoulder, breathing long warm breaths into my hair, before dropping his head again to graze. I saw how the flesh of the wounds was drying, dark red and beginning to crust with scabs. Claw marks ran from his spine to his hock, and from where the edge of his saddle blanket would fall to the base of his tail. One wound ran through his five-pointed brand. All the blood had been washed from him and he seemed more interested in grass than in his injuries, although I noticed how he moved his hind legs stiffly, taking only small steps. I laid my palm flat beside his wounds, with the lightest of touches, and held it there, feeling the slight heat that ran beneath his skin.

'He will be scarred for life; his coat will grow in white,' Batu said, coming up behind me to lean against the wooden rails.

'I do not want him scarred,' I whispered brokenly. 'Before, his coat was perfect.'

'Everyone who saw him spoke of his beauty but from now on they will speak of his beauty and his courage; he is a warrior among horses,' Batu said. 'We are riding out soon.'

I turned then, my palm sliding away from Gryphon. The flat scales, each one hand-carved from hoof, each one sewn on to the leather helmet and breastplate that Batu wore, made him shine like a freshly caught fish. His bow was slung over one shoulder, and his wooden quiver, beautifully decorated with bright paintings, hung against his thigh and held his bronze-tipped arrows. The feathers on their shafts were perfectly aligned; perfect in their flight as eagles when they stoop, deadly and with rushing speed, upon their smaller prey.

'You are riding with the warriors?' I asked, the bottom dropping out of my stomach.

Batu nodded, a gleam of delight in his keen gaze. At the base of his throat, he wore a twisted torc, heavier than mine but of similar design. The eyes on the heads of the leopards were inlaid with carnelian.

'Take me with you! I can shoot a bow, Batu; you know that my mother has taught me! I can ride as well as any of you; you have seen me win games mounted on Swan! Gryphon is excitable, but very fast, and he is sound despite his wounds!'

Batu shook his head. 'Your father would never forgive me, and my father would not allow it,' he said. 'And Gryphon's wounds would break open if he even trotted. You must care for your mother and stay here in safety.'

'But Swan! I must save Swan!'

'I will look for her when we ride through the valley on our way to Ershi. I will make sure she is safe. Now I am going to find Rain, and soon we ride out. Goodbye, Kalli; I will pray that your mother recovers.'

Briefly, his hand touched mine through the rails but I didn't move; I stood speechless as he walked away through the horses, light on his feet, calling to the other warriors as they bridled their mounts. I saw him move close to Rain, his black and white gelding foaled in a spring of floods and now trained as a buzkashi horse. I watched the gelding slip his white face – with its one blue eye and one brown eye – down into the leather thongs of Batu's bridle. Its decorative florets of bronze winked in the light. Gryphon tore at the grass beside me as Batu laid a yellow blanket over Rain's withers and slid it back a fraction, smoothing the hair beneath. He bent to tighten the blanket's belly band, then fastened the tail crupper and the breastplate. The red tassels hanging from the breastplate, and from the edges of the blanket, bobbed like flowers in the breeze. Rain was a splendid sight, and Batu's greatest pride, for the nomads loved horses with bright, unusual markings.

I laid my hand on the arch of Gryphon's bent neck as Batu mounted Rain, and pulled his white face up out of the grass. Sunlight gleamed on the curve of Batu's bow, the scales sewn on his helmet. I laid my face against Gryphon's side and pressed my cheek into his golden hair, and cried in silence as Batu and Rain moved away amongst the yurts, assembling with the other warriors around an altar platform for their god of war. I squeezed my eyes shut as their shaman's chanting drifted through the valley, as the sheep bleated and the foals gambolled on their skinny legs. Everything was shining in the sun; everything inside my eyelids was black as the belly of a great storm.

Gryphon's side moved against my face; my feet moved of their own accord as I kept step with my grazing stallion. Finally I straightened and opened my eyes. The group of warriors was already far down the valley, cresting a swell of the land, a thin plume of dust rising from it. I waited until the last rider dropped from view, then dragged my heavy legs back to Berta's yurt and stumbled inside. My mother's eyes were still closed. I squatted beside her cot, with my back against a loom, but her eyelids didn't flicker. I held my ear to her face, listening anxiously to her shallow, light breathing.

Please, my thoughts urged, *oh please, Mother, wake up! Be strong again! We must ride after the warriors; we must save our horses!*

My calf muscles began to cramp and I stood up slowly to stretch, then sat cross-legged by the fire. A pan held a broth of mutton, cold now and skimmed over with fat. Berta had given it to me last night but I had been too tired to eat. Now the feast delicacy that she had saved, the sheep's eyeballs, were pale and puckered. I pushed the pan further away and began listlessly chewing a piece of flat bread that lay on a stone near the fire. The bread formed lumps in my throat.

Swan shimmered in the shadows of the yurt, a ghost mare, as precious as my own heartbeat. As Berta had reminded me, Swan had been born in the summer of my birth, a foal that made people cry out with surprise and delight; a foal that skittered and drifted across the pastures like down from the breast of a wild swan, light and glimmering. She had matured into a filly with legs so long, so fine, that she seemed all white bone as she ran through the alfalfa, fast and pale as Pegasus in my father's tales. My mother tied me on to her back; I fell asleep at night to the memory of her hoof beats and woke in the morning light to be carried into her pasture again.

As we grew older, my mother began to train us in the nomad way; we spent long hours under my mother's steady gaze, straining to pay attention to her husky commands. Over and over we practised breaking smoothly from walk into trot, from trot into canter, into flowing gallop, into sudden skidding stops. We wheeled through shadows and flowers like two birds changing direction in mid-air. By the time we were seven summers old we could thread amongst poles hammered into the ground as though we were one creature, one long streak of lightning forking between a forest to shoot at last towards the stable door where my mother stood, appraising our progress. My mother taught me to ride without reins, to guide Swan with the pressure of my knees on her pearly sides, to send her one way and then another even at a gallop, shifting beneath me like a sandbank shifting in a spring flood.

Then I learned to shoot arrows, twisting backwards from the waist, tightening the bowstring against my shoulder, forgetting that I was even mounted on a cantering horse as my eyes focused on the straw target, and my fingers notched the arrow against the bow's taut curve. Sometimes Mother would throw a silver coin, minted with the faces of Alexander the Great or Eucratides, upon the dust of our training ground. I would gallop past it, time after time, bending lower and lower over my mare's slippery ribs as I tried to scoop the coin from the ground. On other days, Mother hung rawhide loops from poles and I hurled spears through them as I galloped past. I also learned to hold a lasso pole in my left hand and drop its noose over the heads of other horses running beside Swan. Sometimes we ran relay races far out along the valley, on dusty tracks and through pastureland, and along the edges of vine-yards as the grapes ripened in the simmering heat, Mother and the men from her stable, and I.

At the end of these hard days, we would bathe the horses at a pool, fed from an aqueduct, that stood outside the mud brick walls of our stable. Swan's sweat and dust would slide from her and she would gleam in the thickening purple dusk, a statue of marble in a great square in the heart of a fabulous city. Then I would bring her a bucket of grain, wheat or barley from our own fields, and inhale its sweet smell and listen to Swan's teeth grinding as the poplar leaves trembled in the fading light. Once she had finished eating, Swan would press her muzzle to my face before drifting out to the herd, and I would turn and prepare to ride back to the city, my face burned with sun, my legs so tired they shook beneath me, the inside of my thighs chafed and sore.

My father took great interest in the education of my brothers; they went each day to school with their pedagogues carrying their wax tablets and metal styluses, their extra cloaks in case of cold. Seated behind their wooden desks, they laboured over arith-metic for my father wanted them to be shrewd traders able to check the ledgers and accounts in the warehouses and granaries. Outdoors, my brothers were taught wrestling and gymnastics; back at their desks again, they laboriously wrote out Greek and Latin script and learned to read Homer's *Iliad*. But my father left my education to my mother; asking only that I occasionally wear a gown and smile at his dinner guests, and play the stringed lyre pleasantly on winter afternoons, and be able to read. Beyond this lay my mother's realm. It was in the pastures and stable yard that my mother chose I should learn. Whilst my friend Lila and other girls sat at home working at their looms, I became dirty and disheveled, stained with grass and dust and horsehair. Gradually, I became a stranger in the city, just as my mother was. She taught me how to choose which mare to breed to which stallion, how to blanket a racing horse in layers of felt so that it gained no weight, when to feed a horse the extra nutrition found in mutton fat. She showed me how to first saddle a green young horse; how to poultice a foot abscess; how to deliver a foal, wet and filled with the promise of joy, into a bed of fresh barley straw.

Although my brothers competed with each other to see who could recite the longest passages of poetry, or win a wrestling match, waiting hopefully for our father's delighted belly laugh, it was my mother's approval that I longed for. Sometimes, she would lay her hand along my shoulder as I dismounted, and tell me that I had done well. On other evenings, my fingers cut with bowstrings, my ribs bruised from a fall over a running shoulder, it was to Swan that I went for comfort. It was Swan whose ears flickered as I mumbled my fear that I would never ride as well as my mother wished me to. It was Swan who blew into my hair and comforted me.

Now, I was stuck here in Berta's yurt, and Mother twitched and moaned softly in her deep sleep, wandering far away into her lost days, and the Chinese army was drawing closer, closer, closer to Ershi. To Swan, who trusted me.

I choked on a piece of flat bread and doubled over, coughing. The yurt was a trap; surely Angra had laid his evil hand upon us. I fumbled for the leather pouch of leopard's fur, and clenched it tightly.

There was a shuffle of sound. Someone pounded me on the back. I swallowed the lump of flat bread, and wiped my streaming eyes. Batu swam into focus, his face creased with concern as he squatted beside me. The bruise around his right eye was darker this morning, a squashed grape.

'I have returned; I am not going with the warriors,' he said fiercely, regret and determination kindling in his gaze.

'What? What has happened?'

He didn't answer but searched amongst the pots on the women's side of the yurt until he found a shallow dish. He poured a gurgle of red wine into it from a skin bag, and dropped an arrowhead into the liquid. Then, as I watched in silence, he drew his iron dagger from his sash and nicked the end of his finger; the blood splashed into the wine's clarity in a tiny cloud. Now I began to understand what he was doing. When he handed his dagger to me by the hilt, I turned the point towards myself. It was honed so sharp on a whetstone that I barely had to touch it to my skin to break the surface. Batu held out the bowl and I added my blood to its contents. The arrowhead shimmered in the bottom, like a treasure in a pool.

'Swear,' Batu said solemnly.

'I don't know the right words, the words of your people.'

'I make this oath before Uha Soldong, the Golden Sorrel, light of the dawn, creator of horses. I will not leave you, Kallisto. Horses have bound our families together. We are companions in this war with the Middle Kingdom. We are horses yoked in the same chariot. We are eagles circling in the same sky. May great Tengri, master of all the world, favour us, and look kindly upon us, and show us mercy if we are true to one another in this time of battle. I will be your true companion, Kallisto; I swear it.'

'Before the Golden Sorrel, I will be your true companion, I swear it,' I repeated, and then Batu tipped back his strong brown neck where the torc glinted, and drank from the bowl before handing it to me. The arrowhead shifted as I tipped the bowl up, and the wine tasted sweet and thick, clearing away the flat bread from my throat, filling my chest with warmth.

The bowl was empty when I laid it on the felt carpet. For a moment, Batu's gaze held mine in a blazing grip. I felt courage rise in me. Then the wind gusted in the door, bringing the tang of wild mint and the oiliness of sheep, and my mother moaned softly.

Batu's gaze flickered to her and he frowned. 'She has been cast upon by an evil eye,' he said. 'We must get her into a wagon and ride for Ershi. When my mother and I first came to your mother's door, we were starving to death. Only your mother's kindness saved us. Now it is my turn to repay this. And Swan is a mare of special quality; white as a perfect egg. White is the colour of good omen amongst my people, and how could I ignore that now?'

I lifted my head, bent as I listened to Batu's explanation. Outside the door of the yurt, Rain blocked the sunshine; he swung his head and looked at me with his blue eye.

'Come,' Batu said, 'the horses are ready for our journey.'

'Well spoken.'

We turned, startled, to see that my mother had raised herself upon one elbow.

'We will leave now,' she continued, only determination holding together the weak thread of her voice. 'But I will ride Grasshopper and not lie in a wagon like a corpse going to its sky-burial. Batu, please fetch my horses. Kallisto, bring me my clothes.'

'But, Mother –'

'We must make haste; we must fetch our herd and drive it back here to the nomad camp where it will be safe. No army shall have it.'

And my indomitable mother swung herself free of the blankets, as Batu stepped outside to catch Grasshopper and Tulip.

Chapter 4

'Mother!' I called anxiously. 'Are you well?'

Riding at the head of our small party, she dropped her reins and waved to me with her right arm, but said nothing. Then she ran her hand over Grasshopper's withers, her rings glinting in the light, and picked up her reins once more.

With a chill of fear, I watched her back, slumped and swaying on her horse where usually she was dignified and upright. Her left arm hung against her side, motionless. Her legs dangled slackly and her booted feet, usually held away from Grasshopper, swung and jostled against the mare's ribs. It was horrible to see my proud mother riding like a slave, like someone who always walked and never mounted a horse.

'She is very weak,' I muttered to Batu, riding just ahead of me.

'The evil eye is still upon her,' Batu said. 'It must

be the curse of a powerful shaman. When we reach Ershi, perhaps one of your magi can turn it aside.'

I nodded doubtfully, wondering how we would find time to fetch a priest, and to round up our horse herds, and to drive them out of the valley, before the army arrived. Although we had ridden all yesterday afternoon, and through much of the night, north-wards and westwards under the moon's silver stare, I felt the army of the Middle Kingdom pressing like a cold wind on the back of our necks. We were travel-ling perhaps only a half-day's march ahead of it.

I glanced at Batu's wiry form swaying easily along ahead of me, clad still in his leather armour covered in scales of hoof.

'Batu,' I called softly, 'are you frightened?'

He glanced back; the sun gleamed along the high angle of his cheekbones and the dark slant of his eyes, and burned blue in the mane of his hair.

'No! I have been training to fight our enemies since I was old enough to walk. The cavalry of the nomads, and of Ershi, are more skilled with bows and arrows, and horses, than any other. As soon as we have moved your herd to safety, I shall join the battle! It will be over quickly!'

He grinned fiercely, but then perhaps he felt my eddying fear. 'What is wrong?' he asked.

It was hard to find the right words. I shrugged miserably and stroked Gryphon's black mane, separating strands of it between my fingers; they were as calloused, and decorated with many rings, as were my mother's.

'I can guide a galloping horse with knee pressure alone,' I said at last. 'I can pull arrows from a quiver and shoot them true and straight. My mother has given me her greatest gift: her warrior skills. But no one will let me fight, Batu.'

'Saving your horses, driving them to up into the mountains, is more important for you to do,' Batu said kindly. 'My own mother is a warrior yet now she is at home guarding the flocks.'

I nodded. What Batu had said was true and yet I knew that he didn't live where I did, lost and drifting between separate worlds: the nomads' roaming freedom, my father's opulent home; my mother's foreign tongue, the Persian poetry of my betrothed. Only on horseback did it all cease to matter; only there did I truly feel at ease.

I rubbed my eyes; they felt as gritty as though I'd been out in blowing sand. Very late, as the moon sank, we'd stopped for a few hours of restless sleep. I'd lain awake on sheep fleeces covering the wooden planking of the wagon that Berta had given us, insisting my mother might need it. Then, as dawn stained the sky pink like wild rose petals, we had mounted up and journeyed on.

Now the sun was high overhead. Foothills shimmered in the heat, and the smell of wild oregano rose from the shining grass, making me think longingly of savoury lamb, run through with skewers and cooking over a low fire. At home, our cook often rubbed herbs into meat before preparing it; out here in the mountains, I'd had nothing all day but hard cheese soaked in tea. My stomach griped and pinched as the afternoon dragged past. I stared unseeingly at Rain's black and white haunches moving ahead of me, at the fall of his black tail streaked with white hairs.

Creak, creak, creak. The two high wheels of the wagon bumped and lurched over the rough ground, over fallen tree limbs and dry stones. Lizards flickered out from beneath the wheels' approach like tiny tongues of lightning. In the ears of my imagination, the wheels of the army were turning, turning, turning.

Thud, thud, thud. The hooves of our horses rose and fell in the dirt: first Grasshopper's, then Rain's, then Gryphon's. Behind me came the horse pulling the wagon which was being driven by a manservant; Tulip was tied behind the wagon, and behind her rode my mother's second servant, mounted on a horse the colour of winter grass.

In the ears of my imagination, the thousand hoof beats of the army rose deafeningly. They blotted out the song of birds in the juniper trees, and the jingle of Gryphon's curb chain as he tossed his head, biting at flies on his chest. I felt completely alone in this deafening silence, this roar inside my head. Cold sweat beaded my lip. I wanted to kick Gryphon into a gallop, to run and run until I found Swan and saved her, hiding her in the nomads' high valley under Berta's kind and watchful gaze. Until I found a place where Swan and I would both be free.

Perhaps Batu sensed my fear again for he slowed Rain to a halt, waiting until I was alongside. Rain swung his white face and touched his muzzle to my thigh in greeting before falling into step beside Gryphon. My stallion's golden ears with their black tips pinned back briefly, and he curled his lip at Rain, warning him not to come too close.

'Walk on,' I said sternly with a tightening of my legs, and Gryphon's ears relaxed, flickering forwards and sideways as he listened to the sounds around us, and tolerated the gelding walking at his side.

'Why do the men of the Middle Kingdom want your horses?' Batu asked. 'They already have horses of their own; we saw the cavalry yesterday.'

'In Ershi, people say that the emperor wants taller, faster and more powerful horses to improve his small cavalry mounts,' I replied. 'He is doing battle all the time with the tribes north of his Great Wall.'

'My people's tribes,' Batu interjected.

'The emperor's spy has carried word to him of our Persian horses, that can run many *li* without tiring, that can walk many hours without water. He has set his heart on acquiring them. And also, my father's heard that the emperor has been searching for Heavenly Horses that bring wisdom and long life to their owners. Now he believes that our horses are the Heavenly ones. He wishes to own them so that, upon his death, they will carry his soul to heaven, to the Jade Terrace. There, a goddess will hand him a golden peach, and when he bites into it, he will become immortal.'

'My people believe something like this too,' Batu agreed. 'Horses bring us into the world, and on a horse's back we leave when it is our time to die.'

I nodded. 'In the mounds of my mother's people, the warriors are buried with their legs bent, ready to ride with the spirits. Their horses lie beside them.'

Ahead of me, my mother dropped her reins again. Her right hand reached for her dangling left arm and held it briefly; her fingers moved over her tunic sleeve the way they might feel a horse's injured leg. I glimpsed her hand as it came away and saw that her fingertips were pink, as though she had been picking raspberries in the hills.

'We are moving too slowly!' I said fiercely to Batu. 'We need to be trotting!'

'Your mother is weak, and the wagon could not move fast over rough ground, and Gryphon's wounds would break open.'

'I know all this – I'm not a child!' I muttered, but then I nudged my knee against Batu's so that he would know it was my fear speaking and not my true heart.

Turning in my saddle, I scrutinised Gryphon's flanks and quarters; his wounds were closing over with thin scabs, and only traces of fluid leaked from them. When I laid a palm flat against him, there was only a normal heat running below the surface of his thin skin, his silky golden dapples. At least *he* was beginning to heal, I thought, although the flesh was puffy with invisible bruises closer to the wounds. What did it mean? I wondered. Was the leopard attack a bad omen; had some powerful shaman sent it to strike my mother? Or had the evil Angra sent a deva, a dark angel, to rend my mother's spirit from her body?

'Look!' Batu said suddenly; the excitement in his tone jolted me from my worried thoughts and I lifted my head. Gryphon's neck tightened as he became instantly alert, and his eyes, huge and dark as an antelope's, strained to take in the view.

Before us, the ground dropped away in a final slope and the Golden Valley of Ferghana spread like a lake, calm and broad and flat, stretching far to the north and west, filled with white heat and sky light, a patchwork of fields threaded with the glitter of irrigation canals, softened with the shadows of ash and elm trees. Reining in, I stared at it with delight and relief. There was no end to the valley within sight; it uncurled to the far horizons, hazy and blue. I knew, from my father and other traders, that mountains walled it in: the Chatkal ranges were massed to our north; the Kuramin lay far to our west. Briefly I thought of my brothers with a pang of envy for they had travelled westwards beyond those mountains, to wade at last in the Mediterranean's blue waters, and bring me coral beads and stories of places I might never see.

I stilled Gryphon as he fidgeted beneath me, his tail whisking across my thigh as though to remind me of his mares waiting in the valley below. Of Swan, with whom he had sired two beautiful foals that my mother and I were training.

'We will be home before dusk!' I cried to Batu.

A quiver ran through Gryphon's muscles for he was a horse who could find his way home over many miles. In the autumn of his third year, he had strayed from our pastures and driven a small band of mares up into the foothills. My mother's men had spent days tracking them and searching for them. At last, on a night of fine, stinging snow blowing on a north wind, when the land lay bleak and white and the wolves ran in the forest, Gryphon had driven his mares home into the stable yard and trumpeted at the door, demanding grain and warm shelter.

Now, on this ridge above the valley, Gryphon recognised the smell of alfalfa fields growing lush in the summer heat, the smell of flowers on the grape-vines, the dust and fresh water smells of home. He bunched beneath me, fighting the bit, jostling against Rain. When the gelding didn't move, Gryphon swung his head in impatience, nipping Rain's glossy neck and leaving a trail of wet, ruffled hair but no break in the flesh. I kicked Gryphon sideways, and circled him between Rain and the wagon, making him pay attention to my leg commands.

'Ride on!' my mother cried. Grasshopper broke into a jog trot and, surprisingly, my mother let her go, bouncing weakly down that long track into the valley. Rain and Gryphon trotted too, and I heard the wagon groaning behind us, and the clatter of the servants' horses.

'Look at the road!' Batu shouted as we descended, and I shielded my eyes and squinted through the shimmering air. I knew where to look for the road that ran across the plain, curling southwards from the city and dividing into tracks that led to villages and farms, and running on to the high mountain passes that disgorged weary travellers at last into India. Now the road's surface seethed and crawled as though covered by a torrent of ants. Clouds of dust boiled from it, for our spring had been exceptionally dry.

'Everyone is fleeing,' I muttered, and urged Gryphon on down the track, in spite of his wounds.

We broke into a canter when we reached the level floor of the valley, but even above the drum of our hoof beats I could hear the din of sound rising from the road. Ahead of me, Grasshopper and Rain leaped across a drainage ditch filled with still water, and were swallowed into the road's confusion. I collected Gryphon under me, felt his muscles bunch, felt the moment that he became airborne in a soaring leap over the green water. His hard black hooves thudded on to the edge of the road, beside a camel kneeling in the dirt. A man was frantically tightening the ropes that held a bundle of goods upon the camel's shaggy, two-humped back. The beast roared in shrill complaint. Gryphon dodged around it, while I stared wide-eyed at the melee of people fighting their way both northwards and southwards.

Gryphon trotted past whole caravans of camels, their bells clanging. He dodged a string of donkeys, roped one behind the other and almost invisible under bales of trade goods, trotting with bent heads. Their pale muzzles shone like clam shells. Men shouted orders, women and children rushed along with robes and tunics flapping, some astride horses and asses, some seated in chariots whose spokes whirled brightly, others jolting in wagons. Gryphon leaped and plunged beneath me as a heavy whip cracked over the backs of oxen straining at a wagon loaded with grain.

A trio of small children, their hands linked together, ran screaming ahead of us and I reined Gryphon in sharply and pulled his head sideways, dragging him across the road before his hammering front hooves could knock down the fleeing bodies. He was fighting his curb chain again, trying to break into his smooth canter that would carry us swiftly through this panicked crowd. Sometimes I caught a flash of my mother's pale face, bent over Grasshopper's neck, or of Batu's scale-covered helmet as they rode along.

'The merchants are fleeing the city!' Batu cried once, as we trotted closer together. We dodged rich men in embroidered gowns, and camel drivers running barefoot. The caravans were leaving our city, trying to avoid being trapped there by the approaching army, trying to get their trade goods safely away before Ershi fell into enemy control. Meanwhile, the valley's farmers were abandoning their peaceful villages to crowd towards the safety of Ershi's walls, trying to get their wives and children, their goats and sheep, behind the sandy battlements. But, I wondered, was the city a place of safety, as the villagers believed, or was it a trap that the merchants were wise to flee? I felt a shiver of panic at the thought of being held inside those high walls; my greatest fear was always of entrapment. My friend Lila owned a pair of finches that sang sweetly, hanging in their cage in a shaft of sunlight in the house next door to my father's, but I hated the sight of their folded wings that never lifted into blue sky.

We are only going to fetch our horses, I reminded myself. Soon we will be back in the mountains again, free and safe.

The fear that eddied through the crowd had taken hold of Gryphon, and he no longer paid attention to my voice or to the tight pull of the curb.

'I can't hold him!' I shouted to Batu; he was over to my right, half obscured by dust and a flock of sheep being driven by tribesmen in woolly astrakhan hats.

'We'll meet at the farm!' Batu yelled back, coughing. 'Where's our wagon?' I glanced over my shoulder but could see no sign of it in the pressing throng. Perhaps the servants were still searching for some place where they could cross the drainage ditch.

'I don't know! Try and stay near my mother!'

A herd of horses rushed up behind me, their eyes rolling white, their nostrils flaring, and Gryphon broke into a canter. The horses swept us along ahead of them; we were like a leaf riding on a spring flood. Fields of pea vines, and of melon plants, flashed past, and we clattered through the narrow streets of a village where people threw bundles of clothing, and pots and pans, out of their front doors in preparation for flight. A boy, with a willow crate containing a rooster and two hens, jumped away from Gryphon's hooves. An old woman ran past in the opposite direction, shrieking words that I couldn't hear above the din of hooves, the cries of animals. The wheels of a chariot spun past and I glimpsed the frightened faces of two Parthian women clinging inside it, their veils torn away in the wind of their flight.

Finally, Gryphon and I rushed down to the stretch of road beside the river. The water lay beside us, broad and rippling. This river ran down from the mountains, cold with melting snow, and sometimes swept across the valley in spring floods. Along with numerous smaller streams, it moistened the crops in the fields, filled the troughs where animals drank, and was diverted into aqueducts and channels to provide water for the city of Ershi. The crowd parted and I glimpsed a long procession of white-robed magi wending its way towards a fire altar built upon the riverbank. A white ox was held at the base of the rectangular altar, bellowing as though it knew its fate was to be sacrificed.

The priests are trying to ward off the army, I thought. They are appealing to Ahura Mazda for help, for the intervention of his glorious angel, Sraosha, leader of the forces of light.

Maybe I could push my way through the crowds and find a magus who would sing hymns over my mother, who would have the herbs to heal her from whatever evil power wrestled with her spirit. I fought Gryphon to a dancing walk as we approached the line of stately priests in tall felt hats with lappets that hung down over their ears. Now I was close enough to see their carefully curled hair, their freshly combed beards, the bundles of tamarisk twigs grasped in their hands. Light winked on the brooches pinning their cloaks. I leaned forward over Gryphon's shoulder and opened my mouth. Now I was close enough to see the stern, inward-focused solemnity of the priests' eyes.

Shyness seized me. I struggled to ask for help for my mother, but my tongue stuck to the roof of my mouth and no sound emerged between my parted lips. For a long moment, my stubbornness and my shyness fought inside my throat, the words bunched there, just behind my tongue. Then Gryphon broke into a trot again, and the crowd surged between me and the priests. I could do nothing but ride on in frustration. But anyway, I reasoned, I had already lost both my mother and Batu in the crowds. And Gryphon would not be stopped; he dodged around people and obstacles as though we were competing in a new mounted game. My legs gripped him desperately lest I fall off and be trampled underfoot.

Soon, very soon, we would find Swan!

I thought about how my mother's horses would look, standing knee-deep in their pasture, gleaming golden in the sun like a kingdom's newly minted coins. All our horses, our bays and sorrels, our duns and smoke browns, our chestnuts, all had the same sheen over their coats, the golden metallic shine that drew the eye to them in city streets or in the pastures. It was another special mark of the Persian horses; the Chinese spy would surely have told his emperor about this attribute. It was no wonder, I thought, half in pride and half in apprehension, that this faraway king had sent his troops over the roof of the world, through snow and drought, to bring home our horses for his cavalry to ride, and to carry his own soul to the Jade Terrace.

Now we trotted into the last village before the city. We clattered past low, flat-roofed houses; I saw a girl pulling a loaf of hot bread from an oven and wrapping it in her cloak to carry away. Goats and dogs scattered from Gryphon's flying hooves. Now he seized the bit and dragged the reins from my hands for he knew we were almost home. He broke into a canter, scattering a flock of hens, sending donkeys loaded with barrels of wine into the gutter. He soared around the corner of the last house and swerved into the lane leading to our farm; the sandy walls containing the house and stable block stood dappled by the shade of poplar trees. We galloped up the final stretch of rutted lane, swerving past a flock of bleating goats, spotted white and brown. A guard dog ran out, lips drawn back over his gleaming teeth in a ferocious bark, but when he heard my voice, he yelped with pleasure and turned tail to sprint ahead of us. The wide double doors into the forecourt stood open, their surfaces carved with vines and running horses. Gryphon swerved through the doorway and, just in time, before it was scraped against the door post with its heavy hinges, I swung my left leg on to his neck. We shot into the courtyard and skidded to a halt in a shower of small stones by the water trough.

Swan, I am here! my thoughts cried. *Where are you? You are safe now! Swan!*

Chapter 5

'Bring the horses!' I yelled, expecting my mother's men to come running, but the yard stood silent. I leaped from Gryphon and ran into the stable with the brown dog trotting at my side, thrusting his nose into my hand. Inside the stable, the mud brick stalls were all empty. Only straw glinted in slanting sunshine. Only dust motes turned to gold in its light. I ran back outside and crossed the yard to pound on the house door leading to the kitchen, but no one answered. I ran around to the back, alone now because the dog had gone to sniff at Gryphon's legs. The small door that led to the fields clattered back against the wall as I pulled it open, my heart banging against my ribs.

'Swan!' I cried. 'Swan!'

The pastures quivered with ripples of heat, as though they were turning into rivers. Nothing else moved. Although I squinted against the sun's glare, I saw not a single mare with gently swollen belly, not a single foal with whiskery chin, not a single riding gelding with patient eyes. Not one golden coin of horse gleamed in the flowers of my mother's meadows.

My heart clenched into a fist.

I ran across our training ground but no young horses stood saddled in the shade, waiting their turn to weave between the lines of upright poles, to adjust their strides as they trotted over saplings laid upon the ground at equal distances.

'Help! Help!' I cried but no voice answered me. Where were my mother's horsemen and their wives?

I tore back through the gate, letting it bang shut behind me, and took the stairs leading from the courtyard to the second floor in flying leaps. Below me, Gryphon sucked deeply at the water in the trough; now that we had reached home, he had grown quiet, seemingly unbothered by the fresh blood that trickled from his broken wounds. I pounded on the door at the top of the stairs. There was a long pause. Distantly, I could hear the pandemonium on the road through the valley; donkeys braying, horses whinnying, men shouting, even the faint chant of the magi at their altar by the river. I stared out over the flat rooftop of the stable, crying Swan's name inside my head.

Surely she was there, somewhere, lying in the tall grass, hidden beneath a shady tree. Her pale face and gentle eyes hung before me, ghostly and beloved.

I rapped again on the door. Finally, it opened a

crack and from the dimness inside the living quarters, Mina, one of the wives, peered out.

'Kallisto!' Her weathered face creased with surprise above the coarse cotton of her brown tunic as she pulled the door wider. 'Is your mother here? The king has ordered all the valley's best horses to be taken into the city and the men have –'

'Swan!' Her name broke from me in an anguished cry.

The woman's dark eyes held mine for a heartbeat. 'They have taken Swan too,' she said.

'No, not Swan!'

'The king's men came here,' Mina continued, 'with orders to bring all the elite horses into the city for protection, and for use in the cavalry. So Anoush, Kasra and Ahou have taken the mare herd and geldings; they will be safe at your home inside Ershi. The men must fight, and I am preparing now to flee into the city too. Where is your mother?'

'I am here,' she said, and I turned to see her standing halfway up the stair, her face white as a scrubbed stone. Sweat shone on the angle of her dusty cheeks, beneath her sunken eyes. Her right hand clutched her left arm where a stain of blood was vivid on her sleeve. Mina gave a cry of alarm.

'Leave whatever you're doing, and come with us now,' my mother said to her. 'Time is running short. We will harness the oxen to a wagon of grain, and you will drive it into the city for the cavalry horses. Kallisto, come.'

'But Swan! Swan is in the city!' I cried. 'I won't leave without her!'

'We are not leaving without any of them,' my mother said, and although her voice was flat with fatigue, her eyes were steady. 'We stay together this time. We are going into the city to bring out our mares.' She turned to Mina again and asked, 'The two-year-olds?'

'The men were going to return for them,' Mina said. 'They took the mares and foals, and the riding geldings, then they are coming back later today for the two-year-olds.'

'Good,' my mother said, and turned on the stairs. 'Batu!' she called, and he glanced upwards, the bruise around one eye fading to purple. Rain waited behind Gryphon for his turn at the water trough.

'Batu, there is no need for us to take our stallion any further; his wounds are bleeding. You will take him with you. I have a small band of two-year-old mares in a far pasture, on the southern edge of my land, where there is a pond amongst the willows. Ride Rain, and find my herd. Drive the mares up into the valley where you killed your first wild boar – Gryphon will help you drive them. Hold them there in the valley until we come to join you. Do you remember the place?'

Batu nodded, already turning away from the wagon to fetch sacks of grain from inside the storage wing.

'Water!' my mother said suddenly, sharply, over her shoulder as I followed her down the stairs. 'Find every jar in the place! Fill them and put them on the wagon!'

'But we have water in the city!' I said; then I glimpsed the suffering on my mother's drawn face, and turned to obey her. Mina followed and together we scoured the kitchen, with its familiar smells of barley and mutton, while my mother searched the storage rooms. I grabbed a piece of flat bread and some cold chicken and shoved them, wrapped in grape leaves, into the cloth pouch slung around my waist with my dagger. Perhaps there would be time to eat the food later. I lifted a clay jar from a corner and lugged it to the irrigation channel that ran behind the house, and pushed it down into the water. It filled with a slow gurgle; I wanted it to fill immediately, I wanted to be running through the front gate at home, finding Swan. Mina and my mother bent beside me, filling more jars. Their dusty terracotta turned dark red with wetness. We lugged them to the wagon, stumbling under their weight, while Batu led my mother's oxen from their enclosure and yoked them, patient and unresisting, still chewing their last meal, to the wagon. Mina dashed up the stairs one last time, her tunic flying, and tossed a bundle of clothing and blankets on top of the grain sacks that Batu had loaded on to the wagon. My mother handed Mina the long, black-handled ox-whip of plaited leather, and she climbed on to the wagon and cracked it above the oxen's backs.

I dug through my saddle pack, and found

Gryphon's halter which I pulled on over his bridle, ignoring his tossing head. He was not used to being handled with such haste. 'Stand!' I commanded sharply, and he lowered his head for me but pawed nervously at the baked mud of the yard. I secured the leather strapping by its bone buckle, and led Gryphon over to Batu, already mounted on Rain.

'Don't take the road,' I said. 'Gryphon will not be led along it. You know it is hard for anyone but my mother and I to handle him; he is bonded only to us and suspicious of others.'

'I am going across country,' Batu replied. 'Now give me the rope.'

I handed him the lead and tugged Gryphon forward until his black and gold head was level with Batu's thigh. It was hard to let go of the soft cotton lead rope, to send Gryphon away from me.

'It's only for a short time,' Batu said. 'And he will rest and heal in the valley. Then we can take all the horses back to camp. You can keep them there in safety until the army is driven from the valley!'

When I tried to smile, my lips quivered. I stooped quickly and pressed them to Gryphon's silken cheek in a kiss that was like a plea.

'Nothing for me?' Batu cried teasingly. He puckered his lips, then laughter flashed across his face as he kicked his heels into Rain's mottled sides. In a moment, he and the horses were moving across the courtyard to vanish from view.

'Let's ride!' my mother said, and she slipped her boot into her foot loop and swung on to Grasshopper; I was standing close enough to hear the catch in her breath as her weight settled in the saddle. Then I jumped up, trying not to drag at her waist, and settled myself behind her, on Grasshopper's loins. The mare snorted and gave one small hop, protesting the fact that she was being left behind by Gryphon and Rain, then my mother urged her towards the road.

We overtook Mina driving our wagon, laden with grain and water, and then it was left behind as Grasshopper trotted smoothly through the crowds and the dust. Ahead of us, I could see the two swells of land that marked the location of Ershi. The first hill held a tunnel that carried the main water channel leading into the city. On the hill's far side, the water flowed from the tunnel and along the top of a high arched aqueduct. The second, larger hill was encircled with Ershi's walls, and rose to a gentle peak crowned by the inner citadel where the king's palace sprawled in a mass of plastered halls and reception rooms. To one side of the palace, water glittered in the reservoir that was fed from the aqueduct. On the hill's lower slopes, columned temples and lavish merchant homes stood amongst shady trees. Lower still on the flat land beneath the hill, bazaars and market stalls spread between narrow alleys and crowded, mud brick houses.

As we approached the city, the congestion on the

road grew so great that we slowed to a walk. Heads clad in turbans, felt caps, and sheep fleece jostled past my dangling legs. Children stared up at me, their eyes beseeching and bewildered, their thumbs in their mouths. A camel pressed against Grasshopper, pushing her sideways through the crowd; its long golden coat brushed my arm as it turned its long neck, bellowing, its nose wrinkled around the wooden peg that pierced its nostrils. We came to a halt, wedged between a wagon of trussed sheep, and a group of soldiers in armour, spears carried upright in the crowd. A donkey brayed hysterically. Slowly we edged our way forward, threading between broken bales of fabric strewn across the road.

Now the great, sand-coloured wall of the city rose above us, rearing into the air like the side of a cliff, high above the tops of the walnut trees growing by the east gate. The wall was studded with tall, angular watchtowers with window slits for shooting arrows through, and crowned with rectangular battlements. Men in armour shouted on top of the wall, running to and fro against the brilliant sky. It was hard to imagine that any army could pose a threat to that great wall, so thick, so high, so well-manned. It was hard to imagine how you could escape if you were stuck inside.

People pressed against my legs. Horses snorted and gave shrill neighs of fear. Grasshopper hopped on the spot, nervous and edgy; she didn't like the feel of being hemmed in. A clotted pool of people and wagons was jammed against the gate entrance, and along the base of the wall beneath the walnuts.

'Hurry, hurry,' I muttered under my breath, but my mother heard me.

'Slide off and run ahead,' she said. 'Start getting the horses ready to leave. I will join you soon.'

My feet hit the ground with a thud and I pushed my way into the crowd, feeling as though I were suffocating as bodies and animals squeezed tightly against me. I could see nothing except what was right before my eyes: a woman's gauzy veil, an embroidered tunic, a horse's tail. I caught hold of it, in danger of being swept off my feet and dragged underneath by the crowd. I knew the horse was too confined to kick me, although I heard it give a nervous snort. 'Steady, steady,' I said to it and it quietened, although its rider never even knew I was there. Presently I spotted an opening in the crowd, darted into it, clenched my jaw and struggled on towards the east gate.

Swan, oh, Swan! I cried in my thoughts. *Wait, I am coming for you! Trust me!*

She will be confused and afraid, I thought; *she will wonder what is happening to her, why she is penned up in this noisy, crowded city. She will be happy again though when we reach the valley, when she wades into the cool water.* I imagined the reflection of her white face in the river's surface, and the way that water droplets would spill from her lips. I imagined the long, kind, considering gaze she would give me.

Now I was jostling into the deep shadow lying directly beneath the soaring wall.

I craned my neck, watching doves wheel above the waving treetops and the sandy battlements. The stalls of tea sellers were adrift in the tide of people that crushed towards the gate's high entrance. Then I was under the wall itself, being swept along like a stone grinding through a canyon. Panic tightened around my ribs, and I struggled to breathe. All around me in the long gateway rose a babble of tongues: Turkic and Persian, Greek, Bactrian, Mongol, Sogdian, Kushan, Indian, and others that I couldn't recognise, for traders entered our city from many far places. In any tongue, the language of fear sounded the same.

Now I burst through the other side of the gate, squinting in the sunlight, and the crush of the crowd eased. I drew a ragged gasp and began to run, dodging a wagon heaped high with hay, freshly cut with a scythe. The caravanserai lay to my right, where travellers found lodgings for themselves and stabling for their animals. I skirted the water fountain built against the entrance, fed by an underground spring. The great yard was filling with cavalry units; I glimpsed their masses of shields and spears, their curved bows and shining scale armour. Perhaps Batu's father was in there with his men, and so perhaps were my mother's horsemen and my father's servants, all called on to fulfil their duty to the king and to fight for our city. And perhaps some of our horses were there too, our geldings harnessed in their bright blankets, their decorated bridles. I hoped that there was enough horse armour to keep them all safe.

I took a short cut through a warren of narrow streets where laundry dried on ropes and women shrieked. I struggled across a vast open marketplace; it seemed to stretch on endlessly. The hammering of the tin and coppersmiths was submerged in the din that roared through the entire city.

Swan, Swan! I cried longingly.

I dodged piles of spices from Arabia; skirted a pile of early melons; pounded past a kite-maker's stall festooned with bright ribbons of cloth.

Now I was running slightly uphill along a broad street where merchants' houses basked in the sun behind their high walls. I leaped a covered drain, ran alongside a stone channel carrying fresh water from the reservoir, circled a pool where women could fill wooden buckets. Sobbing for breath, I passed the merchants' grand entranceways, the courtyards, the walled gardens; passed a fire temple, passed a gymnasium. Now I was turning on to another broad street, lined with elm trees.

Swan! Swan!

Here was my father's high wall, and the great double doors of rare and costly wood, carved with geometric Greek patterns. When I hammered upon it, the wood was solid and heavy under my fist. Slowly, Fardad, our old porter, swung open a small, hinged window in the door and peered out, his wispy grey beard quivering. His eyebrows, bushy as caterpillars crawling across his forehead, twitched in surprise when he saw me, bent over and gasping for breath.

'Honoured child!' he cried, rattling aside a bolt.

The door swung open and I fell inwards, clutching the pain in my side. Then, I straightened. A smile of delight stretched my sweating face.

Through my misty vision, I saw that the outer courtyard was filled with horses. Their backs shimmered like gold; they turned their long elegant faces towards me and regarded me with their huge dark eyes. I wanted to weep; I wanted to hug each one of them: the golden mares – Honey and Peach, Apricot, Sandy, and Twist. My eyes ran over the greys: Iris, Thunder and Smoke; over brown Mouse; over the bays, River and Rocky and Brocade; over the chestnuts, Peony and Nomad and Pomegranate. Over Swan's yearling filly, the black Pearl.

Over Swan.

My heart stood still. She turned her long neck as I had known she would; her eyes were deep pools. They considered me with calm kindness. The light ran down over her like poured water. Her face gleamed.

When I ignored Fardad's urgent questions and thrust my way between the horses, Swan's nostrils fluttered in greeting. The tail of a foal flapped against my arm. The shoulder of a mare pressed against my back. I was deep in a crowd of horses and I was happy for the first time since Batu and I had lain on the ridge, watching the army. I laid my cheek against Swan's long head, and breathed in her sweet, familiar scent. My mind filled with flowers and grass, with birdsong, with sky.

The mares and foals turned away from me, jostling to view some new commotion at the door. I craned my neck in time to see Grasshopper push her way inside. For an instant, my eyes refused to believe what they were seeing. Then I accepted the truth of it: Grasshopper had carried my mother home. She lay along the mare's neck, unconscious, and the broken reins of shagreen leather dangled from the mare's snaffle bit. Fardad and I rushed to Grasshopper and caught hold of my mother's body as she slid over the mare's shoulder to land heavily across our feet.

'Marjan!' bellowed Fardad, his voice surprisingly loud despite his age, rising even over my scream of shock.

When my mother's body servant pushed her way through the horses, we all lifted my mother and carried her up the outer staircase, and along the dim hallway to her room. Gasping, we laid her on her high and magnificent Greek bed with its veneer of tortoiseshell, its inlays of ivory. Her head lolled against the round pillows, imported from Corinth.

'Fetch water,' Marjan said, her firm capable hands

already holding a knife, slitting my mother's tunic, rolling the fabric back from my mother's arm and shoulder as Fardad rushed out.

'What is happening?' I asked. My hand flew up to grip the amulet around my neck.

'Look at the wounds, they are festering,' Marjan said, and she laid a hand upon my mother's sweating forehead. 'She is hot; there is strong evil here.'

I leaned closer, noting the swollen flesh around the leopard's claw marks, and the red lines that streaked up my mother's arm and shoulder.

'I will send for a magus,' Marjan muttered. 'We need herbs, and prayers.'

'We're not s-staying! We were only c-coming to fetch the horses,' I stammered but Marjan shook her head gently without raising her gaze from my mother; she had been my mother's servant since they were both young women.

'Your mother will not rise from this couch in time to take the horses anywhere,' she said. 'Go up on the roof and be thankful you have reached home before sunset. Go! You cannot do anything here for your mother.'

I turned away, sick and faint. In the hallway, Fardad rushed past carrying a copper bowl half filled with water; a linen cloth was slung over his shoulder and he was muttering to himself. I passed beneath the tapestries hanging on the walls, their bright intricate patterns brilliant in the corners of my eyes. The thick pile of knotted carpets muffled the thud of my boots.

In the courtyard again, I removed Grasshopper's broken bridle and her sweat-dampened blanket, and smuggled her a treat from the stable: a handful of grain. The other mares craned their necks, eager and curious, catching whiffs of sweetness from my tight fist, but Grasshopper laid her ears back in warning. I checked that the stone water trough, fed from a rain cistern, was full.

Then I stood for some time, leaning against Swan's side and rocked by her calm breathing. Around me rose the familiar sounds of a horse herd: the click of a sinew, the swish of tails whisking flies, the sound of teeth biting an itchy spot, the gurgle of a stomach. There were seventeen elite mares in our courtyard, and six yearlings, and eight foals – for my mother believed in breeding her mares on alternate years and letting them rest in the year between. All the mares were branded on their left quarter with my mother's five-pointed mark. To me, the brand always looked like half of a star, but my mother said it was to symbolise a hand. She said that in her tribe, if a thief was caught stealing another man's branded horses, his hand was cut off.

Finally, I obeyed Marjan and trudged up the stairs, their mud bricks worn in the centre of each step, to emerge on to the flat rooftop. From its centre, I could see into our inner courtyard with its blue-tiled water fountain and its pomegranate tree. Turning, I could see the outer courtyard with its high wall containing the stables, the storage rooms, and the backs of all my mother's mares and foals, the points of their ears, their thin manes falling from their long arched necks. For a moment, my eyes lingered on Swan's cool shine.

Pacing to the further side of the rooftop, I could see into our garden lying between our house and the house next door, where my friend Lila lived. I glanced hopefully towards her rooftop, hoping her tall, slender form might be visible there, but the roof lay empty. Beyond Lila's house crowded the sandy walls and rooftops of many other houses, shops, temples, bath houses and markets. To the north, the walls of the inner citadel, protecting the king's palace, crowned the hilltop.

To the east, I could see what my mother and I loved best about our home: the view over waving treetops, over bazaars and alleyways, into the Valley of Ferghana. I stood there, gazing down that wide tongue of breezy space. In the light of the setting sun, I could see the valley road still choked with people and animals fleeing into the city. And far away, in the blue distance, where the Alay Mountains rose into their snowy peaks, I could see a plume of smoke.

It climbed into the air like a brushstroke. It caught the last sunlight and glowed pale and sandy. It was neither brushstroke nor smoke.

I knew that only a great army could raise such a column of dust.

I knew that I was trapped in the city, like a horse is trapped in a stable when fire takes hold of the straw.

Chapter 6

By morning, when I went to visit Lila and stand on her rooftop, the army from the Middle Kingdom was encamped before the city walls.

'They've been on the move all night,' Lila's father said glumly. 'It's said that we are completely surrounded.' Glumness was usual for him; he was a tall, thin banker who provided letters of credit for the caravan leaders. He moved through life with caution and sternness, as though he had never felt joy.

'This is very bad for business,' he continued. 'Very bad indeed. The caravans cannot come to trade as long as the siege continues.'

'Siege!' Lila's mother gasped and laid a plump, bejewelled hand over her mouth. Despite the grave circumstances and the early hour, she was perfectly made-up with cosmetics: rouge on her rounded cheeks, black kohl lines around her eyes, red on her pouting lips. The fragrance of jasmine floated from her in the wisp of morning breeze. She cuddled between Lila and I, holding our arms as though to protect us and keep us close.

'When will our army ride out?' she asked. 'Surely the siege cannot last for very long! We have such a good cavalry, and so many brave riders! They say that the hippodrome is being used as an army camp, as well as the caravanserai, and that the troops will attack from the east gate. So much commotion in our peaceful city! But what a blessing for you, Kallisto, that the king ordered the elite horses of the valley to come safely inside the city before the invaders arrived!'

As she paused for breath, I thought of the birds in the wicker cage that hung in her reception room and never flew, but I said nothing. Although we had always been neighbours, Lila's mother was so different from mine that I often didn't know how to respond to her breathless chatter. She had three daughters older than Lila, and they had all married into wealthy households; it was partially through them, and their network of servants, that Lila's mother was able to indulge her love of gossip and city news. In my household, it was my father who collected stories as though they were burrs that clung to him.

'The elite horses are the treasure of Ferghana,' Lila's father intoned, squinting into the valley. 'We cannot allow them to fall into enemy control. A good war horse is worth more than its own weight in gold because it protects our country in time of attack.'

I thought of Gryphon, his golden shimmer hidden safely in the valley with Batu, and I felt one quiver of hope. Then I stared into the valley again, where the army crawled and seethed across the fields and gardens. From this height, it was hard to make out details; only here and there, the bright shine of a silken tent, or the lazy lift of a banner. Long lines of wagons were still rumbling towards the encampment like migrating snakes.

'Last time the Middle Kingdom sent troops, many starved to death, and the weakened remainder were defeated,' Lila's father said. 'But this time, they come well-supplied.'

'They say the king will never trade with the emperor who calls himself the Son of Heaven,' Lila's mother said. 'He will not send our horses away, although there are some in Ershi who do not agree, and who wish to open the trade routes to the east. And oh, Kallisto, speaking of the court, you will not have heard yet that Arash's father has met with some difficulty. Some disgrace.'

She savoured the word in her mouth for a moment, like a plump apricot. 'It's rumoured that he had something beautiful, a golden treasure from the past, and he had promised it, and some more treasure besides, to one of the princes. But then, before he gave it, he wagered it in a game; it's said he was drunk at the time. And he lost the wager and the treasure. Some caravan leader won it from him. The prince was very angry, and Arash's father has been demoted from Royal Falconer. He is banished temporarily from the court! What a terrible thing to happen, and now, of all times, when we have so much else to worry about!'

She let go of our arms to wring her soft hands together as though this turn of events had some personal effect upon her comfortable life.

'I hadn't heard all this,' I muttered.

'So hard on Arash – such an ambitious, clever young man! I do hope this will not affect his future.'

'The king will have greater matters to attend to now, and will not need his falcons for the hunt,' Lila's father said. 'The petty squabbles of princes are of no account in a time of war.'

As though she hadn't heard this, Lila's mother continued, 'Oh, and your poor, dear mother! I must go and make sure she is being well cared for, that her needs are being attended to! Servants are so untrustworthy when the mistress of a house is ill and the master is away from home. How awful for you, my dear Kallisto. You must try and be a brave girl in this awful time! I will go and prepare to visit your mother immediately.'

With a final squeeze on my arm she departed in a swirl of azure gown, her small veil drifting backwards from her elaborate headdress and curled hair. Her perfume lingered on the rooftop. Lila's father gave a last grim look at the valley and then followed his wife without a word. Lila and I stepped closer together and wrapped our arms around each other's waists. Hers was much more slender than mine; she was going to be as tall as her father, and far more elegant than either of her parents. It was as well that I had known her all my life, or I might have been intimidated by her beauty.

'Are you scared?' she asked, slanting a glance at me with her dark, almond-shaped eyes outlined in black.

'I'm scared for the horses,' I said, my voice small. 'They are trapped here, the mares, the foals, Swan. The yearling, Tulip, arrived tied to a wagon late last night. We do not have enough food in our stable granary to feed them all for very many days. My mother sent a wagon of water and grain into the city but it was taken by a tribal chieftain as it entered the gate, and is being used for the light cavalry. And my mother was not even in her right mind this morning before I came to visit you. She was muttering and crying in her dreams.'

'I'm sorry,' Lila said softly. 'I'm scared too. Let's go inside.'

In her room, Lila brightened again. 'Look!' she said, shaking out the folds of a new gown of green brocade sewn with tiny jet beads. 'Does it become me?' She held the gown to her body and shimmied across the room like a dancing girl; an exhibition that would have horrified her mother but that reduced us briefly to mischievous laughter. I flung myself backwards on Lila's couch, across a covering of dark sable furs imported from the Baltic lands, and watched while Lila unscrewed caps from various jars of face cream and sniffed at their contents.

'Have you washed since coming home from your nomad adventure?'

'I bathed this morning. Marjan heated water for me.'

'You still smell like horses. But that's nothing new. Oh, try this perfume I bought in the market yesterday!'

She held out a small glass jar with a crystal stopper, her arm bracelets chiming prettily. Removing the stopper, she wafted something smelling like sandalwood beneath my nose and I promptly sneezed. 'I'd rather smell like horses.'

'You're such a barbarian. How will you ever move in court circles?' She flopped beside me on the fur and stroked it absently.

'Is it true, about Arash's father?'

'So my mother believes. Do you think this will affect your betrothal?'

'No,' I said with a sigh. 'Even if in disgrace at court, his father is still a rich aristocrat with lands and power. The king will need his support in this war, and will not risk internal strife when there is a common enemy outside our gates. And the agreement between him and my father is of long standing; they made it when Arash and I were babies, and my father is set upon the match.'

'But it is hard on Arash,' Lila continued. 'I have heard that he is very shamed by his father's behaviour, and wishes to find favour at court himself so that his father's disgrace will not affect him as well. Perhaps he will take on his father's position – think how splendid that would be for you both! I have seen him riding to hunt, when the wild animals are let free from the paradise enclosure and the nobles go out with bows on their shoulders and falcons on their wrists. My mother has heard he has great skill with the falcons. And he looks so handsome riding out . . .'

I listened to Lila with one part of my hearing only; with the other, I strained to hear if the caged birds, further down the hallway, were singing. But the house lay silent, and the roar of the city was a distant murmur, blocked out by the thick mud and stucco walls. My ribcage tightened and I struggled to breathe.

'I must go and check on the horses!' I said, jumping to my feet. In my haste, I banged my boot toe against the foot of a stool, carved in the shape of a lion's paw.

'I will come over and visit you later,' Lila promised. 'Maybe we can go to the bazaar.'

'Maybe.'

Our friendship included the unspoken understanding that I would accompany Lila on her frequent trips to the markets. I kept her company while she lingered over earrings inset with emeralds from Egypt, over shawls and veils of finest Indian cotton, over sandals of turquoise leather stitched by hand with golden thread, over pots of cosmetics from Arabia. In return, she would help me to groom whichever horses we were keeping in our city stables. She had never complained about this, even when she stepped in dung or had a toe trodden upon. My loyal friend, she understood perfectly that without the horses I could not keep my spirit in my body, that it would fly over the city walls and lift off, like a hawk, into a high wind.

Now she rose gracefully from her couch; when she moved around, she made me think of a willow tree. 'If you don't feel like shopping, we will do something else instead. We can play tabula,' she said.

I nodded, and bit my quivering lips, and fled down the pale steps into the courtyard to let myself into the garden that lay between our houses. I hurried between the green rows of onion shoots, the sprawl of cucumber vines, and almost fell through the narrow door into our own courtyard. The mares swung to face me, startled from their mid-morning doze, and I drew a ragged breath and leaned against the wall, waiting for the hammer of my heart to steady. At this moment, they are safe here, I reminded myself.

I moved amongst the mares, running a hand over Tulip's rosy coat, over Grasshopper's long face, over Swan's river of neck. Their coats burned with heat under my palm and I glanced upwards into the dazzle of the sun, rising towards the highest point of heaven. In the pastures, the mares would have drifted under the poplar trees and been standing head to tail, swishing flies from both themselves and each other. Here, they stood pressed together, ribs to ribs, without shade. *It will be too much for them*, I thought. *I'll go and talk to my mother about it.*

At that moment, I heard the voice of Lila's mother, raised in shrill commands in our ground-floor kitchen. Our cook's assistant scurried out looking harassed and headed through the gate on an errand. Fardad's eyebrows, as he let her out, twitched up and down on his forehead in agitation. No, I could not go and talk to Mother; she was very ill, seized in the grip of fever and darkness, perhaps fighting with demons in her stupor. And Lila's mother was making the most of the situation, trying to be helpful in her fussy, breathless manner. I realised then, in that moment, that all those mares and foals and yearlings were dependent upon me alone; if they suffered hunger or thirst, or from the heat, it would be my fault. Mother could not care for a single one of them. Our city groom, and our country horsemen and their wives, were all in the hippodrome where the army camp had been established. In our household there remained only servants without knowledge of horses, and my sick mother, and myself. I stared into the mares' deep, still eyes and felt the weight of their dependency and trust settle on to my shoulders.

Squatting on my heels, I watched for long minutes while the sun beat down. The foals were restless, trying to leap and buck in play. The mares grew annoyed, jostled from their hot daze. They stamped their hind hooves in irritation until the foals finally lay down in the shade beneath their mothers' bellies, and closed their long lashes over their eyes. The yearlings were even more restless, their tails lashing in agitation at the droves of flies. They jumped when stung on the flank, barging into mares, earning themselves bites on the neck and rump, and giving voice to high squeals of pain and surprise. Sandy, our beautiful golden herd boss, shoved her way around the densely packed courtyard, trying to establish her place between the stable door, from whence the grain came, and the water trough.

They are all miserable, I thought; *they miss their cool rivers, their tall grasses. I must do something. When Mother awakes at last, she will be proud of how well I have cared for the horses on my own.*

Our stable had stalls for six animals. I brought Swan inside first and bedded her down in chopped barley straw. Then I led Sandy inside because she would think it her due, and because she was angry at continuously being jostled by mares of lower rank.

Next I led in Peony, who had suffered when her foal was born, and needed rest and special care. Her colt, a shining sorrel with a sickle moon on his forehead, skittered in beside her and began to nurse with blond tail flapping greedily. Finally I led in Grasshopper, Tulip, and Swan's yearling filly, Pearl. The courtyard was less crowded now but the heat was fiercer, beating up from the ground, pressing against the high walls. Not a breath of air stirred in that bowl of sunshine.

I tiptoed into my mother's dim room, the smell of incense and bitter herbs curling into my nostrils along with the sickly sweetness of her oozing wounds. She tossed and muttered in her tangled sheets, although I knew that Marjan had spread them tight that morning. 'Mother,' I whispered, but her eyelids didn't flicker. She would have given her permission though, if she could. I crept to the chest at the foot of her bed and lifted the lid on its bronze hinges, slipping my hand down under the blankets until I found the leather pouch of silver Bactrian coins. After slipping a few into the carrying pouch at my belt, I returned the rest to the bottom of the chest, and smoothed Mother's fair hair from her sweating forehead before running outside, happy now to breathe in the intense heat and the smell of horse dung.

With two of our household servants following, I hurried downhill through the city, passing women at the water fountains filling blue-glazed jars. The market square was as crowded as usual, but people were agitated and noisy, and I had to push my way through them to reach the fabric stalls. Bartering was agony for me, although Lila could spend hours doing it, sweet and fierce by turns, reeling the seller in like a fish on a hook until she had won. Meanwhile, I would hover behind her, silent, fascinated, and envious of her slippery, persuasive tongue. Now, as I stepped up to a stallholder selling bolts of cheap local cotton, my knees quivered with shyness, my tongue stuck to the roof of my mouth. Then I thought about the heat beating upon the mares, and forced myself to speak. My voice, at first small, gradually took on strength as stubbornly I forced the price of cotton lower. Afterwards, the servants carried the rolls under their arms while I purchased long pieces of lightweight rope from another stall. I found two boys of about eight years old kicking a sheep's bladder in an alley, and promised them coins if they would carry stones to my house.

'This big,' I said, gesturing with my hands.

'We will hurry to do this!' one cried, and they tore off, raising puffs of dust with their bare feet.

My tunic was damp with sweat when I finally trudged home again. 'Young ladies should remain inside, taking care of their households,' Fardad muttered as I entered the gate.

'Revered elder one, I am taking care of my household. These mares are the treasure of our valley,' I said quietly but he shuffled off, muttering into his wispy beard. 'And Fardad!' I called more loudly. 'I have a special task for you to carry out. Please?'

He turned back, his deep-set eyes impassive above the seams of his face.

'We will need more grain,' I said. 'And any other food that the mares can eat. If I give you money, can you go and buy food and arrange to have it transported here?'

'Do I look like an errand boy?' he asked gruffly, but he held out his hand. 'Give me the coins.'

'Buy any hay you can find; I saw some being brought into the city last night. Any barley or wheat or millet. Mutton fat. Eggs. Dates and raisins. Peas.' I searched my mind for any other food that our horses could survive on during this war. 'Chicken,' I said finally, and Fardad nodded, committing each item to memory, his bony old hand clasped about the coins.

After Fardad had departed, riding on the household mule, the two small boys arrived with a donkey carrying woven grass hampers filled with stones.

'Pile them here,' I said, and the boys unloaded the hampers while Iris, one of our grey mares, came over to snuffle her lips against the donkey's neck in curiosity. When the boys had left, I began cutting my rope into lengths with my dagger, and tying one end of each piece around a stone. I threw all these stones over the wall, into a grove of almond trees that stood in a strip of wasteground. Then I tied the other ends of the same ropes to the remaining stones, and threw them over into our garden. The ropes stretched tight above the courtyard, at the height of the walls, and formed a lattice. I called two servants from the house to help me, and together we cut up the cotton cloth into rectangles, and then we stood on overturned buckets and stretched the cloth rectangles over the rope lattice and began to fasten them in place with big stitches of thread.

It seemed as though we worked for hours while the mares stamped at flies, breathing softly. The cotton cast blocks of shade over the mares' backs, colouring their coats with mottled patterns of yellow and pink, green and blue.

'Thanks be that my honoured master is not at home to see this mess,' Fardad said when he returned.

'What did you find to buy?'

'One wagon of alfalfa mixed with fescue and feather grass, two sacks of peas, five sacks of grain, two sheep, and a crate of hens,' Fardad said, counting the items off on his crooked fingers. 'And dates and raisins.'

There was chaos in the courtyard as the goods began to arrive. Fardad stood in the middle giving orders while boys dodged around the overturned buckets where we still balanced, sewing. They carried the sacks and bundles of hay into the storage rooms but let the chickens and sheep loose in the courtyard with the mares. Afterwards, when Fardad had gone to the kitchen for a drink of tea, I left the women servants still sewing, and went to survey the store-room. How long would it be before the Middle Kingdom's army was defeated, beaten back from the walls of our city? And for how many days could I feed all those hungry mares with the food that my mother's silver had paid for? And how long would that remaining silver last when we also had to buy food for ourselves to cook and eat?

It was impossible to know the answers; I sighed wearily and pressed my hand to my aching head. Sewing had given me a knot in my neck.

I fetched a soft brush, made of boar bristles, and began to groom Swan. I wished that my father had come home before the enemy sealed off the city; that his booming laughter would fill the silence of the courtyard. I wished that my mother would rise from her bed and start striding around again. I even wished that my brothers were at home; I began to miss Jaison's mischievous teasing and the practical jokes he played on me, and the solemn kindness of Petros.

'But they're not here,' I said aloud, stroking Swan's ears. 'It's just you and me, and we have to look after each other. I'll keep you safe, I promise.'

Then I said no more, because my throat was tight with fear, and because I had already failed her by letting her become trapped in this place that must have seemed so strange to her.

Chapter 7

'Kalli?' called Lila's voice, and she slipped into the storeroom beside me. 'What have you done outside?'

'It's to shade the mares. Can you help with the sewing?' I asked, and soon we were both balanced on buckets, needles and thread in hand, a thin coloured shade falling across our faces.

'It will blow off on a windy day,' I fretted.

'It can be repaired. You had to do something. My mother says the Chinese sent a group to the gate today to propose a treaty, but the king rejected it. Our cavalry is riding out to attack at first light tomorrow.'

'We should go down to the hippodrome and see them leave.'

'Oh, I don't think I'd be allowed to.'

Lila's parents were far stricter than mine; every-thing had to be done according to rules of social protocol. A young girl should be kept mainly at home, unless attended by senior servants or family relatives. Going down to the east gate to gawk at soldiers riding to war was probably not on the list of activities that Lila's parents considered suitable for their unwed daughter. I, however, knew that Lila was much tougher than her delicate face and her antelope eyes made her appear.

'Perhaps we could just go for a morning ride; the mares need some exercise,' I suggested, and Lila's winged brows swept upwards as she smiled.

'Perhaps! I will come over early and –'

A loud rapping at the closed front doors made us pause, turning our heads toward the sound. Fardad came from the kitchen, stroking the long fringe of his moustache, to peer out of the small flap in the door.

'Who's there?' I called, but my voice was lost in the rattle of bolts as Fardad swung both doors wide with great haste before backing away with his eyes lowered.

My mouth gaped open. My knees turned to jelly and for an instant I wobbled on my bucket. Lila jumped nimbly down from hers and smoothed the folds of her gown, but I stood as though turned to a statuette. My voice lodged in my chest when I should have been uttering words of gracious greeting.

The entourage entered, scattering mares, chickens, and sheep that bleated nervously, as though calling for their mothers although they themselves were matronly. The lone rooster, that had been amongst the crated hens, flew upwards, crowing and scrabbling at my roof of coloured cotton. Everyone ignored him.

There followed a moment's silence that seemed to stretch on endlessly, pulled taut as a piece of horse-hair on a two-stringed guitar. And still my voice was lost, sinking deep into the depth of my being, into that dark pool of silence where I hid myself.

'Arash?' I whispered at last, a sound no bigger than the sigh a leaf makes when it lets go of a twig and falls through the air.

High on his palomino horse, he surveyed the chaotic scene without a flicker of emotion in his angled dark eyes. Even a rectangle of blue cotton, casting a coloured shade over him, could not diminish his haughty, aristocratic appearance. His narrow face with its fine, high bones turned towards me and instantly my gaze flickered away.

'Kallisto,' he said formally, 'is your honourable father at home?'

I opened my mouth, closed it, and licked my lips. *You look like a fool*, warned a voice inside my head. *Speak!*

'My f-father is away in the Levant, and m-my mother is wounded and in her bed,' I stammered at last, my voice so low that Arash had to bend his long, supple back, clad in a tunic of red velvet, in an attempt to hear it.

'She c-cannot see you,' I said more loudly, staring at the ground, at my boot toe nudging a pile of horse droppings, at the smooth front hooves of Arash's palomino, pale golden-white as seashells, and perfectly trimmed into curved crescents. I could not raise my head to look Arash in the face although my neck muscles seemed to strain in the effort.

The rough bare feet of one of his slaves stepped forward; I saw a blackened nail, and the dust between each toe. I saw the slave's bent back, and the moment when Arash stood on it to dismount from his horse. Then his boots, of leather so fine and supple that they seemed like living things, appeared in my line of vision as he came towards me.

'I am sorry to hear about your honourable mother,' he said, and his voice was so smooth that the words seemed to drip from him, like honey falling in perfectly formed drops from the end of a knife. I understood why my father talked about how beautifully he could recite Persian poetry.

'I shall send your mother a magus from the court later this evening,' he continued. 'Meanwhile, I have been given the honour of ensuring that the elite horses are indeed safe within the city. I am to carry a tally of them to the treasurer. The horses of our kingdom are its treasure, as even foreign rulers have made clear.'

I watched the feet of a groom as he stepped forward to take the palomino's reins. The slave stood upright again, and used one bare foot to shove aside a sheep that had come trotting past with a mild, inquisitive gaze.

At last, my shoulder muscles burning as though I had been lifting sacks of grain instead of my own head, I raised my gaze higher and stared over Arash's shoulder. The palomino was draped, from withers to croup, in a caparison of red velvet embroidered with gold thread in a pattern of roses, and perfectly matching Arash's riding trousers. Its bridle was of red leather, gilt with silver and inlaid, in the centre of the brow band, with an emerald. The rings of the snaffle bit were silver gilt, and also shaped like roses. In our city, the social status of a person was revealed by the trappings of the horse, the spendidness of its felts and bridle. Anyone could see, at a glance, that Arash moved in aristocratic circles, but it was not this that was holding my attention. It was the mention of our elite horses that had snared my focus.

'My mother is a free woman,' I muttered, my voice finding strength. 'All the horses here belong to her.'

'The treasurer has asked for a census, and I have simply come to tally them – with your permission of course.'

Was he mocking me? I darted a glance at his face but its aquiline profile betrayed nothing; his long narrow eyes held mine for a moment, then slid away. I noticed that he had begun to grow a beard since last I had seen him, and that his skullcap was crusted with pearls.

A servant moved at his shoulder as he paced amongst the mares, staring at them but saying nothing. There was something unsettling about his silence; when presented with a herd of our mares, most people gave exclamations of admiration and pleasure. The chestnut mare, Nomad, stretched out her nose to him but he brushed past it, ignoring her. My fingers curled nervously into fists.

'They are flesh and blood after all, and smell like common horses do,' he said at last, and flashed me a glittering smile that revealed perfectly even teeth. 'I do not see how they will carry the emperor to the celestial gates and the peach of immortality. Now, describe them for my scribe.'

For a moment I almost refused but Lila stretched her eyes wide at me, from where she stood in the shadow of the storage room doorway, and I began to speak. I gave each mare's name, her height, her age, her colour, and the scribe's brush flowed over the scroll of papyrus that a slave held for him, resting on a tablet of wood.

'I remember once seeing you, at some exhibition of mounted games on your mother's farm, riding a white horse,' Arash said when I had named every mare in the courtyard. 'But you were a child at the time; perhaps you no longer have her? Although I am sure that your father listed her in your bride contract. Where is she?'

'She's h-here.'

'And does not belong to your mother?'

'She is mine.'

'But yet, you are a daughter and everything that is yours is actually your father's to give away as he pleases. Only men can own possessions, or disperse them in contracts.'

'Swan is mine,' I repeated, stubbornness making me brave. 'She was given to me by my mother who owns all these mares.'

Arash raised his arched eyebrows as if I was a child, and looked bored. 'Let me see her,' he said, as if I wasn't worth debating with even though, at home on winter evenings, my father loved to hear me debate, on a topic of his suggestion, with my brothers.

Arash followed me into the stable. Swan gleamed in the dim light; her limpid eyes loosened the knot in my throat.

'White as a Pegasus in your father's Greek tales,' Arash said lightly, as though her beauty were an ordinary sight that didn't touch his heart. 'What a pity she hasn't wings to fly away and carry you over the enemy encampment. I hear that you like to ride far off, in the mountains. Is this true?'

I nodded, tongue-tied again. Who had told him about me and what else did he know? I didn't want him thinking about my freedom, my wanderlust; I didn't want him even looking at Swan and making her ears swivel with his smooth voice that was perhaps mocking, perhaps not.

'A mare as fine as this must have many beautiful caparisons,' he said. 'Put one on and bring her outside where I can admire her better.'

He strolled away; his slender strength was like the blade of a costly sword against the doorway's light. My fingers shook as I laid Swan's three best blankets over her withers and straightened them with a deft twitch. On top, I laid her very best caparison. Its quilted golden velvet was embroidered with white birds, blue moons, orange flowers. I myself had embroidered it on winter evenings, warming my feet at a charcoal brazier, when I should instead have been embroidering the covering for my bridal bed.

I ran my hands down Swan's shining face. Her soft nose pushed into my sweating palm as though to reassure me. I set her saddle cushions, covered in blue leather and embroidered with golden flowers, upon the blanket and bent to fasten the surcingle under the pale curve of her belly, the breast strap across her narrow chest, the crupper under her plume of tail. It was like fallen snow lifted upwards again by the wind. I fastened her two neck collars; they were of orange brocade sewn with beads of blue Italian glass. Swan bent her face as I held up her bridle, and opened her mouth as I slipped in the silver plated bit with its jointed snaffle bar. The little silver swans hanging from the cheek straps chimed faintly as Swan tossed her head. I smoothed her forelock downwards.

'Swan, come on, lovely girl,' I said, placing a hand

under her head so that she would follow me outside. She was a mare who could be stubborn, and would not move if you simply pulled on her lead rope but would dig in her front hooves and brace herself, leaning back against the rope. Only when I stood by her and spoke her name would she consent to follow; then, she would go anywhere beside me – into cold turbulent water, through rippled sand, down deep ditches, over fallen trees, through thorn bushes, through drifting snow. She would walk with her face almost touching my shoulder, as though we were companions, neither one leading or being led.

Now she followed me into the courtyard where Arash stood elegantly, surrounded by his retinue of slaves and servants. His palomino stood as though it were a horse carved from sandstone beneath its red velvet. I walked Swan around the courtyard and Arash watched with his eyes narrowed again. I wondered what he was thinking, why he wanted to see her outside. What else my father had listed on my marriage contract?

'Tell me about these elite horses that your family breeds,' Arash said suddenly.

I cleared my throat, encouraging my voice to break free. 'Swan is a f-fine example of all our Persian horses,' I began, my voice a murmur brushing against Swan's neck.

'What?'

I cleared my throat again. 'She has a double spine

like a tiger.' I ran my hand along the double ridge of muscle on Swan's back.

'Everything about her is long and slender,' I said, and my voice finally became strong. It was easy to talk about horses, even to strangers. 'Her body is long and narrow. Her long legs are dry and fine. Her slender neck is set high on the shoulder, and she carries it upright. Her head is elegant as a sculpture, with a straight profile. Her eyes are huge and shaped like almonds. She moves across the ground like a bird gliding on water. Everything about her speaks of endurance, and strength, and fire.'

I halted Swan before Arash, and the palomino's ears flickered forward.

'She is a fine sight,' Arash said pleasantly. Perhaps I had misjudged him, I thought. Perhaps he was trying to be friendly.

Swan took two steps closer, edging in with her nose outstretched towards the palomino. Arash's hand was like a snake striking fast; I barely saw it as he reached forward and slapped Swan's shoulder.

I heard Lila gasp behind me, before she muffled the sound with her hand.

Heat flooded my face.

'Take her back in,' Arash said, still pleasant, still dropping words like beads of honey. 'She is bothering my gelding, Desert Wind.'

I led Swan away, shaking as I walked and as I slid her saddle off. To strike another's horse was the same as striking the person; it was an insulting gesture. I spent a long time leaning against Swan, letting her breathe into my hair and rub her itchy nose on my back, until I felt calm enough to return outside.

Arash's face lit into a glittering smile at my appearance, and for an instant I thought that perhaps I had imagined the whole thing; that the heat and my aching head were responsible. Perhaps it had been a friendly slap such as anyone might give to a horse to make it step aside.

'My dear betrothed,' he said, the smile lingering at the corners of his mouth, his eyes remaining dark and unreadable, 'thank you for the names of your mares. Convey my respectful concern to your mother, and be assured I will send a magus by evening.'

'One has already c-come today,' I said, but Arash seemed not to hear me for he was already stepping upon the bent back of a slave and mounting Desert Wind. I watched as they went through the wide, double doors of my father's house, then Fardad was swinging them shut.

'Most improper when your esteemed parents are not here to receive him,' he muttered. 'Most improper.'

'I didn't invite him!'

Lila stepped out of the storage room doorway, her eyes lit up. 'He's so handsome!' she breathed. 'You are so lucky! My betrothed is pale and pudgy, not elegant and tall.'

'Thank you,' I said, sarcastic with misery. 'Perhaps Arash thinks the same of me: pale and pudgy.'

Lila hugged me, her armlets pressing into my back. 'You are beautiful,' she said. 'Anyone would think so, with your blue eyes and your black curls. And you are not pudgy, just lovely to hug. And I'm sorry.'

'He hit Swan,' I whispered.

'It was more like a hard pat,' Lila hedged, and I stiffened in her long arms. Then I thought that I didn't want to fight with my old friend because, when it came to handsome boys, she was irrational and I had to just accept this. Maybe she couldn't help it; maybe they made her feel the way a really beautiful horse made me feel.

'I should not have let him get away with slapping Swan.'

'Oh, but Kalli! Women must learn to hold their tongues and be submissive in the presence of men!'

'I wasn't hospitable,' I said. 'Was he mocking me when he thanked me? I should have offered refreshments.'

'You could not have invited him inside when your parents were not present!' Lila sounded so shocked that a tiny tremor of laughter licked through me. It was no use talking to Lila about such matters; she was not the child of a nomad who had fought alongside men, nor of a man who preferred to collect the horse myths of other nations, and recite them to his daughter, than school her in social etiquette.

'Tomorrow, come over early if you want to ride with me,' I said. 'I am riding near the east gate, when the cavalry go out.'

Lila nodded. 'I'll be here at dawn. Now I must go home for our evening meal. Do you want to come?'

'No, I must feed all the mares some hay, and then visit my mother.'

I waited until the garden gate had swung shut behind Lila, then fetched a rake and cleared the courtyard of droppings by scraping them into a pile at one end. Fardad said that the boy who emptied the latrines could move the droppings into the garden to rot. I hauled armloads of hay from the floor of the storage room, and dropped them before the mares. The more powerful mares began to munch the hay straight away but the lower ranking and younger mares milled around, nickering gustily, waiting their turns. I carried hay out until each one had her own small pile. Just this one feeding seemed to have used up so much of my supply. Perhaps tomorrow, I could take more coins from my mother's pouch, and send Fardad out again to scour the city for food. If the mares became too hungry, their milk might dry up and then what would happen to the foals?

I closed this horrible thought inside a box in my head, and went to wash the dust and prickly hayseeds from my face before going upstairs to see my mother. A waft of jasmine in the hallway alerted me to the fact that Lila's mother had been visiting; perhaps she had come to spy on the courtyard scene and carry home gossip about Arash. She was a woman who could sense the nearness of a social event in the way that a horse could sense the presence of a ghost.

My mother lay unconscious on straightened sheets. Her head lolled sideways on the pillow, and her skin looked dry as an autumn leaf. I stared in shock for she seemed to have aged many months in the space of a few days. When I touched her cheek with my lips, there was no response. 'Mother,' I whispered. I wanted her eyes to snap open, and for her to start questioning me sternly about my care of the horses. I wanted her to fling aside the covers and pull on her boots before striding outside. Would any of these things ever happen again? *Yes, they must!* How could I live without her? And how could her bold spirit remain caged in a sick body? I held her sweating hand, twisting her rings and feeling helpless, until Marjan came and told me that my evening meal was prepared.

After eating the rice, flavoured with basil and garlic, and skewers of braised lamb, I wandered though the house, restless and frightened. Our grand rooms with their high stuccoed ceilings seemed to echo my footsteps. My fingertips ran across the bright wall paintings of court life: tribute being brought to kings, a party of nobles hunting from horseback. An appaloosa showed off its spots as it reared up in the path of a roaring lion. Between the wall paintings, many precious objects reposed in wall niches: a copper hookah, candlesticks carved from the white bone called ivory that came from a huge animal in a country called Africa, and silver-chased drinking rhytons.

My favourite things in our house were the objects depicting horses that my father brought back for my mother and me as gifts from faraway places: the vases with chariot scenes, a bowl showing the god Poseidon riding a hippocamp, a wheel from the winning chariot at the last Olympic Games. Tonight, although I ran my fingers and eyes over all these objects, my thoughts strayed away in anxious turmoil.

Why had Arash come here today? Was he truly making a census of horses for the treasury, or had he lied to me? Why had he slapped Swan? Did he mind the fact that I liked to ride in the mountains, feeling no walls but grasses and sky? Was it true that his father had fallen from royal favour into disgrace? What was going to happen to us all?

Finally, to calm myself, I fetched a terracotta lamp filled with sesame oil, and looked in my father's chest of book scrolls until I found my favourite: *The Art of Horsemanship* by a man named Xenophon. My father had had a copy made for me in the city of Alexandria where there was a library with a great collection of texts. Stretching out on the rooftop, on my summer mattress, I pored over Xenophon's thoughts on training horses, by using kindness, until my vision blurred.

When I blew out the lamp, stillness settled over me. I could sense the hostile army, waiting out there in the darkness, gathering its strength. I wished that Swan indeed had wings like Pegasus, or like the great winged Heavenly Horse that the nomads talked of and that they believed was a protector of the people. My father said he had once seen a carving of a winged horse in an Indian temple, and once on a stone seal from the ancient civilisation of Mesopotamia.

When Swan galloped through the grass with me, it felt as though we both took wing and soared. I hoped that we would have that freedom again in our lifetime.

Chapter 8

The cavalry came down the road to the east gate with a thunderous roar of hooves. It was packed so tightly that the riders' knees were pressed between a moving mass of horses. Swan flung up her head in excitement, her nostrils sucking in deep breaths as she smelled all those strange horses. She sidled and danced in the side street where we had been waiting for sunrise so that we could watch the cavalry ride out. I gripped her with my knees, feeling her warmth through the quilted blanket, and the clasp of Lila's hands around my waist as she balanced behind me. All around us in the street, crowds of people jostled together, craning their necks to watch, and gave a great cheer as the massive east gates swung ponderously open.

The light cavalry was the first to pass by. The tribesmen wore leather armour sewn with scales of hoof and bone, and carried recurved bows slung over their shoulders. Their wood and leather quivers, painted with wild animals locked in mortal combat, bristled with arrows. Some of their sweating horses were protected with layers of heavy felt blankets stretched from the poll at their ears to the croup above their tails. Other horses wore leather and scale protection, and looked like strange monstrous beasts from foreign lands, or as if they were turning into marine creatures like hippocamps with scaly tails and horses' heads.

'There's Batu's father!' I cried to Lila, reining in Swan as she plunged restlessly around in the crowd. I flung out my arm, pointing as the black horse, Starlight, surged down the street; briefly I glimpsed the hawk profile of his chieftain rider. An image of Batu, waiting and waiting alone in a valley, flashed through my mind. Perhaps, in his bones, he felt the earth shiver as the cavalry of his people rode to battle; perhaps the skin on his face tingled as the sun touched it this morning. Part of me wished he was here, rushing fiercely down the street in the torrent of riders, but another part of me felt glad that he was far off in a place of safety.

I stared, fascinated, at all the horses trotting past, noting a strong leg, a cracked hoof, a nervously tossing head, a foaming mouth holding a cruel, spiked bit. Spotted, sorrel, black, golden bay, they passed me by, all those hundreds of horses with their bronze bits, their decorated bridles, their brightly embroidered blankets, their woollen tassels and jewelled neck collars. Their strength and willingness in the face of death.

I stared into the faces of the warriors swaying higher, above the horses' backs; some were fair-haired and pale-skinned; others were dark, swarthy, and tattooed with the strange black markings of various tribes. Several times I glimpsed the blue eyes and fiery red hair of Yeu-chi tribesmen. Women rode in that long procession too, their hands calloused on the reins, their bows slung over their shoulders, their eyes alight and intent. This is how my mother would have looked, I thought, and felt an ache of pity for her, trapped in the sweet stench of pain-relieving opium and her own feverish sweat.

Pouring beneath the high arch of the east gate, the tribesmen shook tambourines of horse skin, and gave long, high battle cries that stopped my heartbeat and made the hair stand up on my scalp. Lila's hands tightened on my waist, and Swan swung around so wildly that her hindquarters collided with a doorway. Someone in the crowd gave a shout of alarm.

Now the rising sun glittered on the chain mail that protected both the men and the horses of the heavy cavalry, and on the tips of their long lances. These troops were mainly aristocrats. 'Look for Arash!' Lila shouted in my ear but I didn't see him although I strained for a glimpse of his golden gelding. The heavy cavalry passed out through the gate, beating kettle drums that made their horses plunge and jump in nervous excitement, and that made the doves on the battlements take wing, scattering across pale blue and golden sky like flurries of almond blossom.

The infantry marched in the cavalry's wake, rank upon rank of peasants and serfs armed by their masters with swords and daggers. Camels rocked past, bellowing in complaint, and laden with extra supplies of bronze-tipped arrows.

'We will be free by sunset!' shouted a man standing at Swan's shoulder, and the crowd around us took up the shout. 'Free by sunset!' they roared, as the east gate swung slowly shut again behind the last troops, and as the doves drifted back upon the battlements to strut and coo. The sunlight poured over the city walls, bathing us all in warmth, and shining upon the cheering faces.

'We will ride down later and watch them come home!' I shouted to Lila above the din, and then I wheeled Swan around and we began to ride through the marketplace. When we slid off Swan's back in the courtyard at home, Lila's mother rushed out of the house with her gown fluttering in agitated waves around her plump legs.

'My dear girls, where have you been?' she cried shrilly. 'The city is filled with strange troops, wild men from the tribes! Traders! Stranded caravan leaders! You must stay safely at home in these dangerous times! Lila, go home immediately and do not leave the house again today! I forbid it!'

Fardad turned away impassively, his eyebrows still for once, and rattled home the bolts on the front doors. Lila slid her hand down Swan's face and slipped a ring of dried apple between the mare's soft, wrinkled lips. Then she smiled at me and darted away through the garden with her mother trotting after her, still scolding.

Later, in the heat of the afternoon, when I knew that her mother would be dozing on the cushions of a high, padded couch, I slipped quietly into Lila's house to find her. We climbed to the rooftop which offered the same view down the valley as did my own.

'They are fighting through all the city's gardens, and in the surrounding fields,' Lila mused. 'It is true that Angra's dark forces make the land barren, and curse the crops.'

Side by side, we leaned our elbows on the walls encircling the roof, and stared into the shimmering heat haze and the golden dust that rose above the battlefield. It was hard to discern details: only the surge to and fro of dark blocks of fighting men, the wheeling sweeps of cavalry like the sweeps that birds make against a pale sky. Lila was right; they were trampling the millet shoots, splashing through the rice fields, flattening the early wheat. Even if our forces beat back the Middle Kingdom's army, it would leave a swathe of destruction in its wake.

'No one is winning,' I said softly, my hand rising to grip the pouch of leopard's fur that hung always at my throat. For a moment, I remembered the warm roughness of Berta's hands as she fastened it there.

'I don't want to watch any more,' Lila said. 'Let's play a game.'

We sat on the beautiful red and yellow flowers of a knotted carpet, and laid out the tabula board on a low wooden table with an inlay of mother-of-pearl. Lila said it had come from India, and for a moment I traced a finger over the picture of birds with huge tails. Then we laid the tabula board, with its pattern of black triangles, on top of the birds, and began to play with the ivory pieces.

'A hair comb against . . .' Lila raised her thin, arched brows.

'Your brooch with the foal,' I wagered.

For a long time there was only the rattle of dice in the wooden box, their clatter as they fell on to the board, the click of the gaming pieces, the shriek of a bird, and the muted, distant roar of the army fighting far off below the city walls. Sometimes a breath of air rustled through the topmost leaves of the apricot trees standing in the wasteground beyond my house, and briefly made the cotton awnings above my courtyard billow. Sometimes the breeze carried the note of a trumpet or the scream of a falling horse, and I would feel the sick lurch of my stomach. Then the wind would die again, and my fear would grow heavy and dull, leaning its weight on my sweating shoulders.

We waited and waited all through the long afternoon for the moment when the great rabble of the Middle Kingdom's army would be pressed backwards, away from our walls, and would flee out of the broad, shining bowl of our golden valley. But it didn't happen.

'Maybe tomorrow,' Lila said wistfully as the sun sank into the emptiness of the west where our valley opened out into shining sky. The Alay Mountains on the southern horizon had become stiff purple walls against the waning light, like mountains painted on with a brushstroke, and the haze above the battlefield was cloudy as a bruise. From the edge of the roof, I could see how the bright threads of irrigation ditches were clotted with bodies, and broken chariots, polluting Ahura's sacred water beneath the drooping willows.

Lila stacked the ivory gaming pieces back into their case. 'You lost your wager; you owe me a hair comb. Are you going down to the gate?'

I nodded. 'I'll come over later and tell you about what I see. Which comb do you want?'

Lila considered; I knew she was thinking about the various items tossed haphazardly inside the jewellery casket that stood, on its golden feet, inside a wall niche in my bedroom. Not even the war could dampen her interest in acquiring something pretty and new.

'The comb with the amber stones along the edge, the one from the northern sea,' she said at last, and I nodded in relief. For a moment, I had feared that she might ask for my favourite, the ivory comb with the head of a white mare carved into it.

The streets were crowded as Swan and I rode down to the east gate, weaving between goats, children, dogs, slaves, traders, and women carrying jugs of water from the fountains. Although Swan was accustomed to running free in my mother's pastures, skimming clumps of flowers the way that a bird skims clouds, she was an excellent mare to ride through the crowded city. She and I had spent so many years together, twisting and turning across the flat dust of the training grounds, threading through poles and executing spinning turns, that she could be ridden now without even a bridle if I chose. Every portion of her sides was sensitive to me; to the slightest squeeze of a leg muscle, the slightest nudge of a boot heel. At mounted games, she was an expert: swift, attentive, capable of stopping so fast from a gallop that her hocks bent beneath her; able to spin so quickly that her tail hair was still flowing in one direction when her body had already taken off in a new one. Now, in the crowded streets, I guided her easily, as though we were playing a different game together. Her elegant pricked ears swivelled constantly, listening to sounds from all around us: the hammering of blacksmiths, a man shouting at a dog, a donkey braying mournfully.

When we competed in games, Swan's ears waited for the shouts of applause. She loved to win, and would arch her neck and toss her long face.

We found a position against the walls of the caravanserai, as the crowds thickened in anticipation. Quietness hung over the mass of people waiting; the exuberant cheers of the morning were silenced, and the faces below me were sombre. Women clutched at amulets hanging from their necks, and muttered prayers beseeching for the safe return of loved ones. The great gate swung open slowly, creaking, revealing a tiny portion of purple sky, the first wink of starlight. The troops entered in clots and groups, light and heavy cavalry mixed together; exhausted infantry staggering amongst them. Camels limped alongside. Horses bled from shoulder and neck wounds, staining their felt blankets with blossoms of red flowers, and stumbled with fatigue in a lather of sweat. Reins hung slack from their mouths. The warriors drooped on their backs, quivers empty of arrows, bows lost or broken. Some warriors carried tails, cut from the horses of dead enemies and tied into their sashes or on to their saddle blankets. Once I glimpsed a horse trotting along with neither a rider or bridle, its saddle blanket strapped on backwards to signify that its rider had died. Some comrade on the battlefield must have taken a moment to do this last act in honour of a tribal brother. In peacetime, no one would ride such a horse ever again but I knew that in time of war, all traditions changed.

Swan stood still beneath me, watching the ragged flow of the troops pass by with her eyes sombre and her head low. Perhaps she smelled the dust and fear in the sweat of the horses; perhaps she had listened all day, in the safety of her courtyard, to the surge of their panicked hoof beats. As the gates swung shut, she carried me home at a slow trot, her pale neck a shimmer in the lamplight falling from windows and doorways. An owl hooted in a walnut tree as we turned into our own street and for the first time, I was glad to hear the bolt rattle shut behind us as we rode into the courtyard. I was glad that Swan had nothing to do now but eat hay, and sigh sleepily through the long afternoons; that the worst that could befall her was boredom.

After that first day inside the besieged city, my days fell into a strange routine that blurred one into the next. Every morning, as the sun rose into a clear sky, I raked the horse droppings into a pile for the latrine boy to haul to the garden. The horses that had spent the night in the stalls, I led outside. Other mares were led in, to spend the day in the chopped barley straw. In the cool of the morning, the mares were lively; they whickered greetings to me, brushed my arms with their whiskered noses, and pushed each other around as they waited for their breakfast.

I rationed out the food; on some days, the mares chewed hay, grinding it slowly with their wide back teeth, looking as though their thoughts were drifting far away in other places. Sometimes I fed them dried peas soaked in weak wine, or handfuls of dried dates that made them slobber brown, sticky juice. Lila complained that my mares were ruining all her gowns because they kept wiping their mouths across her shoulders. Our cook killed the hens, and made kebabs for the servants and me to eat. The chicken bones were boiled to create a broth, and I soaked millet in this and fed the mares a thick porridge in copper buckets and in ceramic bowls that I took from the kitchen when our cook wasn't watching.

As the sun rose higher, and the mares finished their food, they became dozy. By midday, the sun hung high in a sky burnished like a bronze mirror. Heat held us all, human and animal, as though we were shamans entering a state of trance. Heat distorted our vision: buildings and trees shimmered as though turning to water, and heat pressed upon us, making us thin and insignificant. It was the hottest month that I could recall, and the driest.

'My mother says that Apaosha, the demon of drought, has come with the enemy army,' Lila said one day. We were sitting side by side on the carpet, with our legs pushed beneath a vertical loom on which was stretched a rug with a floral design. Lila was supposed to be finishing it to add to her bride-wealth, and I was helping her out of friendship, although sitting there made me feel fidgety and gave me a backache.

'Perhaps your mother is right,' I said, and I imagined Apaosha mounted on his black stallion, galloping up and down our golden valley in a cloud of angry black dust, such as desert storms raise into the air. I thought of how the kettle drum of that stallion's hoof beats would ring from the mountains.

'Wind, Rain, Clouds, and Sleet,' I recited the names of the four grey horses of the goddess Anahita, divinity of waters. These greys pulled her heavenly chariot; I thought that perhaps now, as Lila and I sat weaving, those pale and beautiful mares were being stampeded over the horizon by the demon's angry black stallion.

I called their names again later in the day when I climbed on to our stable roof to check on the water cistern. I called softly, as though I were cajoling shy young mares in from the pasture, as though I longed to run my hands down their dappled faces, over their smoke-soft muzzles. The level of water in our cistern, usually replenished by rain, was sinking lower. Surely Anahita's four chariot mares would take pity upon their sisters trapped in the courtyard, and would bravely sweep over Ershi, dragging the clouds around their hooves. I climbed down from the roof and watched helplessly as the mares sucked up long draughts of water from their trough, dribbling it on to the baked mud of the yard. For how much longer could they drink this water, when no rain was falling to fill the cistern with its cool sweetness?

'Wind, Rain, Clouds, Sleet!' I called softly again, like a prayer, and tipped my face to the sky. In the cracks between my cotton awnings, it remained a hot, brassy blue.

In the late afternoons, I stood amongst the mares with a fly whisk. I flapped and swished its long plume, made from the hair of horses' tails, across the legs and bellies of the mares. They stamped and fidgeted, tormented by stinging bites. One windy afternoon, my lattice of ropes and cotton broke loose as ropes became untied from stones, and cotton became unstitched from rope. Three servants balanced on the walls, holding it down, while Lila and Fardad and I worked from below, making everything secure again. The spooked mares circled the courtyard at a trot, snorting nervously and stirring up clouds of gritty dust that filled our mouths and stung our eyes.

Then it was time for the evening feeding, for me to pace the length of the storeroom, gripped by fear as supplies diminished. Fardad complained, when I sent him into the city, that there was no more hay to be found, and that the prices of all foodstuffs were spiralling upwards even as the coins dwindled in my mother's pouch. One evening, Fardad slaughtered a sheep, and we all ate mutton and vegetable stew. The next day, when the meat had cooled, I cut off white, congealed fat and mixed it with barley and raw eggs to form balls that I could feed to the mares.

By the time that darkness fell, the sky turning purple above the battlements of the city wall, it was time for me to rake the dung from the courtyard again, to rotate the mares from the stalls into the yard. When true darkness fell, I stood alone on the rooftop, watching the myriad fires burning in the enemy encampment like fallen stars. I thought about Batu, wondering if he and the two year olds were safe in the valley, and how long they would wait there for me. How Gryphon's wounds were, if they had healed. I ached for Batu's fierce, flashing joy, and for Gryphon's elegance and speed.

Often, I would sit beside my mother, holding her hand. Sometimes she opened her eyes and stared at me without knowledge, sometimes she tried to speak to me but the words made no sense, or were in her childhood tongue. On other occasions, she slept in a drugged stupor, burning with fever. The magus that Arash had sent came every day, chanting hymns in my mother's room and waving his bundle of larch twigs while Marjan sat patiently, waiting to smooth the sheets.

Outside in the city, crowds flocked to the fire temples, while the magi in their white robes made sacrifices before the sacred and eternal flames, symbol of Ahura Mazda's power of light. White doves, unblemished oxen, crates of chickens, donkeys, bleating lambs; all were brought to the altars and sacrificed as the priests entreated Ahura for power and help in defeating the enemy that encircled Ershi. The smell of burning hung heavy in the still air.

In peacetime, the human dead of Ershi were carried outside the gates to lie in the ground of sky-burial where the grave maker dogs, and the vultures, could pick their bones clean and let their spirits rise into high heaven. Now, in this time of war, this was no longer possible. A temporary sky-burial ground was created in unused land beneath the aqueduct's many-legged shadow on the city's western side. Columns of vultures rode the afternoon air in great looping spirals above it like campfire ash rising aloft. The grave maker dogs ran in ragged packs through the alleys, bloated and drooling.

Then there came the day when the water stopped running.

I had ridden Swan, with Tulip alongside on a rope, to the hippodrome for exercise. The great oval track was packed all night long with troops, with felt tents and campfires and lines of exhausted horses, but today the army had ridden out to harass the enemy, and to destroy their catapults. The hippodrome's expanse lay quiet. I circled it, keeping the mares to a steady trot that raised a light pinkish sweat on their necks and shoulders. I remembered the races that were run here in peacetime; the flash of chariot wheels, the blur of horses' legs eating up the ground, the roar of the crowds, the frenzied betting. I remembered the great moan that rose from the crowd when a favourite horse went down, or a chariot veered from the track. Even my brothers, who cared little for horses, knew the names of the winners. Now only the shadows of my mares drifted alongside me, and only the drumbeat of their eight hooves marked the passage of the afternoon. Swan's hot smell wafted into my nose; to someone else, she might have simply smelled like a sweating horse, but to me she smelled distinct and individual. I could find her in a horse herd in darkness simply by pressing my face to her neck and breathing her in.

At home again, I put her into a stall to cool down, and wiped her off using a sponge from the Mediterranean Sea, and a leather bucket holding water scooped from the trough. I fetched her a handful of millet from the storage room, and noticed how low our supply of food was running. Fardad was asleep in the kitchen, sitting on a stool with his back against the wall, his toes poking into the ashes of the cooking fire, his moustache rising and falling in the light breath of his snores. I smiled to myself, and slipped out of the front gate to run downhill to the market and bargain for grain. One hand clutched the few small coins remaining in my supply; only the price of slaves was falling in this city because no one wanted the expense of feeding them.

At the bottom of our street, a crowd of women had gathered at the fountain. I ducked my head in shyness and hurried around the fringe of the group with my eyes averted. When someone called my name, I hesitated. A servant from Lila's house broke free of the crowd and rushed over to me, her face creased with agitation. 'The water has stopped running; the fountain is empty!' she cried, and then she turned abruptly and began to hurry homewards. I craned my neck, looking past the other women's bright tunics and robes, and saw that the stone basin, which usually brimmed with fresh water, was empty and only slightly damp. The stone dried in the hot sun even as I stared at it, becoming chalky and pale. The women scattered like wind-blown leaves, their high voices carrying the news through the streets. I hurried on, my skin crawling with fear. Everywhere I went, the same alarm met me.

In every street, stone channels usually rushed with clear mountain water that was carried into Ershi by the aqueduct, and was stored in the reservoir before pouring like life-blood down through the city. This water was carried home in jars to cook stews, wash babies, water goats. But now, in every street I ran through, the stone channels were all empty. A strange silence replaced the usual gurgling rush of the water, the splash of fountains. I hadn't realised, until now, how water's music was a sound like a warp thread on a loom, holding the city's tapestry together.

'The enemy has stopped the water from running over the aqueduct into our city!' cried a man in the marketplace, grasping at the long curls of his beard as people crowded around him. 'The water that is in our reservoir now is all we have left! The king's guards have surrounded the reservoir to protect it.'

After that, I ran home and climbed on to the roof of the stable block and stared down into the water in the cistern. My distorted reflection stared back: the dusky oval moon of my plump face, the tangle of my black curls, the bright chips of my blue eyes. The ripples of worry that crawled across everything. I jumped down, sweating, feeling the sun suck moisture from me.

'What has happened?' I cried, bursting into the kitchen where our cook was slicing cucumbers from the garden and dropping the pieces into a bowl of goat yoghurt.

'They say the enemy has diverted the river's flow, and changed the course of the irrigation canals,' Fardad said, looming in a corner, his eyebrows shooting up and down in agitation. He pulled his dagger from his belt and began to trim his fingernails, nicking himself and starting to bleed.

'Is it true, about the water?' I cried, bursting into Lila's house and interrupting the evening meal. Her father nodded glumly, reclining on one elbow on his couch in a tunic of green and purple stripes. He wiped his lips with a piece of flat bread.

'There is no more water flowing into Ershi,' he said. 'Even the small river flowing along the western wall is nothing but a bed of dry gravel. The aqueduct is empty. The king's guards will ration out the water that remains, so much for each household.'

'What about the wells?' I cried.

'There are only a few, along the base of the hill,' he said. 'They are already low from this dry weather, and will soon run dry especially now that there is no other source of water. Soon, there will be so little water in this city that even gold will not be able to buy it. People will die for water, and for its lack.'

He nodded gloomily over his salad of chickpeas, his thin face carved with lines. Lila flashed me a terrified glance from her couch, and her mother wiped her sweating forehead with a linen cloth and dabbed at her trembling mouth.

'This is terribly frightening,' she whispered. 'This is a terrible time for us all.'

'But the spring! Outside the caravanserai there is a spring!' I cried.

'Only the troops may use that water for their horses. The king has posted guards around it,' Lila's father said.

I spun on my heel and flew home. The mares stood patiently, back feet lifted, as they dozed with lower lips hanging, and waited for their evening feed. Their trusting gazes turned to me. I stared into the water trough, and felt weak with fear.

'They will have drunk this water by morning,' I whispered. 'Mother, I don't know what to do.'

Chapter 9

I could smell myself as I rode Grasshopper behind Lila through the marketplace. I felt as though everything with which I had come into contact in the last two days had left a scent upon me. In my hair lay the bitterness of herbs from my mother's room; on my hands the sweat of mares and the sweetness of foals; in my tunic clung the cooking oil from the kitchen; all over me lay a miasma of dust. Water flowed through the stone channels, from the reservoir, for one hour each sunrise and sunset. Soldiers guarded the fountains and, at the decree of the king, each household could fill only two jars for its cooking and drinking needs. For bathing, there was nothing left over, and the city's bath houses stood silent and empty. Households with elite horses might fill buckets so that the horses had just enough to keep them alive, at least for the time being; no one from the mighty king to the lowest slave knew when the siege would end. Or who would be victorious and might claim the horses, if they had survived that long. It was fortunate that our Persian horses were renowned for their ability to survive on small rations of water, even to endure several days without it.

'I need perfume,' I muttered. Lila, riding ahead on Iris, laughed, turning her head.

'And I used to complain when you smelled only of horses,' she said, reining around a man trying to sell carpets from a stack beside the stall of a coppersmith.

Now that the mares had little to drink, I no longer trotted them around the hippodrome for exercise, for I didn't want them to lose moisture through sweating. Instead, if a mare was restless, I took her out for a slow amble through the streets, stopping in the shade of walnut trees to rest. Today, Lila had won her mother's permission to accompany me, and was wearing her prettiest trousers and tunic in an attempt to be cheerful despite the columns of vultures wheeling so high overhead that they were black specks in the brilliance, and despite the stink rising from the city drains. Lining every main street, they were normally flushed with waste water but now they were clogged with debris: bits of rotting flesh, dry bones, fallen leaves, dog faeces, droppings from donkeys, bird feathers.

She must hate this even more than I do, I thought, watching Lila's tall, slender back as she rode along.

The sun shimmered on her blue brocade tunic and on Iris's quarters.

'Wait!' I called, spotting the stall I had been looking for, and Lila reined Iris in under the shade of an awning. I slid from Grasshopper and began to bargain for a jar of sesame oil. I had used all the oil in my terracotta lamp, reading Xenophon's *Art of Horsemanship* on the rooftop when I was too frightened to sleep in the dark silence of my room. *'The horse should trust people, knowing that they are the providers of food and water,'* I would quote in a whisper, drifting off to sleep at last beneath the stars.

While the stallholder haggled over his price, clutching two different sized jars of oil, I saw something move furtively in the corner of my eye. A skinny brown arm came out slowly from beneath the stall. Bony fingers reached tentatively towards Grasshopper's legs. The mare stamped at a fly and the fingers froze into stillness. Then they reached out again, further, straining to touch the mare's black knee.

'Which jar, young lady?' the stallholder demanded, and I stared at his swarthy face, his dark eyes burning deep in their sockets like coals from a fire.

'Your price is more than I can afford,' I muttered, trying to muster my bargaining courage. I cleared my throat. 'I will find another oil supplier,' I said more loudly.

I glanced downwards again; the fingers had reached Grasshopper's foreleg and were stroking it with a touch so light, so gentle, that I understood why the mare was now standing absolutely still despite the flies.

'For you, this large jar for the price of the smaller one – a gift in this time of need, a great gift and one I can ill afford with my many children to feed, may Ahura take pity upon them and –'

I bent down and peered beneath the stall. The thin arm shot backwards. In the gloom, the face of a slave girl tilted towards me, her lips sucked in as she waited for my reprimand, or perhaps for a slash from the plaited riding whip hanging from my right wrist. Even in our cosmopolitan city, her appearance was strange and foreign. Her hooded eyes were chips of blue in her sallow, pointed face, beneath the matted tangle of her dark hair.

'You like my horse?' I asked in Persian.

She ducked her head, her eyes cast down, her bony fingers tracing patterns in the dust. Was it her strange eyes, or her silence, or the gentleness of her touch on Grasshopper's leg that intrigued me the most? I squatted, the embroidered hem of my tunic trailing on the ground, and stared at the girl.

'You like my horse?' I asked again, using a Turkic tongue. Her gaze flew up at me, a brief shine like a glimpse of sky on a cloudy day, and then she bent over again. I saw that she was tied to the stall's wooden supports with a rope, and that it had chafed her ankles raw and dry. Flies crawled in her hair.

Was it because my mother had once been a slave in the markets of Tashkent that I straightened, and gripped the startled oil seller by one of his own wrists?

'I will take the slave child,' I said. 'She must be worth as much as a large jar of oil.'

'But my wife, my honourable wife, needs her to help in the kitchens!' the man protested, clutching at his skullcap. His deep-set eyes blazed with the thrill of a new bargaining tool. 'My wife is run off her feet with work, may Ahura bless her and keep her, for she has so many children! And this girl is a great necessity and cannot go with you.'

'And yet I hear that it is very hard to feed slaves in this time of war,' Lila said sweetly at my shoulder, her face bright with a dazzling smile. 'Surely this is a good time to take coins home to your wife, and to save your oil for another buyer.'

The man paused, caught off-guard by Lila's sudden appearance and her wide, limpid eyes with their fringes of thick lashes.

'My lady friend is in sore need of a slave, for her dearest mother is fighting with demons, and her honourable father has abandoned them.'

I stifled a snort of laughter, and bestowed upon the oil seller what I hoped was a smile at least half as dazzling as Lila's. There was a scuffle at my feet as the slave girl pulled herself out from underneath the stall and began to stroke Grasshopper's face; I could feel the love that made her dirty hands loose and soft, and that warmed her flat gaze. She scarcely looked at me as I pressed the coins into the man's hands, or as I hugged Lila in thanks before leading Grasshopper into the shade of an elm tree. Untied now by her oil seller, the girl followed us with one hand laid against Grasshopper's ribs, and I realised, seeing her standing upright, that she was older than I'd thought. Her head reached to my shoulder although she was as thin as a stray dog.

'How many birthdays have you had?' I asked and she lifted her brittle shoulders in a shrug.

'Eleven? I don't know,' she whispered, staring at the ground.

'Where is your tribe? Speak louder so I can hear you.'

She cleared her throat and began to speak like a child reciting a lesson. 'My mother was a subject of the Son of Heaven, and taken from the border of the Middle Kingdom and sold as a slave. She journeyed through the northern sea of grass and gave birth to me but my father was a chieftain who disowned me. I was taken in a tribal war two summers ago and brought here to Ershi to be sold.'

I nodded, understanding her strange appearance and those hooded, angled eyes. 'And now the army of the Middle Kingdom is at our gates,' I said. 'Do you wish to join them and return home?'

'I have no home,' she said listlessly, but I saw how her eyes lit up again when Grasshopper swung her head around and sniffed curiously at her bare arm and the shoulder of her ragged tunic.

'Fardad is going to kill me,' I muttered to Lila, and she laughed and climbed on to Iris from a stone mounting block at the roadside.

'You still have to buy oil before you return to face his wrath,' she said. 'Let's hope you haven't yet spent all your mother's money. You know your mother won't have slaves in the household.'

I nodded, and swung on to Grasshopper who gave a small leap, almost overturning the stall of a tea seller, his urns shining in the bright sun.

'Watch out for my wares!' he cried in alarm.

The slave child did not jump away in fright when Grasshopper leaped; she moved quickly beside the mare, as if she were a foal keeping pace with its mother. I gave her a puzzled stare.

'You can ride?' I asked.

She nodded, gripping my saddle's leather foot loop in her fist, her blue eyes flickering over every detail of Grasshopper's saddle blanket, the saddle's leather covering embroidered with stars and heads of grain, the bridle with its reins of shagreen leather that I had repaired myself using a bronze needle. Her fingers traced the mare's five-pointed brand.

'From your herd?' she asked and I nodded. 'My father's people had many horses, horses like the wind,' she said, and then her mouth folded in a tight line, and her soft eyelids swept down.

'Walk on,' I said to the mare, and we wound our way after Lila, with the slave girl keeping step. She was still gripping the foot loop when I rode Grasshopper through the open gate at home.

'Honoured child!' Fardad bellowed, rushing from the storeroom with his tunic flapping as I dismounted. For one moment in time I thought that he was bellowing because of the ragged stranger standing stiff as a twig at the mare's side, and then I realised that his cheeks were ashen above his wispy beard, and that his eyebrows had disappeared beneath his skullcap.

'I couldn't stop him!' he wailed, clasping his old hands, with their tracing of blue veins, together. 'Your father's household guards are all away fighting! Marjan tried to rouse your mother but she wasn't able to! And you were not here to prevent it! She has been taken!'

Something like a bolt of lightning flickered through me. The taste of sulphur burned my tongue. The light dimmed as though a storm cloud passed before the sun. I knew then, before Fardad said another word, that something had changed in my life, that something terrible had occurred.

'Swan?' I whispered, my throat closing around her name as though I could keep it safe there.

Fardad nodded; behind him, our cook and two servant girls and Marjan stood in a semicircle, staring at me with long, compassionate faces.

'It was your betrothed, Arash. He came with his

retinue this afternoon while you were in the market. And took Swan away.'

'Where? Where did they go? Where?'

My voice, usually so soft that people had to ask me to repeat myself, bounced around the courtyard like a pebble ricocheting off the mud walls. Doves rose in protest from the rooftop and spiralled upwards. The slave girl moved away from me, drifting amongst the mares with her hands touching each one of them: fondling their muzzles, their silken tails, their shining coats. In all that golden gleam, there was no flash of white, no shine like cool water, no eyes to greet me.

Oh, Swan!

Lila had her arm around my shoulders but I barely noticed.

'I don't know where he took her,' Fardad said, tugging at his thinning beard in his agitation. 'I don't know why he wanted her.'

I snatched at Grasshopper's reins so fast that the mare swung her head up and away, her neck tense and her eyes rolling white. I leaped into the saddle without using the foot loop, my heels kicking into her ribs even before my weight had settled fully on to her back. I wrenched her around in the courtyard's confines, scattering mares and foals. The stricken faces of the servants, Fardad's wild rheumy eyes, Lila's open mouth as she cried out, and the slave girl's curious, flat gaze all spun around me in a whirl. Then the mare's front hooves were through the door; I heard her tail lash against the frame as we shot past and as I pulled her head northwards and drove her uphill at a gallop. The hard pounding of her hooves alerted people ahead of me so that they scattered to the sides of the street, calling out alarmed questions. Their voices were like bird calls, meaningless, insignificant.

I kicked Grasshopper onwards as she faltered and she gave a soaring buck across a drainage ditch, and galloped hard and fast, her back flattening out, across a stretch of wasteground beyond. We careened around the corner of a fire temple, the pillars on its portico flashing by, pale as the trunks of trees in a birch forest. Hens scattered around us like leaves. The mare snorted loudly but kept galloping, her powerful hindquarters driving us uphill between the houses of merchants and bankers until we were against the very walls of the inner citadel. We shot through the archway into the outer courtyard of the Royal Falconer's sprawling house, knocking aside two porters who ran after us with their daggers drawn. The mare skidded on her haunches, her nose inches from the solid doors that led to the second courtyard, and I leaned over her shoulder and hammered upon the door with my whip handle.

The porters with their drawn daggers were beside me, reaching for the mare's reins. I swung my whip in a circle. 'Keep your hands off!' I shouted, and collected the mare under me, making her hop and leap sideways across the courtyard. They stayed outside the range of her slashing hooves.

'Open the door!' I shouted. 'The honourable lady Kallisto of the House of Iona is here to see your master's son!'

I kicked the mare hard as the doors began to move and we barrelled through the crack like a fish going between rocks in a canyon's torrents. The porter sprawled backwards, clutching his cap as it slid over the back of his curly black hair. I wheeled Grasshopper in a tight circle on the paving stones laid in a pattern of golden and black around the pomegranate trees. My voice echoed from the stuccoed walls painted in brilliant colours – red, white, yellow – and carved into flowing designs. The porters and guards, still with their hands on their dagger hilts, stared at me, dishevelled and desperate in my grubby tunic, my oldest boots, and alone without a single servant or family chaperone.

'Our master and his son are fighting with the cavalry,' one said at last. 'Will you wait in the reception hall and take a cool drink?'

'Arash is not fighting, and I will wait,' I said, glancing upwards to where the last rays of setting sun kindled the palace's rambling facades into brilliance. They led Grasshopper away after I gave instructions for her to be groomed and fed; then I stepped inside the first reception hall through which I had entered this house once before, on a feast day, with my parents. I paced the hall's cool length. I stared at its walls with their paintings, tapestries, and niches filled with marble busts of kings and statuettes of goddesses.

A servant woman brought me a tray holding a bowl of melon soup flavoured with cardamom seeds, and a damp cloth to wipe my hands. I ate and drank in a daze for I had become a stranger to myself. I was freezing cold as though it were winter and the wind was blowing down over the Alay Mountains with snow in its wings. My skin crawled and shivered.

Swan, oh Swan.

My heart pounded, slowed, raced onwards. My boots paced past the leg of a couch piled with cushions and bolsters. I skirted a great wooden chair carved with stags' heads and twining antlers; I rounded a table inlaid with sheets of coloured Italian glass. I ran my hand over the wall hangings depicting hunting scenes and the coronation of the king; foreign princes waited to give him a tribute of horses. They were smaller than our Persian horses, I thought, staring at them for a moment, noting their short legs, their height in comparison to the chariot they pulled, four abreast. Then I paced on again.

Swan!

Night crept in the doorway, lay down over the pomegranate trees. The light of oil lamps fluttered over the black and golden tiles. My head spun with fatigue and fear, and time stretched out endlessly, a sea where I was adrift; alone and lost without my white star, my white mare. I clutched dizzily at my shoulders, my arms hugging myself.

'Kallisto?' Arash strode in, his bodyguards at his

heels. His head was high, his back stiff and straight in a robe embroidered with semi-precious stones. Light winked on the gilt scabbard of his dagger slung on a belt with a golden clasp. His beard seemed darker in the flickering light.

I flew at him. 'Where's my mare?'

'Calm yourself. Be seated on the couch.'

I ignored him. 'Where's Swan? Tell me! You have no right to take her.'

'His Magnificence, King of Ershi, Crown Jewel in the Golden Valley, has need of her,' he said smoothly. He folded himself elegantly on to a couch and took a dried fig from the tray that the servant woman held out. I spun around in my restless pacing.

'His Magnificence, the king?'

'We are at war with the rabble from the east. All over the city, our magi are sacrificing to the Great Holy One, to Ahura Mazda, creator of every good thing, keeper of the light. What greater sacrifice, dear Kallisto, than a white mare without blemish? Imagine her, clad in her costly caparisons, led to the altar flame by the priests of the king's temple in the palace courtyard! Such a sweet smoke would arise to heaven, don't you think? Surely then the king and his cavalry would win the support of Aruha Mazda, and we would win this war.'

I stumbled against the table, knocking over the bowl from which I'd eaten soup. The thin ceramic, fired to a high temperature, shattered at my feet, sending fragments flying in every direction. I tried to speak. My voice was lost. I clutched at my throat with both hands, and stared at Arash in stricken silence.

'You understand, don't you?' he asked at last. 'You and I, Kallisto, can give the king what he needs most at this moment. We can bring great honour to him, and obtain great blessings from the Supreme Being. Perhaps we can bring victory to the city, and we can find favour. All I need to accomplish this is Swan.'

My throat pulsed beneath my clutching hands. My voice broke free in a shriek. 'She is not yours to take, or to give!'

'But she is. She is part of your bride-wealth, listed by name in your marriage contract. So she is mine to take, and mine to give to the Most Revered King so that he might sacrifice her. I will speak to the magi tomorrow and make the arrangements. You do not have to trouble yourself with the details.'

'She is not yours to take!' I shouted, my voice breaking into sobs. 'You cannot do this!'

'But I already have, and when your father returns from the Levant he will give you to me in marriage, and you will have to obey my wishes. In the meantime, Swan is housed in safety until the sacrificial ceremony.' He gave me a mocking smile and continued, 'You know what your nomad friends say? *If you have two days more to live, take a wife and a horse. If you have only one day left, take a horse.* Who knows how many days we have left to live in this war? So, I have taken a horse.'

He jumped to his feet as I rushed at him with my fists up and dodged me, shouting for his bodyguards. Although Jaison had taught me to wrestle, and although I could shoot an arrow through a straw man at fifty paces from a galloping horse, I could not fight off three men grabbing my arms from behind. Although I struggled until I thought my blood would explode from my head and my heart burst from my ribcage, I was steered out of the door and lifted on to Grasshopper. She lurched forward, snorting, as men hauled on her reins. At the front gate, someone smacked her across the quarters with a whip. She surged out into the street, already galloping as I fumbled for the reins and braced myself for a downhill plunge under dark trees. The high walls around opulent homes threw the crashing echo of hoof beats back at us, and the face of the half-moon lifted clear of the palace and shone down, pale as a white mare.

At home, it was the slave girl with the blue eyes who took Grasshopper's reins, who led her away into the rustling barley straw to feed her and stroke her into calmness. It was Marjan who guided me upstairs with her hand pressed hard in the small of my back, who kneeled on the rug to yank off my boots and push me on to my bed, throwing the covers over me. All night, while the moon rode the sky, I tossed and moaned, fighting with demons of fear and grief the way my mother fought in the room down the hall.

Chapter 10

'But perhaps this is the Great One's will,' Lila said, sitting on the end of my bed with her brows creased in a worried frown. Her long fingers smoothed the damask coverlet edged with fox fur, and her earrings glinted in the morning light. 'You know that a horse sacrifice is the most powerful one of all. And that a white horse without blemish is the greatest offering one can make.'

I nodded, my face swollen with crying.

'The army of the Middle Kingdom is ravaging the valley, laying waste to all the crops. And Ahura Mazda has commanded that we till the land and make it fruitful. It is the forces of Angra, the evil one, that make the land barren. And the evil one has brought the drought to us. All of the horses in this city will die if we don't get water soon. Perhaps you can stop this from happening if you give up Swan.'

I wiped my nose across the back of my hand, smelling the sweat in my tunic sleeve. I tried to think about all the horses milling restlessly within the confines of the city walls, growing thinner, hungrier, thirstier. I tried to visualise all their foals, tugging at dried teats, flapping their fuzzy tails in agitation as their bellies shrank and pinched.

All I could see was Swan's face, her pools of eyes.

A fresh sob broke from me. My throat was raw with crying. Lila moved closer and put her arm around me. 'Maybe giving up Swan will win you a place with the great angels,' she whispered.

I moaned. 'I just want – I want Swan free and safe, I want her resting beneath the poplar trees in my mother's pastures. I just – *want her*!'

Lila stroked my tangled hair. The slave girl, bought yesterday from the oil seller, hunched on the red and black rug at the foot of my bed and sneaked glances at me. Perhaps she had slept there all night; I hadn't even noticed her until now.

Something tugged at my mind, like a fish nibbling at bait. I tried and tried to catch that slippery thought but it kept darting away. It was a memory of something that Arash had said last night in the reception hall. Suddenly, it flashed into my mind, hooked, bright and shining.

'This is not about Swan, or about saving the city!' I exclaimed. 'This is not about pleasing Ahura Mazda, or about right thinking. This is about Arash's desire for power in the royal court.'

'*We can find favour,*' he had said in his voice like beads of honey. I knew, suddenly and with firm conviction, that this was what Arash wanted. He didn't care about saving the horses walled in Ershi. He wasn't concerned about appealing to Ahura Mazda, Creator of All, so that the tide of war would turn and sweep the enemy from the valley, or so that Angra's demon of drought would be chased away by Anahita's four grey mares, Wind, Rain, Clouds, Sleet.

'It is *favour* that he wants,' I said, staring into Lila's eyes. 'He wants to win his way back into the king's favour because his father is in disgrace. Arash is clever and ambitious, your mother has said so. And now he thinks that giving Swan as a gift to the king will ensure his own rise to power within the court. He thinks that Swan's sacrifice will wipe out the stain of his father's drunken wager. I am sure of it!'

I kicked my feet free of the coverlet and strode to the window, almost tripping over the slave girl's legs.

'I must go to Arash again and demand Swan's return! My father is still master of this house and Arash has no right to take Swan before I am married to him!'

'I don't know,' Lila said with a sigh. 'Perhaps Arash is only doing what he thinks your father would have done if he was at home. Perhaps offering up your most precious thing is what is required. My father says that the people of Ershi must fight hard to ward off the evil forces, and to struggle against them. Perhaps Swan is a weapon in this battle between angels and demons . . .'

I turned on my heel. 'She is my mare, she is my protector and my totem; Berta said so! No one can give her except me, and I do not choose this sacrifice!'

I stared out of the window, trembling with doubt and anger. I waited for the sky to break open, for a thunderbolt to strike me dead for my rebellion, my selfishness, but the sky remained a clear, tender blue above the rooftops of the city. A gentle breeze wafted through the apricot trees, carrying with it the muted roar of battle. Did I hold the power to turn aside the destruction of the valley? Perhaps it for this very reason that Swan had been born in the summer of my birth, a foal so beautiful that people cried out in delight as she drifted through the flowers like a white petal, a swan's feather. I clenched my fists against the pain of these memories.

Swan!

'Perhaps the angels are trusting you to make this wise decision,' Lila said.

'Swan trusts me! Swan needs me to save her! And Arash has done this household an injustice.'

Lila rubbed her forehead, perplexed and troubled. She knew, as well as I did, that falsehood and injustice were part of the evil Angra's great Lie. If Arash was part of this, how could my sacrifice of Swan set the balance right?

Beneath my window, the cotton awnings – becoming faded in the bright light – flapped gently in the breeze. The slave girl scratched at a scab on her arm.

'The white horse comes from heaven,' she whispered, her head bent over her knees. 'It is your protector. So it is believed in my father's tribe.'

I stared at the knobs of her spine and the sallow skin on the back of her neck. 'What is your name?' I asked her.

The knobs on her spine moved as she shrugged. 'In this city I have been called Sayeh.'

I knew she would not tell me her true name, her tribal name. 'Ask Marjan for some salve for your sores,' I said.

'Even if Arash's thinking is not true, your own could be,' Lila persisted. 'Even if Arash wishes to win favour, you yourself could still give up Swan to help in this fight against the evil one and his dark forces.'

'I do not choose to give her,' I said stubbornly. Lila stared consideringly at the set of my jaw. She had known me all my life.

'Poor Swan,' she mumbled, for she had known Swan for as long as she could remember too. We had often ridden on Swan together, our four legs hanging over her satin sides, our faces filled with wind as she stood in the irrigation ditch behind the valley stables, drinking long draughts of mountain water. Once, Lila had come off over Swan's shoulders at a gallop and Swan had stopped so fast that she scored long lines in the dirt, and she had bent her neck down and breathed gently on Lila's face until she broke into laughter despite the bruises on her chest.

Now Lila's eyes brimmed suddenly with tears. For a long moment our gazes locked together.

'You cannot go to Arash looking like this,' she said finally with another sigh. 'You are not doing this the right way. You must go to him wearing your finest clothes, and your jewels, and with your hair combed, and you must speak softly and prettily to him. You must beseech and cajole him. I'll help you get ready.'

She swept across to the wall niche, hung with a covering of embroidered fabric, and began to look through my clothes. 'Nothing but tunics smelling of horses,' she complained, but then she found a tunic and trousers so new that I had never worn them yet. My father had bought them from a trader returning from India through the high passes of the Hindu Kush, and they were made of lightest silk, that magical fabric guarded by the kingdom far to our east. We had no trade routes to the east for silk, and could obtain it only when it was sold into India first. No one knew how silk was made, whether it came from an exotic plant or the hair of some fabulous, foreign animal. It was a fabric so light, so liquid, that it lay upon the skin like water or like summer air.

'This is what you will wear,' Lila decided, holding the clothing up and inspecting it, running its folds admiringly through her hands. The silk was dyed palest green, like the green of new leaves unfurling to hide the singing birds, when the apple trees blossom. The collar, front and hem of the tunic were embroidered with silver thread, and sewn with hundreds of tiny blue beads and with white pearls, forming a pattern of vines and stars.

'Prepare your mistress a bowl of warm water, and a cloth,' Lila said to the slave child.

'There isn't enough water to wash –' I protested, but Lila clapped her hands together gracefully, and Sayeh hurried from the room. 'You cannot go to beg for Swan smelling like drains,' she said. 'You must wash your hair too. And you must beg and not demand.'

By the time that I had gone downstairs and washed in the bath room, Sayeh and Fardad had fed the mares a portion of millet each, and the girl was running a curry comb over Thunder's grey dappled sides, sweeping it in gentle circles.

'She must go and wash too,' Lila commanded. 'You cannot go riding around alone – it doesn't look right – and you must take her with you to Arash.'

The sun was already high in the sky before everything was arranged to Lila's satisfaction and I climbed upwards through the city again, riding on Nomad and with Sayeh following behind, seated obediently on the household mule.

'Slaves must walk!' Lila had exclaimed in shock when Sayeh led the mule, curry combed to a high gloss, from the stable.

'My mother will not allow me to keep a slave,' I had reminded Lila. 'So I have given this girl her freedom, and she is to be my body servant. You know that my servant left this spring to marry a camel driver. Sayeh will replace her.'

Nomad's hoof beats, and the hoof beats of the mule, fell muffled and dull in the dusty streets. They echoed from the fire temple's pale pillars that had gleamed in the moonlight last night like birch trees. My headlong rush on Grasshopper seemed like something that had happened a long time ago; now, it was like the confused memory of a frightening dream. I had felt filled with burning courage then, and an anger that lifted me up the side of Ershi's hill towards the palace complex as a wind lifts an eagle aloft towards the highest crags. Today, in the glaring light, I felt drained and emptied of everything but fear, despite my pale green finery, my swinging earrings and necklaces of silver and lapis lazuli that Lila had lifted from my jewel casket, and the forehead jewellery that trembled over my eyebrows as I rode along. Lila had combed my hair, curling my ringlets around her fingers, and given me jasmine perfume to rub on my neck, and had spent far too long dabbing cosmetics on to my face.

'Look!' she had cried finally, holding up a bronze mirror. My face had floated in its dull sheen, the face of a beautiful stranger, coloured, jewelled, and with huge blue eyes filled with trepidation.

Now the smell of my perfume mingled sicken-
ingly with the stench of the dry drains, and a lizard
scuttled from beneath Nomad's hooves into a crack
in a high wall. The closer we approached to the house
of the disgraced Royal Falconer, the worse I felt.
Everything seemed to float around me, and I was
turning into a mirage, a shimmer of fear. What would
I say when I came to the gate? Could I make my
voice clear and high like Lila's as I asked for entrance
to the reception hall, and could I make it sweet and
soft when I begged Arash for Swan's life? And what
would I say, what words could I use? Shyness seized
me, like a stray dog seizing a hen. *I cannot do this*, I
thought, *but I must.*

For Swan.

I glanced back over my shoulder; Sayeh had
washed in my leftover water, and Marjan had cut the
tangles from her hair and combed it out straight, and
found an outgrown tunic of mine, faded but clean,
for her to wear. She rode the mule without thinking
about it, her body flexible and loose, although when
she stood on the ground and was spoken to, she was
as stiff as a twig. I saw her lean forward and fondle
one of the mule's great ears with its pale fringing of
long hair.

We were almost there now. I wiped my sweating
palms on my thighs, and then gripped Nomad's reins
more firmly. Her mane had been shaved off to reveal
the splendid arch of her neckline, and her jewelled

neck collar glinted in the light as she paced towards the high arch of the first courtyard.

Two guards stepped in front of us, and I saw, as I reined my mare to a halt, that they were not the same men who had witnessed my humiliation the previous night. For a long moment we stared at each other, my tongue frozen against the roof of my mouth.

'I wish to speak . . .' My voice was a sigh of summer wind against the stuccoed walls. Heat flooded my face and the jewels trembled on my forehead. I cleared my throat and took a deep breath in.

'I wish to speak with the honourable Arash, your master's son,' I said more loudly.

The men shook their heads, their long black beards scratching across their tunics. 'He rode out on a sortie at dawn with the heavy cavalry. He is encamped in the hippodrome and will not return to this house tonight.'

I stared at them; were they lying? Should I ask them about Swan? What could I possibly say that would make them disloyal to their master?

'You are s-sure he is not here?' I asked at last, and they stared back at me impassively, sternly.

'He is encamped in the hippodrome,' one repeated.

Behind them the walls surrounding that great house soared skywards, throwing the heat on to us. Nomad pawed restlessly at the ground, and I tugged on her reins, wondering whether Swan stood some-where very close, straining her ears to hear her stable mate, fidgeting restlessly in a stall, wondering when I would come and bring her home. If Nomad neighed, would Swan hear the sound? If I called her name, would she respond with a gusty whicker of recognition, a high joyous whinny?

'I have come about a horse,' I said softly, and smiled at the guards although my lips trembled. 'Arash has said that I might visit a mare that is in the stables here.'

I smiled again, but the guards stepped towards me, their hands on their dagger hilts, and Nomad shifted two steps backwards.

'We cannot allow you to enter,' one of the men said. My gaze flickered across the grim line of his mouth beneath the great plume of his black moustache, and fell to the tips of his shining black boots.

'I will-wait for-the honourable Arash in the-hippodrome,' I said, my words running into each other in their reluctance to fly free of my mouth. Nomad wheeled around, and the mule swung its ears and fell into step behind the mare. All the way down through the city my heart beat heavy and slow, like the sound of hoof beats when a horse is very weary. The hippodrome's expanse was quiet; women sat cross-legged on the ground by small, smouldering fires, and shaped dough into flat bread or stitched at embroideries. Here and there a lone horse, perhaps too lamed or injured to ride out, stood with its head hanging. I found Arash's tent at last; it was crimson and splendid, and deserted save for an old servant who sat on the ground outside, stitching at broken harness, and who said that I might wait for his master's return. Sayeh and I tied Nomad and the mule to a tent peg, and ducked inside to where it was slightly cooler and dimmer. Cross-legged on the thick carpets, I stared at the wall hangings, at the bed of a fine, shining wood inlaid with mother-of-pearl. I wiped at my sweating face with the back of my hand, smearing the black lines of kohl that Lila had applied so carefully around my eyes.

The afternoon trickled past, sand moving grain by grain. Occasionally, a dog barked. A horse stamped. A baby cried fretfully to be nursed. The old servant man laid aside the leather and his needle, and fell asleep in the tent's shade.

Had Swan been watered this morning? Had someone run a brush over her, lightly and with love? Or roughly and in haste? Had she been fed; was she cool and comfortable or tied up outside in the blistering sun, plagued by flies?

What was the point of it, all those hours that I had spent training her, teaching her to wheel and spin, to gallop flattened out, to canter collected beneath me, her muscles coiled tight? Why should it all come to this, her death at the base of a flaming altar in the king's courtyard, where nobody knew her stories, her skills, her memories?

My mother said that a horse could remember

everything as well as a person could; that if you struck or mistreated a horse it would remember you all of its life and mistrust you. She said that a horse had only to be ridden once along a mountain track and, years later, it would know its way there, would know where to place its hooves to avoid crevices and fissures. She said that a horse had only to find its way to a pool of water on a hot afternoon, or to watch the running of wolves down a ravine in winter, to know those places again. The water it would always know how to find, and the wolves how to avoid.

But I was the keeper of all Swan's memories, and now we had been separated. The magi in their long white robes would not know anything about her. They would not know that they must speak her name to make her walk forward towards the moment of her death. And would she look around in that moment, searching for me, for my familiar figure that had run to her through so many years of dust or rain, through drifting snow, through summer's ripples of heat? Would she wonder why I had deserted her before blackness engulfed her?

I bent over my knees and clasped my ankles, gripped with anguish.

But what if Lila was right, what if this was Swan's destiny and mine? What if it was to save the city from Angra's wrath that we had both been brought into this world, and what if we had some role to play in the great battle between the armies of darkness and light? If I withheld Swan, if I failed in this moment of sacrifice, would the enemy kill all our brave riders, all our galloping horses? Would they scale Ershi's high walls, break its massive gates? Would they be the victors at last, and take all the elite mares, the fiery stallions, the trusting foals, homewards with them over the roof of the world, past the dread Taklamakan desert where nothing lived, nothing flew?

What would my fate be then? When I died and my soul stepped over the bridge to paradise, would the great angel Sraosha cast me down into the abyss to be tormented for ever? Was the sacrifice of Swan what the great Ahura needed and desired? Did I believe this was the right thing to do?

I remembered the words of a hymn that the magi chanted on feast days:

> Hear with your ears what is best, perceive
>   with your minds what is purest,
> So that each man may, for himself, before
>   the great doom cometh,
> Choose the creed he prefers.
> May the wise ones be on our side.

But what was the best thing for me to choose, trapped in the heat and torment of this moment?

'We are all turning on the great wheel,' my father had said once, stroking the long curls of his beard, and sprawled on a couch after an evening meal. 'We are all trying to find our way to the power in the middle. There are many religions on earth, just as there are many spokes on a wheel. You can walk in any way, but the purpose of them all is the same. I do not care whether a man walks in the path of the Buddha, or the great Ahura, of the Tao, or the prophet Abraham. Or whether a man follows the spirits of his tribal rivers and mountains, or the Hindu gods and goddesses. The ways are all spokes on a wheel, carrying us towards the power in the middle of life.'

Oh, Father! I thought, as the light faded across the hippodrome, and a hen clucked near the door of Arash's tent. *Father, where are you now when I need you, when you should be here to speak for me, to save Swan?* I ached for Father's great belly laugh, his huge ringed hands laid warmly on my shoulders; even for his deep voice calling me his plump dove, his ripe peach. I had no doubt, suddenly, that my father would have saved Swan if he had been here. He would have gone to the Royal Falconer and persuaded him, with the finest imported wine from the island of Rhodes, with purses of chinking coins, with food and dancing girls and laughter, and even with Greek philosophy, to return my mare. My father would have done this because I trusted him to.

The way that Swan trusts me, I thought.

In that moment, all my doubts dissolved,

snowflakes on hot rocks around a fire. I knew suddenly that Swan's trust was more important to me than the desires of angels, than the spokes of wheels.

I rose to my feet and went past Sayeh, curled asleep on the rugs, to the tent doorway. The old servant stooped over a small fire of dried camel dung, cooking skewers of meat. 'They will return soon,' he said, glancing up, and even as he spoke there was a commotion near the entrance. Straining my eyes through the purple dusk, I saw the slow swell of troops and horses. They eddied in amongst the tents; voices called, harness chinked, a horse neighed. Fires winked into brightness all around as the moon rose. Still I waited and waited for Arash. The old man removed the crisp meat from the flames and the fire began to subside into embers that pulsed in the velvet night.

'Arash?' I asked uncertainly.

He ducked into the tent, a dark figure, alone save for a slave boy who squatted by the dying fire. Sayeh slipped from the tent to join him. The glow of a lamp blossomed and the tent shone like a pale red flower. When I entered, Arash was seated on the bed, staring at the floor, his shoulders drooping in lines of fatigue beneath the glint of chain mail. I had never seen him look this way; his handsome face was dusty and stained, his eyes bloodshot, his hair matted with sweat. A long, dull indentation lay across the shoulders of his armour as though he had been struck a heavy blow with a lance.

'They have taken him,' he said listlessly. 'They unseated me, and Desert Wind has been taken by the enemy.'

Even his voice was flat and dull; there was no honey in it.

'I am sorry,' I said softly, and he glanced up, startled; perhaps he had thought it was his old servant who had followed him inside. His eyes widened, his glance flickering over my pale green tunic, my necklaces and earrings, my best riding boots with their pale blue leather stitched with overlays of green leaves and orange birds.

'What do you want?' he asked.

I knelt at his feet, the lamplight flickering over us, over the wall hangings with their still figures, over the crimson creases in the tent walls, over the length of Arash's aquiline nose.

My mouth opened, closed. My voice was lost.

'P-please,' I said at last, staring at the toes of Arash's boots. 'Please.'

I could not speak another word; the one I had released trembled into the peak of the tent like a little bird fluttering in a blind panic. Arash raised his thin brows and stared at me.

I gathered my courage 'Please, g-give Swan back to me. I cannot live without her.'

The lamp guttered in a draught of night air, and the tent shook around us like a poppy in a field of bending grass. Arash gave an impatient gesture, and his chain mail made a tiny scraping sound. I could not raise my head to meet his proud, fierce eyes; I could not force another word through my tight throat. The night and the tent seemed to hold us as though a spell had been cast upon us.

'Please. I beseech you.'

He rose, paced the tent, sat again. 'He was my best horse,' he said. ' I will miss him very much. I'd had him since a colt, and trained him myself. He went out with courage this morning. We rode on a sortie from the south gate, but the enemy was waiting for us with huge crossbows that could shoot arrows continuously. They had a great range. Many men were killed today, many horses. It was not splendid, Kallisto, not like hunting lions, not the way the poets tell of it.'

I risked a glance up; his face was in profile, and his eyes were far away like the eyes of my mother when she thought of her lost tribe. Grief made him look much younger, like the little boy he'd once been and who I had shared a pomegranate with, speechless with shyness, at a feast day. Now light shone on his high cheeks, bright as tears. Pity fluttered through me.

'My father is in disgrace,' he muttered suddenly. 'You know this?'

I nodded, unable to speak.

'I must find a way to return my father's house to favour. If we fall from grace, what will become of us all, my parents, me? To you, Kallisto? The gift of Swan will restore us.'

'What – what did your father do?'

'He had come by a golden treasure, a wonderful chariot harness with bridle and traces and belly straps and chest collar. It was all covered in gold, and in carvings of wonderful animals, and it was inlaid with precious stones. It was very old. The merchant from whom he obtained it owed my father his life, because my father had saved him from a lion while out hunting. Thus the merchant parted with the treasure. Then, my father promised the harness to one of the princes, one of the king's royal sons. But before he had the harness delivered to the prince, my father lost it in a drunken wager. And so the prince was cheated of what he had been promised, and my father was disgraced.'

Arash sighed, and rubbed a long hand across his face, and squeezed his eyes shut above his narrow, beautifully shaped lips. The red tent walls reflected in the metal links of his chain mail with a dull glow.

'What if we could f-find the other harness?' I asked.

'What? What other one?'

'S-surely there must be another, a m-matching one, so that the chariot could be pulled by a team. If we could find the other harness, we could give it to the prince, and your father would be forgiven, and you would find favour and –'

My throat squeezed my voice into silence.

'And what?'

'And I c-could have Swan back again. You would not need her then.'

He gave me a stern, searching look that lasted for many minutes. Hours even. My legs shook, folded beneath me, and the blood rose to my face.

'How would you find this treasure?'

'I don't know . . . I could t-talk to the merchant that your father obtained it from . . .'

Outside, a horse and man walked by, and the half-moon rose into the tent doorway where Sayeh squatted in the dirt, watching and listening. The old servant man coughed and spat, and Nomad shifted her weight restlessly from foot to foot.

'If I give you the merchant's name, and you can find the treasure and bring it to me, I will give Swan back,' Arash said at last. 'But only if the prince is pleased with the gift. And only if you can bring it to me quickly.'

'And Swan?'

'She will be safe and well cared for until you bring the treasure. I will not speak to the magi about her sacrifice yet.'

'Swear it!' I cried, my voice suddenly strong, my fingers gripping the toe of one of Arash's riding boots. 'Swear you will not harm her, and you will return her to me if I can bring the treasure!'

'Let go of my boot.' He kicked out suddenly, the

tired lines of his face hardening into a more familiar haughtiness; I felt the burn of leather across my fingertips.

'Swear it, Arash. Please.'

'Before Mithras, god of oath-taking, I swear,' he said. 'The merchant's name is Failak and he came from Kokand. Before the war, he was lodged in a household below tower number ten on the east wall. But I don't know where he is now. I will give you five nights from this night to obtain the golden chariot harness – if it even exists – and bring it to me here.'

'Eight,' I whispered, my voice quaking.

'What?'

'Eight nights to bring the golden harness.'

'Five.'

'Seven.'

He glared at me, his eyes narrowed. 'Seven nights. After that, your mare will be sacrificed. Now, go away; I am very tired.'

Chapter 11

Although it was fully dark as I mounted Nomad and rode from the hippodrome, with Sayeh following on the mule, I wanted to begin searching for the merchant.

'Your own household will be worried about you,' Sayeh muttered.

'I can't help it!' I replied obstinately. 'Finding this golden harness is my only hope of saving Swan's life! We will ride to the street beneath tower number ten on the east wall.'

The streets grew narrower as we rode downhill. Lamplight spilled from doorways, and dogs barked and fought over refuse. A smell of dust and drains filled my nose, and Nomad picked her way fastidiously, snorting at children who dodged past, shouting and playing. Now the city wall rose up on our right hand, a looming mass that blocked out the stars, its mud surfaces still radiating the afternoon's heat. And on the other side, I thought, the enemy waited, starving us out, prowling, impatient, implacable. Soon our last water would run dry; soon we would have to surrender unless our troops could rout the enemy and send them eastwards into the mountains without our horses. I shivered, and the hair stood up on my arms. Here, at the base of the wall, the enemy seemed very close.

I could see the watchtower now, its high rectangular shape rising against the face of the moon. The arrow slits covering its facades were invisible in the darkness. I swung Nomad into the street running towards the tower, and became aware of a roar of grinding, smashing noise.

'What's happening?' I asked suddenly, reining Nomad in. The mule's pale muzzle bumped against her hindquarters as Sayeh and I peered ahead. Torchlight flared and bobbed over the backs of men shovelling bricks amid swirling clouds of mud dust. The sound of pounding and smashing filled the air. Buildings gaped open, their roofs destroyed, their walls tumbling down as men attacked them with vigorous blows. Wooden doors splintered. Three camels strained in their harness, roped to roof beams, and a wall suddenly gave way, its mud and bricks pouring into the street in an avalanche of rubble. The camels coughed and roared as the roof beams crashed downwards. Dust obscured them.

'They are destroying this street!' I cried, dumb-founded. People jostled around Nomad; women's wailing cries pierced the crashing of walls, and children blubbered in their mother's arms.

I turned in the saddle and leaned out to grasp the shoulder of an old woman shuffling past, her arms filled with a cloth bundle. 'Please, what is happening?'

'They are breaking down our houses, and destroying our temple!' she cried. 'The enemy is tunnelling beneath the wall, trying to make the tower and the wall crumble down so they can breach it and enter Ershi. But our men are filling this street with rubble. It will be piled against the wall on the inside, strengthening it against enemy attack. I must find my daughters!'

She hobbled away into the fluttering darkness, and I continued to sit on Nomad, watching in horrified fascination as men attacked homes and craft shops with swinging mallets, pickaxes and shovels, battering them into nothing but heaps of broken dirt. A string of donkeys jostled past me, their panniers laden with rubble that would be shovelled against the base of the city wall.

How thick was the wall? I wondered. How far from me, at this very moment, were the enemy troops? I imagined them digging down into the sandy soil, like mountain marmots, tunnelling underneath the wall's bulk and into our city, into our safety. I imagined the enemy men pouring inside like water pouring through an aqueduct into a pool.

Chills ran down my spine and I wheeled Nomad around in a tight circle. 'The house I'm looking for is gone,' I said, my voice stricken. How would I find this merchant, Failak, now? And where had he gone to lodge?

'It is too late to be out,' Sayeh said, her small face pinched and tired. 'We cannot keep searching tonight. The streets are dangerous.'

I nodded and nudged Nomad in the direction of home, past clusters of soldiers staggering along with their arms around each other's shoulders, singing a ragged, drunken chorus. I averted my face as they blundered past, one of them running a hand familiarly across Nomad's shoulder and then my leg. I kicked out with my boot, my beautiful pale blue boot with its leather embossing of orange birds. The soldier's eyes widened in greedy admiration and he gripped my boot and tugged, laughing wildly. Torchlight shone like sparks in his red beard and long tangled hair. He was a Yeu-chi, I realised, and remembered that the people of his tribe believed they would be horses in their second life.

'You are touching an elite Persian mare,' I said, leaning over Nomad's shoulder to catch the man's swinging blue gaze. His grip on my boot eased as his eyes focused on Nomad's arched neck, and his touch suddenly became gentle and calm as he ran his hand, calloused from bowstrings and reins, over her flanks. Then we had passed the soldiers, and they descended the street with ribald laughter. I nudged Nomad into a trot, dodging drains and elm trees and shadows until at last we reached the safety of our courtyard where Fardad bellowed an angry welcome. 'Half the household is out searching for you!' he cried. 'And this mare is in a sweat!'

'I will tend to her,' I said. 'Stop fussing. We are not harmed.'

Sayeh and I twisted barley straw into wisps and rubbed Nomad and the mule dry and clean before staggering into the kitchen for a late meal of stew made from stringy goat, onions, and pumpkin. Afterwards, I lay in my linen sheets, my body humming with fatigue, but my brain whirling with thoughts of a golden harness, a tumbling wall, a wave of enemy troops rising over it. With thoughts of Swan; her pale face somewhere in the gloom of a secret stable with guards posted at the door. *Seven nights*, I thought over and over.

Seven. I cannot fail.

For two days I searched the city for the merchant called Failak. I knocked on countless wooden doors, some smooth, others carved in geometric designs; some painted blue or yellow, others plain wood weathered by sun and dusty wind. With Sayeh beside me, I waited in endless reception rooms and court-yards; thirsty, impatient, and clutching on to my hope as it shrank in my grasp, becoming weak and small, and frightened as a mouse. Over and over again I forced my stuttering tongue into action, forced words from my tight throat, forced myself to stand tall, to raise my chin, to create words as loud and clear as bird calls. I spoke with merchants and bankers, wives and serving girls, grooms and porters and caravan leaders and tinsmiths and sheep herders. I ventured into warehouses filled with trade goods: brocade fabric, barrels of wine, jars of imported olive oil, crates of precious objects wrapped protectively in wool, chests filled with embroideries and camel blankets, caskets of jewellery. I asked questions in tea shops, I chatted with stallkeepers and artisans.

But still the merchant's whereabouts eluded me as I laboured through the streets in the suffocating heat, following threads of rumour and gossip, of hearsay and speculation. Meanwhile, the city grew more desperate around me. The vultures darkened the sky, wheeling and turning on the updraughts or settling earthwards like a flung cloak. Disease crept from street to street in the dust; wailing and shrieks of raw grief pierced the air as children died on their bedrolls. Houses stood shuttered in the mounting heat. A woman killed her neighbour, fighting at a well over the last bucket of silty, dirty water being hauled from its dry depths. A grain thief was knifed in the back as he climbed a stable wall, seeking fodder for his horses.

'Our days are numbered,' Lila's father intoned on the evening of the second day of my search. We were on the rooftop of the house again; Lila had asked me to play tabula but I was too tired. My head pounded as I stared over the rooftops into the valley, where the enemy campfires spluttered into brightness.

'Last night,' her father continued, 'Ershi's wall was breached on the western side with a narrow tunnel. The enemy was burning bitumen and sulphur crystals, creating a poisonous gas. They forced this gas through the tunnel into the street outside the hippodrome, using bellows.'

Lila's mother made a small moaning sound from the couch where she reclined amidst a pile of satin cushions, but her father did not pause in his pacing around the rooftop's perimeter. Lila, seated by her mother and listlessly embroidering a tablecloth, looked up to watch his pacing.

'I have made enquiries for this merchant you seek, Kalli,' he said suddenly, and my eyes flew to his narrow face.

'There is a man called Habib who claims that this merchant left the city on the evening when the army of the Middle Kingdom marched down our Golden Valley. He claims to know where this merchant lives, in a valley to our south-west, two days' ride into the mountains. So whatever your business is with this merchant, on behalf of your father, it will have to wait until after the siege. But by then your father will have returned and can transact his own affairs.

'If business will ever be done in Ershi again . . .' he muttered glumly, trailing off into a dark stare that was not focused upon me, or his wife and daughter, but seemed to travel ahead of us into a time when all was lost to us.

I turned away and began pacing on the other side of the roof.

The merchant, Failak, had left the city!

Such a possibility had not occurred to me. My stomach lurched and griped. I swallowed hard, tasting the bitterness of acid climb my throat. He had left! And now, only five days remained until I had to bring the golden harness to Arash, and when I failed to do this, he would send for the magi in their tall felt hats, and would offer them a pure white mare without blemish, to be sacrificed on the king's behalf for the salvation of our stricken city.

At some moment, when the enemy roared at our wall and our soldiers rained arrows upon them, at some moment as the small green stones of the apricots ripened and the lizards ran along the walls, my mare would die. And I would go into darkness, in a two-storey house where my mother fought for her life, and where I would stop fighting at all.

Two days' ride to the south-west, I thought. *And I have five days left.*

'And now I hear too that the enemy has been seeking to enter Ershi through the tunnel that carries the main watercourse,' continued Lila's father, the weight of imminent disaster creasing his narrow face into deeper lines. 'A few spies made it all the way across the aqueduct before they were discovered and killed. Now our men are knocking down walls around the great homes standing near the reservoir, and using the rubble to block off the aqueduct so that the enemy cannot use it to enter the city. The area is heavily guarded.'

Five days left.

Tears spilled over my cheeks and I turned my face away from Lila and her mother until my eyes were dry again.

'This merchant, Habib, where does he live?' I asked Lila's father.

'In the street running to the fire temple,' he said. 'But you do not need to concern yourself with matters of business when your father is away from home. This seeking of merchants is most improper.'

'My honoured husband is right,' Lila's mother agreed from her cushions, and I gave an inward sigh and was thankful that I hadn't shared the real reason that I wanted to find the merchant.

'Young women are becoming most wild and forward during this war,' she continued. 'And half the servants are missing. I am thankful indeed that all my daughters are married except for Lila, who stays at home as she should. And today my cook has gone missing! And I am told that people are growing so hungry they are buying dog meat in the market, and eating the horses that return rider-less from combat!'

'It's terrible,' I muttered, staring at Lila's head bent

demurely over her embroidery. I was quite sure that her eyeballs, under her downcast lids, were rolling. I wished that I could feel a giggle rising up in me, like a bubble in a pool, but there was nothing inside me tonight but a stone of fear.

'There is a rumour in the palace,' Lila's mother continued. 'I have heard that some nobles are pressuring the king to make a treaty with the Chinese, and agree to trade our horses. But he will not hear of it. And I have heard –' her voice sank to a whisper – 'that there are other nobles who think it is time for a different king in our city.'

'Do not speak such words!' Lila's father said, sounding aghast. 'You will get us all imprisoned or worse.'

His protest was followed by a long silence during which I wondered about what had been said. Perhaps even the king would not survive this battle; perhaps his worst enemies lay within the high security of Ershi's walls. As mine did.

'The cavalry is preparing to ride out on a sortie tomorrow,' Lila's father said finally. 'The enemy has built siege engines and our men must destroy them before they can be moved against Ershi's walls. You would do well to stay at home, Kallisto.'

'I must go home now,' I agreed meekly, but Lila's parents both shot me a stern glance as they said farewell. Perhaps they were beginning to feel that I was a bad influence upon their sheltered daughter, and not as shyly docile as they'd once believed.

I trudged down the stairs into the courtyard below. The garden lay in darkness but I felt the rasp of a cucumber vine against the back of my hand as I passed through. A bird gave a sleepy cheep of alarm in the pomegranate tree before subsiding into its feathers. A quick peek into the kitchen showed me that Fardad was sleeping. I felt my way between the mares, running my hands along their silky necks, until I found Nomad again. She was the oldest and quietest of our herd, and had experienced so many different situations that I could trust her to follow me into the dark streets without protest. I bridled her by feel, slipping the bit between her velvety lips and the headstall over her flickering ears. Without bothering with a saddle blanket, I led her out through the door, gritting my teeth as the bolts rattled in protest. Then I mounted, and rode for the house of Habib who thought that he knew where the merchant Failak lived in the mountains.

A servant let me in, and roused his master from poring over his accounts. After listening to my plea, the merchant shook his head ponderously. 'No, no,' he said. 'You have been misinformed. This Failak whom you seek does not come from the city of Kokand as your betrothed believes. He lives in a mountain valley . . . how to describe it? I shall make you a map.'

He spread a roll of birchbark upon his desk, and I leaned over his shoulder to watch as he drew a map upon it. 'Here is Ershi,' he said, 'this dark circle. Here lie the mountains.' He drew little points of ink as uneven as waves. 'Here is a river, I do not know its name,' and he added a thin line of coolness to the birchbark. 'Here lies a green valley, aligned south-westwards, two days' ride from our walls. Here is the village, where the river begins in the high slopes, and where the merchant Failak lives.'

I stared at the dot on the map as I thought about this man who could tell me whether or not there existed a second golden harness. The man who could help me save Swan, if I could find him, if he would trade with me.

Taking the map with many thanks, I rolled the birchbark and slid it into the leather pouch that I wore at my belt, then mounted Nomad again. It was very late when I stumbled at last up the stair from my courtyard to the upper floor, and crept along the dark passageway, running my fingertips over the texture of tapestries and the smooth gloss of wall paintings. The sweetness of opium drifted from my mother's room and on an impulse I turned and pushed against her door. It swung inward and I stepped to her bedside. The sesame oil was growing low in the terracotta lamp that sat on a table inlaid with tortoiseshell. It cast flickering shadows across my mother's sunken cheeks. I laid a hand gently on one of hers where it lay slack across a satin sheet, stained now with blood and seepage from her wounds. Gently I pulled the sheet back and stared at her shoulder and left arm. They were puckered and shrunken, but I thought that some of the evil was leaving them for the wounds were not as puffy and fiery as before. My mother would have many scars if she lived to heal from the dark eye that had been cast upon her, that had loosed the leopard on to her like an enemy spear.

I smoothed the sheets over her again, and collapsed into the chair where Marjan often sat, and laid my head against its smooth back of walnut wood where carved antelope fought with long, thin horns. My head pounded. Despair seemed to swirl around me in the room; was it only the shadows fluttering in the lamp's dying light, or was my eyesight clouding with horror? I could feel the stiff track of dried tears on my face. Now my eyes were dry, staring into the future, the unthinkable future that I was too weak to face. The future without Swan, and perhaps without my mother.

I clutched at the leather bag containing its tuft of leopard hair, the amulet that Berta had given to me. But I didn't know how to wrestle with that rushing feline strength and make its power my own. Perhaps Batu could have helped me but he was missing from my life; I was sure that he wouldn't have waited in the valley all this time for our return.

'What can I do?' I muttered. 'Mother, wake up and tell me what to do.'

I stared imploringly at her face but no muscle twitched.

'Ershi is a trap. I must get out. I must find this man, Failak, and get the golden harness, and save Swan.'

But I was trapped here in Ershi, for even the aqueduct and the tunnel were closed off now and guarded, and I could see no way to ride south-westwards with the wind and the sun on my face.

'Swan and I are both trapped,' I moaned in anguish, bending forward into my hands so that I didn't have to stare at the shadows whirling through my mother's room. 'Trapped. We have lost our freedom.'

Her fingers were light and dry, like dead leaves, as they touched my face. I held very still; perhaps I was dreaming. Perhaps I would awake and find this was all unreal: the enemy assault, the dying city, the threat to Swan, my weakened mother, my anguish and terror.

'You . . . are . . . a warrior,' my mother whispered.

I stared at her between my laced fingers. Her words drifted out through her dry lips, and sweat broke out on her forehead with the effort of speaking. Her fingers fell away from my face and I clasped them on the fine wool coverlet embroidered in scarlet thread.

'A warrior does not . . . give up her . . . freedom.'

I waited, while the lamp guttered and smoked, and the stars climbed westwards, but my mother sank deep into her opium-induced dreams and said nothing more. I lay on the bed beside her with my face against her chest and listened to the light catch of her breathing, my ringed fingers threaded through hers.

Yes, I thought, a warrior was what my mother had trained me to be. And now, at last, I would become one.

When I awoke, the lamp had sputtered out and darkness filled the room. Faintly, far off, a rooster crowed and I knew that dawn must be seeping over the Tien Shan mountains. My mother's breathing was even and deep. Her cheek was cool when I pressed my lips to it. Then I rose and strode softly into my room, lighting a lamp. In my wall niche stood the rectangular golden casket that my father had brought back for me from a trip to Isfahan; it had a lid decorated with golden grape leaves, and four small feet shaped like a lion's paws. On its shining sides was engraved the white horse, Pegasus, his great wings held above his curving back. The reins hanging from his bitted mouth ran to the hands of a man, and all around them were engraved sunflowers and grass-hoppers. Rotating the casket in my hand, I stared at the goddess Athena standing by a spring of water, her arms outstretched towards the white horse as she gave him as a gift to help the man slay the fire-breathing dragon.

I hefted the casket in my hand, and wondered how its weight compared to the weight of a golden chariot harness complete with breastplate, bridle, and crupper. On the trade routes running through

Ferghana, all goods were traded by weight; a thing was worth only its own weight in gold however fine or glorious its craftsmanship might be.

The twisted golden torc that Berta had given me, with its bright blue eyes, still lay against the base of my throat. I fingered it thoughtfully before opening the jewel casket and looking inside. Here were my favourite earrings and forehead jewellery, the silver ones inlaid with lapis lazuli that I had worn to beg at Arash's booted feet. Here were my finest rings, my armbands, my necklaces of amber and coral. My father traded in luxury goods – frankincense from Arabia, precious stones from the Mediterranean, Italian faience glassware, perfumes and ivory and marble statuettes and drinking horns of solid silver – and he had been giving me jewellery since I was a stumbling toddler. I had never considered its value, until this moment. *Thank you, Father*, I thought now, as the early light gleamed in the amber's golden depths and sparked in the facet of an emerald.

There was surely enough wealth here to turn a girl into a warrior; surely enough to purchase an ancient chariot harness, and the life of a white mare.

Chapter 12

'This is madness!' Lila protested, her eyes stretching wide beneath a curtain of shining hair. 'I am going to tell my parents and they will stop you!'

I stepped closer to her bed and caught hold of her slender hands. 'No! I must do this because it is the only way I can escape from the city! Come to my house after daybreak, and make sure that Fardad and the other servants will help Sayeh care for the mares and foals while I am gone. Please.'

She stared at me for a long moment while the grey light preceding dawn lapped at the window sill. A shiver ran through her. 'What will I tell your mother?' she asked at last.

'You don't have to tell her anything. I have left a piece of parchment beside her bed. You know her tribe had no written language, and she has never learned to read Persian. So I have drawn pictures on the parchment so she will know I have gone out with the cavalry. And give this to Fardad to buy food for the mares.'

I slid three golden armbands over my wrists and pressed them into Lila's hand.

'But what will you use to purchase the harness?' she asked.

'I have my jewel casket here, under my tunic,' I explained. I patted the bulge that lay across my stomach, its weight pressed into my skin beneath the strips of linen that I had used to tie it in place. If I bent over, the corners of the golden box poked uncomfortably into me.

'May the great angels ride on either side of you!' Lila said fervently, and I turned away on my booted heel and left before the tears rising into her eyes could spill over. Silently, I rushed down the stairs and through the dim garden. In my own courtyard, I dived into the granary where I had assembled my pile of equipment. I pulled leather leggings on over my roughest trousers of dull, worn linen; they were the ones I used when training young horses and they had been washed, and repaired with small stitches, many times. My fingers shook as I fumbled to tie the thongs, holding up the leggings, around my waist. Next I fastened a wide leather belt, with a buckle of red and white stone, over my tunic. To this I fastened a leather drinking flask filled with water, and a pouch containing a flint for making fires, and a little food: dried apricots stuffed with almonds, dried dates, rings of dried apples, golden raisins.

Then I lifted the light chain mail armour from the dusty floor where it lay shimmering with a dull gleam. It belonged to my brother Petros and he had almost outgrown it before he travelled away trading with our father. The many, finely-wrought rings of iron slipped over me in a cool, hard cascade and the folds shook themselves straight under their own weight. The armour hung from my shoulders, close fitting across the bulge created by the jewel casket tied beneath my tunic, slightly longer than need be, and heavy. I felt braver, just for a moment, although my fingers trembled as I secured my dagger in place, then tugged a leather helmet over my plaited hair.

A cock crowed again, far off, as I ran into the harness room and, closer to home, a dog barked. I was breathless with panic. At any minute, our servants would rise to stir the fire into life in the kitchen and to go out into the street for the morning ration of water. I must not be discovered by them!

Most of my mother's weaponry was stored at our farm in the valley, but I found an old quiver, with a faded pattern of running antelope stitched upon it in red leather, and fastened it around my waist over the chain mail tunic. The strap holding it in place was soft with age and wear; I hoped that it wouldn't break before this day was over. Bows stood stacked against one corner and I sorted through them, running my palms down their double curves, strumming my fingers over their strings of gut to feel for weaknesses or slackness. I hefted several bows in turn to my shoulder and pulled on them, testing their tension and spring as I notched imaginary arrows. This one would suit me, I thought, choosing a bow with a weight and tension that I knew I could manage to handle whilst fitting arrows to it at a gallop.

I slung the bow over my shoulder and then turned to the basket of woven grass where my mother's supply of arrows was usually stored. My heart lurched. The basket stood empty; only one stray white feather, broken from a shaft, lay in the bottom on the woven coils. Perhaps my mother's horsemen had taken all the arrows to use in the war. Perhaps already their finely polished shafts of willow wood lay strewn across the trampled gardens outside the city walls, or broken in the long grass of the plain. Perhaps they had pierced enemy armour, or were being burned in enemy campfires.

'What are you doing?'

Surprise jolted through me. I spun on one heel and met Sayeh's blue gaze. For a long moment, we stared assessingly at each other. Would she still serve me, I wondered, now that I was riding out against her mother's people? Would she keep my departure a secret?

'Sayeh,' I whispered, 'I need your help.'

'You're riding to find the golden harness that your betrothed spoke of in his red pavilion.'

Surprise jolted through me for the second time. 'Help me,' I entreated. 'I am going to ride Nomad down to the hippodrome and then try to buy a horse. I don't want to take one of my mother's mares to war. After I buy a horse, you can bring Nomad home again. And while I am away, I am entrusting all the mares and foals to your care, Sayeh.'

Her eyes widened in wonder and I heard the quick intake of her breath. 'Truly?' she asked. 'All the mares?'

'Lila will make sure that the servants help you. It is only for a few days.'

'All the mares,' she repeated, and I knew that she would devote her every waking hour to them; that she would sift the grain with her own hands to remove stones; would brush their flanks with loving strokes; would stagger twice daily into the court-yard to pour the precious rationed water into the stone trough from pottery jars.

'Hurry!' I whispered. 'Bridle Nomad!'

Eagerly she snatched at the bridle that I held out, its iron snaffle bit ringing as it swung against my armour, so that in the courtyard the mares pricked their ears and blew through their nostrils. I took another bridle, an old one with plain undecorated leather, and a worn felt blanket, and my own saddle with its dangling toe loops and the handgrip of leather thong fastened to the wooden supports at the front. We had had fun, my mother and I, experimenting with those thongs and loops as our horses galloped across the training ground, raising puffs of dust as we swung on and off, or hung upside-down from our saddles.

Today, it would not be a game for me. And my mother would not be there to help me if I fell, if I was dragged, if I failed to dodge an arrow.

My heart bounded in my throat as I hurried into the courtyard and slung the saddle on to Nomad's back. My fingers fumbled under her belly, fastening the band, and under her tail with the crupper. Sleepy voices sounded in the kitchen and I led Nomad through the mares, saying goodbye to them with my eyes. Perhaps I would never see them again: black Pearl's whiskered chin, Peony's sleek gleam, or Iris's eyes, huge in her grey face.

Sayeh was at the door ahead of me, dribbling sesame oil on to the bolt so that it slid across without a sound. In a moment, we were in the empty street. 'Get up behind me,' I whispered and the servant girl swung nimbly on to Nomad's loins as I nudged the mare into a trot. The streets became crowded as we neared the hippodrome, filled with soldiers in armour, horses, strings of goats, wagons carrying the last dwindling supplies of grain, files of servants carrying water.

'W-when do we ride out?' I called as a band of

horsemen jostled past; although my voice quivered with fear, they barely glanced at me and their faces, beneath their helmets, were hollow and strained.

'As soon as we are all assembled,' muttered one man; he had a tattoo of antlers across his cheeks.

Nomad snorted as we entered the great arched gateway in the stone wall surrounding the hippodrome for now we were being swept along in a jostling throng of servants and slaves, all rushing with arms filled with harness, armour, boots, and weapons. A sea of battle standards rose near the far side of the hippodrome amongst a clattering expanse of lances, and over a sea of tossing heads. Voices shouted and yelled, horses gave high whinnies of nervous excitement.

A great fist squeezed my heart. For one moment, it stopped beating. Was I truly going to do this? Perhaps Lila was right, and madness had stolen my mind. I licked my dry lips and pulled Nomad to a halt, surveying the chaos all around.

'A horse . . . I need a h-horse,' I stuttered.

'And arrows,' said Sayeh. 'I am going to walk now, for no warrior would have a servant girl riding behind.'

She slid down into the crowd and caught at my foot loop for balance. As the sun rose, casting brightness upon spears and decorated bridles, I moved as if I was in a terrible dream; I swayed through rushing waves of noise and a babble of tongues, through the hot dark fear that sucked at me, through the roar of smithy fires and the ring of hammers on glowing spearheads, through the trampling of horses. Dust clogged my nostrils. I couldn't breathe, and the jewel casket was heavier and heavier, flattening my stomach against my spine.

From far away, I heard my young, hesitant voice stammering over requests for arrows, over questions about horses. Warriors' faces blurred in and out of my vision; they all seemed to be dark and lined with fatigue, scowling, shouting through stretched mouths. I stared over their shoulders, shaken by shyness, unable to meet their fierce gazes. I saw that now the cavalry was hundreds of horses deep, massing at the hippodrome's far side in preparation for riding out of the city's southern gate; somehow, I learned from the voices around me that we were riding out against siege engines, just as Lila's father had said the previous evening. Our task was to cut a swathe through the enemy lines and clear a space around the great towers so that they could be set alight and burned.

Now I was pushing my way through the crowd towards a string of kneeling camels being laden with bundles of new arrows; I purchased enough to fill my quiver. Their shafts were of peeled willow but rough, made in great haste overnight in city workshops where men bent their backs to their tasks all through the long hours. All night, in the forges, the smiths had worked by their fires, hammering the iron arrowheads as slaves worked the bellows, sending hot air fanning across the embers.

Now I was asking for a horse, bartering, bargaining. Searching. I was buffeted, hemmed in. I was going to be sick. I clamped my mouth shut and rode along the lines of tents and picket ropes. Now my voice was raised in a cry, a despairing cry for help, for a horse. At last a tribesman led an animal forward; a raw-boned appaloosa with a dark head but a blanket of spotted white across his sides and hindquarters. His eyes rolled wildly, ringed with white.

'We were going to eat him!' shouted the man holding the lead rope. 'But you can make me an offer for him!'

I reached under my chain mail, up inside the rough sleeve of my tunic, and pulled out three golden armbands inlaid with Egyptian emeralds.

'I can't eat these!' the man shouted with an oath but he took them anyway.

'Horse armour?' I asked, holding up a fourth armband, and he turned away, muttering, to a tent. After a pause, he reappeared with a long thick felt which he threw over the appaloosa, covering him from poll to croup. I took the horse's rope and led him away to where Sayeh waited with Nomad. We unfastened my saddle from the mare and fastened it on to the appaloosa as he swung heavily around, almost knocking a slave down. I bridled him with my extra bridle, the one of plain leather, and attached a weighted tassel beneath the reins so that, when I dropped them to shoot arrows, they would not fly around and trip my horse but would hang taut from the bit. I boosted Sayeh on to Nomad's bare back.

'Take her straight home, and water them all!' I cried and for one moment her eyes locked on to mine.

'Yes,' she said, as solemnly as if she were taking an oath, and then the crowd swallowed her small straight back and the mare's golden gleam, and I was alone with the hard-mouthed gelding and my devouring fear. I kicked the horse towards where the cavalry was already beginning to move through the hippo-drome's far gate into the street beyond. With a dull roar of voices, with a thunder of hooves, with a clash of spears upon shields, we poured through the streets of Ershi towards the south gate.

I am riding to war, I thought. *I am going to faint and fall off.*

The appaloosa surged along; he was strong and sturdy and willing even though hard in the mouth. *But untrained*, a voice in my head kept repeating. *Untrained by me, by my mother. A horse that has never learned to gallop straight ahead whilst his rider jumps on or off, hangs from one side, hangs upside down from a loop in the saddle. He is a horse I have no bond with, a horse whose trust I haven't won. But we are trusting each other now with our lives.*

The walls of Ershi loomed above, broken only by

the open gateway and a patch of clear blue sky. A hot breeze puffed in off the plain, and the battle standards lifted and snapped, red and purple and golden, and decorated with the symbols of the noble houses: eagles and stags and leopards all soared and ran above our heads as the kettle drums boomed and the tambourines rattled.

Now we were flushing through the gate, faster, the appaloosa's wide shoulders breaking into a rough trot, wind filling my mouth. I wasn't breathing. My heart had stopped. I couldn't swallow. Darkness filled my eyes, then brilliant sunshine, then darkness. I swayed in the saddle, faint with fear. Before me swung the trampled fields, the stripped gardens, the far-off blue thread of a river.

The great mass of the enemy, filling the valley.

I lifted my head, fighting to breathe. Over the appaloosa's dark pricked ears, I glimpsed the line of the mountains, clear and blue with the snow-capped peaks turning to gold as the sun licked them. Strength poured into me and my vision cleared. I gripped tighter with my thighs and urged the horse on faster, neck and neck with the men on either side of me. The edges of my eyes filled with cavalry, with the magnificent plunging gallop of brave horses, with the flap of saddle blankets embroidered with bright patterns, with red tassels flying from reins, with the glitter of silver inlay and glass stones on bridle straps, and the wink of gold-plated bit rings.

The roar and whoop and wild yells of the tribes-men lifted me upwards, out of my dark trap of fear. I soared over the ground. The valley vibrated with our headlong rush, our streaming power. A whoop flew from my own mouth and the appaloosa's stride lengthened. Everything became a blur.

We plunged down and over a drainage ditch, dry and cracked; we hammered between the long avenues of trees in an almond orchard; we sprinted over the hard packed ground of a roadway. Sheep scattered. Far ahead, the enemy gathered itself like a wave, a dark wall, and began to move towards us. I screamed again, a long high note that was swept into the river of the cavalry and surged forward with it.

Now I could see the siege towers rising from the plain; their frameworks of wood stood as tall as the valley's elm trees had once been, before the enemy felled them. The frames were covered in oxhide to protect them from flaming arrows, and at the top of the towers were long pivoting beams ending in sharp metal claws. When the towers were pulled forward by oxen, and rolled up against Ershi on their many wheels, the great claws would dig and gouge into the city's walls of packed mud. Then the cloud ladders would be rolled forward, with their tall tower and high ladders, and with enemy soldiers packed inside them. The men would scale the walls and enter the city through the holes that the claws had broken open.

Get on the flank, I told myself. *Get on the flank!*

Only if I could break free of the main thrust of the cavalry, and make my way to the edge, could I ride away towards the mountain valley where I hoped that Batu still waited. Only then could I ride south-westwards searching for the merchant called Failak who perhaps owned a second golden harness.

We pounded on. Horses were pressed to me, their riders almost touching my knees on either side. I hauled on the appaloosa's bit but he braced his thick neck, and his strong legs didn't waver in their galloping. He opened his mouth, setting his jaw against my pull, and thundered on. Now I could see the enemy soldiers ahead, massing around the bases of their siege towers, sun shining on pikes and the heavy shafts of their deadly crossbows. The bowmen stood behind the kneeling pikemen, covering them, and the sun shone on their armour of lacquered oxhide and of iron. Silken banners rippled in the hot wind. We were wheeling now, turning sideways on to the enemy, horses straining to swing around, legs flashing, necks bending, nostrils flaring wide and red, eyes rolling. Foam flew back from horses' mouths and spattered my cheek. I was pulling the appaloosa around, trying to work my way slowly across the oncoming rush of horses, finding small openings and breaks that I could shoot through like a mouse shooting into a tunnel. Gradually, stride by stride, I manoeuvred for a place on the far flank.

Now everything seemed to be happening at a

speed so blinding I could barely follow it. A shower of glinting arrows, fast and bright as summer stars, flew through the air ahead of me as the lethal enemy crossbows unleashed their volleys. I had heard, in Ershi, that some of the bows were so huge it took twenty men to release them, and that their arrows flew, without feathers on the shafts, for many, many paces. I had heard that the tips of those darts were tipped with a poison so strong that even a scratch from one of them would kill a man.

Just ahead of me, a horse screamed and went down with an arrow embedded in its chest. The appaloosa's front hooves skimmed against the fallen horse's thrashing legs; for a moment, I thought he would be entangled in the reins. Then he jumped strongly upwards, and we were past. A woman beside me took an arrow in the arm; I saw the pain flare in her eyes and whiten her cheeks. Then I dropped my reins and pulled an arrow from my old quiver with its red leather patterns, and began to shoot. I was alongside the enemy now, could see their eyes beneath their helmets, and hear their wild foreign cries as they loosed their shining hail of arrows. I kneed the appaloosa, making him twist and dodge through the shadows of the great siege towers standing like a nightmare forest against the sky. He was neither as nimble as Swan nor as fast as Gryphon, and it took most of my strength and concentration to guide and control him.

Shooting arrows, though, was something I could do without thought; one hand gripped them by the shaft and pulled them smoothly from the quiver; then my other hand notched them to the bow, drew its springing tension back against one shoulder, felt the thrum of the gut as the arrow flew away, released.

Now we were beneath a great siege tower taller than the city wall of Ershi; carpenters were still scrambling down through its framework, seeking the safety of the ground behind the enemy soldiers. I saw a man take an arrow in the leg and fall through the wooden beams, yelling as he plunged head first. Then the appaloosa tripped and I tightened my legs and clung on. He surged to his feet again, and a fresh volley of crossbow arrows flew towards us, hissing like serpents.

I'm going to be killed here, I thought. *I will never escape to the mountains.*

I threw myself over the appaloosa's back and lay along his off-side, one hand gripping the leather thong at the front of my saddle, and my leg bent beneath me in the foot loop. The horse's blanketed shoulder surged against my face; I could hear his breath whistling. Now we were swinging around again, out of range of the crossbows, and I hauled myself back into the saddle. We dodged motionless bodies and fallen horses writhing on the chewed ground. I wrenched the horse's head around and shot southwards, still trying without success to work my way on to the cavalry's flank. Once more we came around, shooting arrows at the troops beneath the siege engines, and as we wheeled away this time I saw a tower blossom into flame; our second wave of warriors had been able to come close enough to set it on fire with flaming arrows. Black clouds of pungent smoke billowed into the valley's pure air.

We were wheeling past again, shouting, shooting. We were much closer now. Too close. *Mother!* I cried inside my head, the word echoing. *Help!*

The pike men were on their feet, and I saw a great shaft of iron slicing through the air towards me. I kicked free of the saddle, and threw myself from the appaloosa's off-side, my supple boots hitting the ground so hard that the shudder ran through my body. The horse shied and I hauled on his reins, running beside him for three paces with my hands gripping my saddle loop. When I leaped astride again, he was still galloping and the pike man was left behind.

A swell of land lifted up before me, scattered with the stumps of walnut trees; the horses dodged amongst them and opened up into a looser pattern so that I was able to work my way across the slope between them. At last I was riding on the very edge of the cavalry. The appaloosa had slowed to a laboured canter but I lashed him on with the reins into a frenzied gallop. I hoped that he would hold true to his pace and direction when I dropped the reins. If he circled back to join the other horses, or if he slowed to a walk, my plan would not work.

I waited for several strides until his hooves touched the down slope on the ridge's far side, and then I dived backwards from the saddle, one foot hooked in the leather loop on the far side. Ground rushed at me. Sky spun. My body swung loose, my arms trailing. It had been the hardest thing to master, on the training ground with my mother: the looseness, the ability to let every muscle and bone swing slack as the ground rushed up to meet my head, as my hands brushed against protruding roots and the heads of grass.

I was a dead rider now, being carried along by my crazed horse, one foot tangled in the leather. No one would worry about shooting me, or stopping me.

A last volley of arrows hailed down, making the horse snort and renew his efforts. Then we were dropping down off the ridge, my head inches from the rough slope of a sheep pasture. My right hand banged across a stone. The horse's legs, his great bones stout as tree limbs, rushed past my eyes; my torso twisted and snapped against his ribs. His tail slapped my face with a sting like a whip. I closed my eyes as blood filled my head and everything turned to blackness. Hoof beats replaced the crash of my heart.

When I felt the appaloosa's stride slowing. I kicked upwards with one foot, thumping him behind the forelegs, and he surged on again. I opened my eyes a crack and saw only a blur of ground rushing past, with green grass and sheep droppings. There were no other horses' legs in view. The world became quieter until only the horse's laboured breathing, and his hoof beats, remained.

'Whoa, slow down, easy!' I called soothingly to him, and then jerked myself, with one long convulsion of muscle, up towards the saddle again. The horse, unfamiliar with my voice and unused to this manoeuvre, shied violently and I lost my grip and plunged towards the ground, my head snapping on my neck. After this, I waited until the horse slowed of his own accord to a trot, then a walk. Finally, bruised and dizzy, I pulled myself into the saddle long enough to kick my foot from the leather loop and scan my surroundings. A clump of willow trees lay to my right, and I jumped down again and hauled the horse behind me into its shade.

Doubling over my jewel box, I retched into a patch of raspberries. For a long time afterwards, I leaned against the appaloosa's shoulders, panting and shaking. Beneath my armour and tunic, my skin was slick with sweat and my blood tingled in my arms and legs. Roaring filled my ears. The horse blew, his head hanging, and foam dripped from his mouth. I was too breathless to praise him but I ran my hands down his sturdy legs from shoulder to fetlock, noticing his striped hooves.

When I tied the reins to a tree, and crept to the

edge of the willows, I could see down into a shallow valley where dusty stones lay in a dry riverbed. Perhaps this had once been one of Ershi's water sources, and had been diverted by the enemy. A peasant drove a flock of sheep across the far slope, guarded by huge mastiff dogs with drooling jowls. Further down the valley, an enemy encampment of tents stood in a ring, and when I stepped out of my shelter, I could see that many more tents were pitched over the hillside, pale as mushrooms in the trampled alfalfa. I was on the very edge of the army camp, I decided. If I shed my armour, surely no one would stop a girl riding southwards, for only warriors and nobles would be of interest to the men of the Middle Kingdom. I struggled out of the chain mail, glad to be free of its slithering weight, and feeling anonymous in my rough tunic and trousers. Lifting the linen, I retied the sashes holding the jewel case against my stomach.

The appaloosa snuffled at grass and I uncorked my water bag and dribbled a stream into his wide lips, giving him just enough to wet his tongue. He stared consideringly at me afterwards, as though noticing me for the first time, and when I told him he had been brave, he pressed his heavy face against my chest.

'You need a name,' I murmured. 'I will call you . . . Mountain, for your size and strength.'

I tipped the flask back and took a swallow of

tepid water, then ate a handful of dried fruit, savouring its sweetness. At last, my muscles stopped trembling. Sunshine fell in dapples through the willows, adding more dark and light to the pattern of Mountain's coat. I tilted my face to the light, and breathed a deep lungful of clear air. *I am free*, I thought, and for a moment I imagined those finches in Lila's house, how they would stumble into the air if someone opened their cage door, how they would grow strong as they realised that freedom lay all around them.

I removed the felt and the saddle from Mountain's back, and then used the felt to rub sweat from his chest, his flanks, and his belly. Then I sat down, holding his reins, while Mountain tore at mouthfuls of grass. The smell of oregano wafted from amongst the crushed stems. Flies buzzed, and birds called, and sometimes, far off, hooves thundered past and men shouted. The afternoon crept by, golden, hot, secretive.

As shadows lengthened, I stared at my saddle, unwilling to abandon it with its shaped cushions, its blue leather covering appliquéd with yellow flowers, its carefully crafted leather loops. Yet no peasant girl in the valley of Ferghana would have owned such a saddle, and it might only attract unwelcome attention. At last, reluctantly, I laid it at the base of a willow, along with Petros's armour and helmet, the felt blanket, and my bow and quiver. These objects made a small, sad pile against the tree's craggy bark; who knew whether I might ever be able to return for them?

At dusk, as wolves began to sing under the first faint prick of stars, I rode the appaloosa out from the trees and headed at a trot towards the foothills, making my way by memory, by a feeling in my gut, by the smells of herbs and stones, by the sound of water trickling from a spring or of antelopes grazing. Occasionally we stopped and hid behind trees or the walls of abandoned farms as strangers rode by. We avoided paths and tracks, and headed across country, dodging enemy fires, hunting parties, and supply wagons.

Oh, Batu, I thought as I stared ahead at the great black wall of the Alay Mountains. *It has been many long days since we said goodbye, and surely the valley where you killed your first boar lies empty. Where, in all these layers and folds of slope and shadow, are you sleeping tonight?*

It was late as I walked the gelding up the lower reaches of the valley; late and chilly, with my body stiff and aching, and the gelding's head drooping although he ploughed sturdily onwards. We picked a cautious path across a bed of gravel. The gelding lowered his head, the reins slack in my hands, and sucked up a long draught of water from the rushing stream whose chatter filled the dark air. My thoughts drifted as we moved on, the horse's steady walk lulling me into a doze. My chin nudged my chest and strands of my hair, escaping from their plaits, tickled my cheeks.

Suddenly Mountain shied violently, almost unseating me. Long muscles closed around my chest. Tendons strained against my face, muffling my shout of alarm. I pitched from the snorting horse, and landed hard with the wild thing pressing me down. Stones grated against my shoulder blades.

Leopard! my foggy mind cried in alarm, but then I felt the knife blade held across my throat.

Chapter 13

'Don't – d-don't hurt m-me!' I croaked as the pressure was released over my mouth. My eyes strained to see the attacker who sat on me, pinning me in place, but he was only the silhouette of a wild-haired man against the face of the moon.

'The starry sky at night –' my assailant said roughly, in a Turkic tongue.

My mind, slow and dragging with fatigue, reeled in amazement. This was the first half of a phrase that Batu and I had used as a password, for many years, when we played at bandits and warriors in the summer grasslands.

Dry with fear, my tongue stuck in the roof of my mouth. My assailant shook my head, one hand tight in my plaited hair, and I felt the point of the knife pierce my skin. A convulsion of fear twisted through me so that I writhed on the gravel.

'The starry sky at night –' he repeated.

'– is a b-black horse decorated with pearls,' I replied.

The man grunted in surprise. His grip on my hair eased slightly but the knife was steady at my throat and I could feel the warmth of blood as it trickled across my collar bone. 'What comes next?' he demanded.

'The r-rays of the sun in the afternoon –'

'– are the tail hairs of a white horse,' he finished. 'Who are you and what are you doing here?'

'I am the lady Kallisto of the House of Iona in Ershi, and I am searching for a tribesman named Batu, from the clan of the Fierce Eagles.'

The man gave another grunt of surprise, and the pressure of the knife blade eased at last. I lay very still, listening to the slight shift of gravel as footsteps approached. 'Catch the horse,' my assailant said over his shoulder, and I heard Mountain snorting. When my assailant stood up at last, a dull pain throbbed along the backs of my legs and in my ribs. 'Kneel,' the man said, and I obeyed, and held still while he tied my wrists behind my back with leather thongs. Then he prodded me with the hilt of his dagger. 'Stand up, and walk.'

The valley closed in around us as we moved higher, its steep sides cloaked in a dense forest, and the rush of water growing louder. I stumbled between the two men, my legs weak as those of a newborn foal. The white, spotted blanket across Mountain's quarters was a dull gleam behind us. My nostrils twitched, catching at a drift of woodsmoke, and abruptly my assailant shoved me around an outcrop of rock into a narrow ravine that arrowed through the mountain flank to meet the main valley. The mouth of a cave glowed like a bowl in a potter's kiln, and the flicker of campfire light danced on the rocky ceiling. At our approach, the men seated around the burning logs looked up, their hands moving to the hilts of their daggers, their hawk noses casting shadows over their thick moustaches and uncombed black beards. The boy turning the body of a quail spitted upon a spear gazed at me for a long, calm heartbeat. I saw the flames reflected in the pupils of his black eyes.

'It is a good thing that you practised the password for so many years,' he said gravely, his face perfectly still. Then it split open in his wild, delighted, flashing grin, and the firelight licked the high slope of his cheekbones.

'Batu!' I fell forward into the cave, my legs giving way, and he leaped to his feet to catch me. I smelled the horses, smoke, and mossy forest scents in his orange tunic of padded Indian cotton. His hair hung down across my face, and it smelled like wind and mountain sunshine. A sob of exhaustion shook me as he kissed my cheek, and undid the thongs that chafed my wrists.

'Sit by the fire,' he said in the voice he used for tending injured horses, and he lowered me on to a warm rock as the other men shifted to make room. Batu pulled the spear from the flames, and used his dagger to slice pieces of moist meat from the golden and charred body of the quail; he gouged a stuffing of millet and wild chives from inside its small body cavity, and heaped all the food on a copper plate. The steam rose into my nostrils and I thought that I had never before smelled anything as delicious. My mouth filled with saliva and I moulded the millet into a ball with my fingers and ate it, burning my tongue in my haste. I ate and ate while Batu spitted the body of a second bird and turned it slowly over the logs, waiting until I was ready to talk. At last, I had emptied my plate twice, and he handed me a mug of wild mint tea sweetened with mountain honey.

'You will be safe now,' he said reassuringly. I ducked my head, suddenly shy beneath the gaze of so many wild strangers, but the men were paying little attention to me. They moved around the cave; one was sharpening a dagger against a whetstone, the rhythmic rasp blending with the crackle of burning logs. Another man held a guitar and began to play, running a bow across the two strings of horsehair.

'Who are all these people? What are you d-doing here? Where are the two-year-old mares?'

Batu grinned triumphantly. 'The mares are with my mother's herd. I waited four days for you, but then I heard from a farmer in the valley that the enemy had laid siege to Ershi and that no one could escape. I knew, when you didn't come back, that you were trapped inside. So I drove the mares to my mother's camp. Then I returned here, thinking you might escape after all. See, I left you a mark in case you found your way here some day when I was not around.'

I followed the line of his gesturing arm and saw, inscribed upon the rock wall of the cave, perhaps with the point of a dagger, the rough drawing of an eagle, a mare, and a stallion. The horses looked as though they were galloping joyfully across the rock, striated with ochre and orange. Their tails flew out behind them.

'Then,' Batu continued, 'I began to meet other men who had not got inside Ershi before it was sealed off; tribesmen, and farmers from the valley. We have formed a raiding band here in the mountains, and we ride out and strike the edges of the enemy encampment swiftly at night, then melt back into the shadows. We destroy their supply lines, and burn their tents; we cut the tracing on the harnesses, and undo the lynchpins in their wagon wheels and throw them into the river!'

Batu's face gleamed with a mischievous excitement that I knew well. He had looked the same way when we were eight years old and had, on a wager, managed to steal two hound puppies from another tribe's dog at a summer festival, and play with them for an afternoon before being caught.

'And Gryphon, is he recovered from his leopard injuries? Where is he?' I asked eagerly.

'We have a small band of horses, pasturing on the lower slopes of this valley, and guarded at all times by two men. They are mainly workhorses from the farms, that are more used to threshing grain and pulling ploughs than being ridden. Rain is with them, and Gryphon too. His wounds have knitted back together. I thought that if you came here you might need him. No one else can ride him; he is loyal only to you and none of us can even catch him.'

I smiled. 'He has never liked strangers. And I do need him.' I described Swan's fate, and my urgent mission to bring back the golden harness so that I could save her. Batu's face darkened with anger as he listened. From one of my leather pouches, I pulled the parchment map and Batu held it open in the firelight, peering at its squiggly lines of ink.

'You must sleep for a few hours,' he commanded, 'and then we will ride for this village. Along the way, you can tell me how you managed to escape from Ershi. Here, use this bedroll.'

I lay on the lumpy mattress stuffed with sedges and Batu threw a sheepskin over me. The firelight played and danced inside my closed eyelids, and the quail meat warmed my belly, and the rock wall of the cave was rough and hard against my spine. I thought of the horses there, galloping for ever on their orange legs, and a smile slackened my mouth. When I opened my eyes a slit, Batu was sitting crosslegged by the fire, scowling as he used marmot fat to oil a bridle's leather straps. Gryphon's bridle, I thought, his bridle with the decoration of blue clay beads, gleaming like drops of water in the cave.

'I have brought another horse for your herd, an appaloosa,' I said, and Batu's eyes lit up for, like all the nomads, he loved a colourful horse. I watched him for a little longer, scowling again, rubbing at Gryphon's bridle, and then my eyes drifted shut in sleep.

It was not yet dawn when Batu roused me, shaking my shoulders. Outside the cave the moon was sliding over the western mountains, and the water of the stream was pale as moth wings as it crashed downhill. Batu and I slipped along a faint track to the horse herd, and muttered the password to the men guarding it.

My heart bounded with excitement. 'Gryphon, Gryphon!' I called softly, and gave the special whistle, like a bird's call, that I used to summon him when he was far out in my mother's pastures, grazing the alfalfa and shimmering like a flung coin. Now my eyes scanned the slope, flitting across the dark bodies of horses as they rustled through the shrubs and grass. Twigs broke, teeth ground together. The smell of the herd rose around me, and I saw the pale blanket of the appaloosa as he passed by, following a chestnut mare. Something moved behind my shoulder. Warm breath gusted on to my neck. Whiskers tickled me. I felt his presence coiled like a whip, his muscles tensed to spring away, spooked in the strange half-light. Very slowly, I turned around.

'Gryphon,' I whispered, and he bent his head, pressing his muzzle into my open hand. My magnificent stallion, flame and smoke. His black legs, long, hard, dry. His golden chest, and his high-set neck. His coat sleek as rare Chinese silk beneath my fingers. I laid my face against him and let his heat soak into my aching muscles. 'I am so glad to find you,' I whispered. 'I am so glad you are safe.'

I ran my hands over his quarters, feeling the lines where the leopard claws had raked him; the skin in those lines was knotted, but cool and firm, and hair was beginning to grow over them. Batu had been right; my stallion would carry white scars in his coat for the rest of his life, in a pattern like a spider's web netted with morning dew, or like foam upon a fast river. 'It only makes you more beautiful,' I comforted him, holding up the bridle.

Gryphon slipped his muzzle between the supple oiled straps, and I fastened the cheek piece on the near side with the buckle of bone, and smoothed his forelock between his narrow ears. He snorted softly with excitement as I laid the blanket, which Batu had given me, across his back and smoothed it straight and flat. Then I led him to a rock, and vaulted on, and he bounded across the slope, snatching at the bit and longing to gallop.

Daylight met us at the mouth of the valley, and we turned away from it and rode with its rising warmth upon our shoulders. Gradually the aches and bruises in my body softened, and Batu and I ate dried dates and flat bread as we rode, and I told him how I had come out of Ershi's south gate with a cavalry sortie. He flashed me a delighted glance, and laughed aloud. Then we let the horses ease into a steady trot on a loose rein, and Gryphon swept along, his shadow swooping across the grass as fast as the flight of a bird, his hard hooves striking the ground rhythmically, his mane lifting in the breeze. I turned my face to the blue sky and echoed Batu's laughter.

We rode through the foothills all day, following the map, and occasionally asking directions from a sheep herder or a merchant caravan. Despite the siege of Ershi, trade was continuing between Samarkand and India, and we passed heavily laden camels and strings of donkeys. By evening, we had left the Golden Valley behind and were heading into the deep shadows of high ridges. We rode until the moon began to climb the sky, and then we stopped at an isolated farm and asked for shelter. Leaving the horses fed and watered in the stable, we entered the one-storey, mud house and sat on the floor while our host brewed tea, and his wife laid the tablecloth upon the faded carpets.

'Do you know of this village?' Batu asked, showing our host the map. The man studied it for a moment, and then nodded once, sharply. A cloud seemed to pass across his face.

'Do you know this man we seek, a merchant called Failak who might have once come from Kokand?' Batu persisted.

Our host nodded again, and a troubled frown

creased his forehead beneath his skullcap. He took a long sip of his tea.

'This man Failak came from the south,' he said. 'He is not from Kokand.'

'But he does live in this village now, this village on our map?'

The man took another long sip of tea and seemed to ponder Batu's question, his deep eyes hooded under his shaggy brows. At last he spoke with a strange reluctance. 'This man Failak has taken over the village you seek. Or so I have heard. He drove the villagers away or enslaved them, in the spring when the snow melted in the high passes. He and his people came from deep in the Pamir mountains. He wanted the turquoise mine that lies on the edge of the village. Now he controls the mine, and the mountain pass, and all the trade in that area.'

Alarm shivered through me; when my gaze flew to Batu, I saw it mirrored in his eyes.

'This man Failak is a warlord,' Batu said softly, and our host nodded.

'His band has taken over the summer pastures around the village, and the tribe that had used them for many generations has been driven eastwards, and been dispersed; their flocks starved without spring grass. This village is a very bad place for you to go seeking anyone, especially this man calling himself Failak, though he is not a Persian but a man of the tribes living in the mountains. You must turn back, and ride home in the morning.'

At the doorway, three small children stared at me with serious, round faces, smooth as river stones. Their bright eyes took in every detail of my hair and clothing until their mother shooed them away and brought platters of food to set upon the embroidered cloth. Batu and I chewed roasted hare in silence. *A warlord*, I kept thinking. *A warlord!* The dark meat stuck in my throat.

In the morning, in the stable, I smoothed my hand across Gryphon's shoulders. 'Will you still come with me?' I asked Batu in a small voice.

'I have sworn to be your companion in this war, and we will find Failak together by nightfall,' he replied, leaning his shoulder against Rain, his jaw set in a determined line and his eyes a steady, fierce gleam in the dim light. 'I am not afraid, Kalli.'

We rode on whilst our host and his wife, with the three small children pressing against their trousers, stood in their doorway and watched us leave, their faces long and frightened between their black hair and earrings. Gryphon and Rain were fresh after their night confined to a stable, and trotted hour after hour until at last the track grew too steep and narrow and they were forced to walk. The thin air sang in my ears. Beneath us, long ridgelines and rocky scree fell away in vast expanses of grass and stunted junipers. The track was marked now with piles of curved ibex horns and the bleached skulls of mountain rams; in winter, these cairns of bone would mark the way for travellers in the drifting snow. We skirted a canyon, and came at last down the slope from a high pass, and saw a village of one-storey homes clinging to the far side of a valley in a jumble of stone terraces. Blankets, draped over a rope to dry, snapped in gusts of cold wind. The shadows were purple and deep as we rode towards the village, skirting a herd of shaggy yaks. I felt the village's many windows staring down at us like eyes. My skin crawled.

A warlord, I thought.

'You must turn back and ride home,' said the voice of our host.

Swan, Swan. *I am doing this for you.*

I pressed my lips in a tight line and rode on, silent behind Batu, although my knuckles were white on the reins. The leather-clad men, mounted on shaggy ponies, seemed to appear on the wind like snow-flakes, riding along on each side of us and to our rear, cutting off our escape. Rough dogs with glinting eyes and open mouths trotted beside the men.

'Ignore them,' Batu muttered ahead of me, and I stared at Rain's black and white quarters, and willed myself to keep moving towards the houses of that village, built like a fortress in the side of the mountain.

The horses waded through a rushing stream, and then Batu reined in, and turned to me. 'We should walk from here,' he said, and I nodded; it was a sign of respect to lead one's horse towards a nobleman and, in the tribes, if you failed to show this respect to a chief, you might lose your horse.

We walked, my legs stiff and tense, and with our mounted guard drawing closer, flushing us into the village like a hunting party flushing pheasant from the grass. I could hear the dogs panting. Gryphon snorted gustily, uneasily, his ears laid back and eyes rolling. I laid my palm upon his withers, and then clasped the amulet of leopard hair, in its bag of golden leather, lying at the base of my throat, below where the knife had nicked me the previous night.

We were halted at the edge of the village, where the track led into the first dusty alley, and faces – their cheeks glazed dark with sun and wind – peered out from doorways with sills painted bright blue. 'We seek the honourable Failak on a matter of business!' Batu cried clearly, standing very tall, to the man who had halted us, his battleaxe held horizontally to block the street.

'Give me your names, and wait,' the man commanded. He disappeared up the street with long strides, and our mounted guard closed in around us, eyeing us with suspicion and muttering to each other in their harsh, foreign tongue. I bent my head, staring at the ragged hem of my oldest tunic of brown linen. I remembered the days I'd worn it before, long ago before the war; I had worn it to train Gryphon, a hot-blooded colt, eager to run. Now, beneath the tunic, my jewel casket was a hard, heavy rectangle.

I turned my thoughts quickly away from it, as though the men guarding us might follow the direction of my thoughts and strip me of my wealth before I ever reached the warlord.

The hooves of the shaggy horses stamped and shuffled restlessly in my line of vision; at last, the boots of the man with the axe reappeared.

'Give me your weapons,' he demanded, and a terrible chill slid over me. My eyes flew to Batu's face; it was set in proud lines, but he unbuckled his dagger from his belt and held it out stiffly, followed by his quiver and bow. After I had done the same, the men took the reins of our horses and led them away to a stable. We walked on, feeling naked, and climbing upwards past the houses' flat roofs, and women toiling in patches of garden surrounded by stones.

At the top of the village, we came into a flat space before a high wall, beyond which rose the facade of a three-storey house with wooden beams, and a watchtower reached by a ladder of poles. In the midst of this dusty flat space, a man stood waiting for us, a tall pillar of brilliance. Although I was too shy to steal more than quick glances at him, I saw that he was clad in a brocade tunic of azure blue, trimmed with the costly fur of the black sable and held with a belt encrusted with turquoise stones. His cloak of black sable hung elegantly over his shoulders, and his trousers were stuffed into knee-high boots of four different colours of leather. I noted, in my quick glances, that everything he wore was clean and perfectly cut, and richly embroidered. His hands, clasped loosely before him, were as hard and lean as talons, and rings of turquoise flashed on every finger. His face too was lean and smooth above his oiled beard, and his hair was a cascade of perfectly curled waves. In the streets of Kokand, merchants and artisans, and even wealthy traders, would have made way for him.

The earring in one of his ears glinted in the setting sun as he considered us intently for a long moment and, although his face remained impassive, his eyes were sharp points of interest. Then a muscle twitched at one corner of his mouth, as though he might smile.

Perhaps he is not a warlord after all, I thought, but merely a rich trader who prefers not to live in the city. He does not seem like the leader of a bandit horde.

'The honourable lady Kallisto,' he said at last. 'What a great and most unexpected pleasure to welcome you here. I know your father; we have traded together in the past. Perfume, I believe it was, that I obtained from him. And coral beads.'

His voice took me by as much surprise as his appearance already had, for it was mild and soft. A glimmer of hope rose in me and I flashed a glance at Batu but his face remained set in stiff lines. Perhaps all would be well now, I thought, and by tomorrow we could ride home. We must ride home tomorrow! There were only two days left of the seven days that Arash had granted me to bring the treasure and save Swan.

'My guests, you look weary. You shall dine with me, and only later need you state your business. Come.'

Failak's sable cloak swung as he turned to a door in the wall; we followed him through it. Inside, on the second floor of the house, I stared in wonder at the furnishings: the tapestries and thick knotted carpets, the couches with satin bolsters, the stools of inlaid wood. A glance out of a window showed me only bleak slopes dotted with yaks, and I heard the cold wind gusting against the wooden poles of the ladder leaning against the watchtower.

We ate shortly, our host sprawled on a striped divan, and guards posted at the doors. Women carried in dishes of chased silver, heaped with rice and braised lamb in a creamy sauce flavoured with cumin. Over the table's low surface, Failak watched us with the same intent, expectant look with which he'd considered us outside. It was the expression that a cat wears, waiting for a mouse to venture from its burrow. He wiped his ringed fingers fastidiously clean on a linen cloth, and picked his teeth with the point of a very narrow dagger, its handle encrusted with pearls and turquoise.

'And what is it?' he asked softly at last. 'This matter of business?'

Batu stared at me, his eyes sending me strength, as I struggled to find my voice. 'It's about – about a g-golden harness,' I stuttered. Failak bent his head encouragingly towards me, his gaze impassive now, and sipped wine from his golden drinking horn as I explained how I knew about the harness in Ershi that had been given to Arash's father after a lion hunt, and then promised to a prince, and finally lost in a drunken wager. 'Is there – is there another harness?' I dared to ask.

Failak ran his hand down the drinking horn's golden curve, as though he were stroking a pet. 'I really don't know if there is another harness,' he replied. 'Just after my men found the first one, I was called away on a matter of urgency, and I have only returned home within the last few days. Matters to do with the war, and involving business ventures, detained me. So now I too am anxious as to whether there is a second such golden harness. Shall we ride out and search in the morning?'

'Ride where?' I asked.

'To the tombs,' he said. 'Where else do you think that such an ancient treasure could have come from? There are burial chambers all along the ridge behind us, where the nomadic peoples – who used to pasture here – once buried their dead. You are not afraid of ghosts, are you?'

And he smiled at me in the lamplight, a slow smooth stretching of his lips like a cat stretching after the mouse has come out of its burrow at last, and been devoured.

Chapter 14

'You cannot do this!' Batu insisted, his hands a tight grip on my shoulders as we stood in the hallway outside the room where I had slept.

'I must do it, for Swan. You know it's my only chance to save her!'

'No, Kalli, we must ride home, right now. You cannot go into the abodes of the ancestors and rob them! The ancestors are our spirit guides, watching over us, sending us wisdom and blessing. To be a tomb raider is a most terrible thing. Great evil will befall you if you do this!'

I shook myself free of his hands and stepped away. 'I did not come this far to turn back. In Ershi, we do not worship the ancestors as you worship them in the tribes. I am not afraid,' I lied, although my legs quivered.

'I am afraid,' Batu said hoarsely. His high cheeks

were blanched pale, and in his eyes there was a grim flatness that I had never seen before. I stared at him, feeling blood drain from my heart.

'I have never heard you admit to fear in all your life.'

'But it's true,' he insisted. 'Listen to me! This house is filled with ghosts. All night I heard them rustling in the darkness. I heard the tramp of booted feet going past my bedroom door, but when I opened it, no one was there. I heard the neighing of horses and the clatter of weapons in the courtyard below, but when I went to the window, the yard was empty, bleached by moonlight. This man Failak lives in a haunted world. He thinks that the power of the turquoise will guard him against the evil eyes, but all the stones in his mine will not be enough to protect him if he is robbing the ancient ones. And so, I am afraid, Kallisto, and you should be afraid too. You should flee this place while you still can.'

I stared at Batu, my eyes stretched wide. On the wall behind him hung a tapestry worked in crimson wool and showing men mounted on elephants, hunting tigers in the long grass. Against the picture's brilliance, Batu's face remained set in hard lines, and his uncombed hair was as ruffled as the wing of a bird in a contrary wind. I laid my hand upon his arm but he shook it off.

'*He who does not venture into the lion's lair will never steal her cubs*,' I quoted, a proverb in the tribes, but Batu's stony gaze did not change. I sighed. 'If I do not save Swan, I will walk with her ghost all my life. I must do this, Batu.'

'I will not come to the tombs with you. You will ride alone.'

A great stone dropped into my stomach, and I staggered against the tapestry at my back; the weight of that stone dragged my shoulders down over my ribs and made my legs shake harder. A silent cry poured from my dry lips. For a long, terrible moment, Batu and I glared at each other, our jaws set in obstinacy and pure fright.

'Have it your way!' I cried. 'Stay here. I don't care!'

I brushed past him and strode to the stairway; despite the hot tears welling in my eyes, I ran down those packed mud steps two at a time, and did not falter even when Batu called my name, an urgent cry. I was knuckling the last traces of dampness from my eyes as I burst into the courtyard, and found Failak pacing the dusty expanse and staring out over the rooftops of his stolen village.

He turned at the sound of my footsteps, his sable cloak swinging open over a robe of velvet from Samarkand, embroidered with gilt thread and decorated with imported jet beads. 'Ah, the honoured lady Kallisto,' he said smoothly. 'And where is your tribal bodyguard this morning?'

'He is n-not interested in c-coming t-to the tombs.' My tongue almost tied itself into knots, and my eyes darted around the courtyard, unable to meet Failak's gaze.

'Indeed, it is hard to find loyalty,' he murmured. 'But we shall ride to the tombs nonetheless. Perhaps your boy might like a day of hunting instead. I shall arrange it.'

He turned away, his boots plainer than those he'd worn yesterday, and his trousers covered with leather leggings for riding in, and shouted for men and horses. I remained rooted to the spot, staring over the valley with its grazing yaks and camels scattered along the thread of a cold river. Behind my shoulders, I could feel the ridges of the mountains rising up, looming over me like a great wave about to drown me; I could feel the brooding presence of the burial mounds marching along the watershed. Every fibre in my body strained to run, to flee, to cry for Batu, to gallop away on Gryphon. I gritted my teeth and remained perfectly still, pressing the soles of my boots deeper and deeper into the hard dirt of the warlord's courtyard. At any moment, I thought, Batu would join me. I waited for his footsteps in the dirt, his hand on my shoulder; I ached for his joyful grin, his fierce whoops of laughter.

It was not until I was mounted on a shaggy chestnut pony, and riding up the grass track carved into the side of the mountain, that I understood at last that Batu had meant what he said: he was not coming with me.

'Your stallion will be glad of a rest after your long ride from Ershi,' Failak said as we rode. 'He was stabled overnight and given grain but now he is out on the pasture, loosely hobbled, and I have set a man to watch over him.'

I stared down into the valley, hoping to catch a glimpse of gold, a gleaming flash, but we were high up now, and the herds were merely specks below us. My chestnut pony was sure-footed and strong; he went steadily up the steep grassy track, where once the funeral chariots had pulled the dead, their organs removed, their bodies packed with fragrant herbs and stitched back together with horsehair thread. Then they were covered in honey, and wrapped in felt blankets, and bound with woollen ropes. Slowly they had wound their way upwards, laid upon their chariots, accompanied by their grieving kinsmen, their lamenting children, and their fast, slender horses. They had ascended, in their last journey, towards the great heavens filled with blue daylight, and the dark burial pits that would hold their mortal remains while their spirits rode onwards, mounted on their horses, into the afterworld.

A shiver racked my body, and I felt Failak watching me from the corner of his eyes, but he said nothing. We rode on, breaking out of the valley's pool of shadow and into the warmth of the rising sun. The track levelled out as we attained the crest of the ridge. And now, ahead of us, lay the long barrows of the dead. They were grassy swells, longer and higher than small houses, with sloping shoulders built of stone and soil heaped over the central burial chambers.

'For many long years they have been here,' Failak said softly at my shoulder, drawing rein. 'But what need have the dead for jewels and weapons, horse harness and knotted carpets? Why should the living be deprived of riches that can be taken without a battle, without a coin? From the Scythian dead, I have obtained some fine treasures, long forgotten by anyone now alive.'

His black horse stamped a foreleg nervously, and the sun gleamed on its bridle inlaid with turquoise stones. We rode on. The chestnut pony's breath came in anxious snorts, and he shied violently several times, almost unseating me, but when I looked around I could see nothing that might have frightened him. I knew that there were many things in the world that horses could sense when their human riders saw nothing. Now the barrows rose around us, and the teasing wind died into utter silence. Only the fretful breathing of the horses could be heard and the high, far-off whistle of a mountain bird. The silence pressed me down, smaller and smaller, shrinking me until the weight and size of the barrows grew enormous, and I was trapped between them. A cold sweat ran between the bones of my spine.

Failak drew rein at last, and smiled pleasantly at me, and stroked the curls of his oiled beard; I could smell the costly perfume of myrrh in the oil. 'This barrow is the one that my men were working upon before I rode to Ershi on business,' he said, gesturing at the largest mound we had yet ridden past, lying in the centre of the line of tombs. 'It was from here that the golden harness was obtained. Indeed, there might well be more than one harness for why would there be only one horse pulling? A team is more likely, and thus the existence of more than one harness. It is as well for your mare, Swan, that she has a mistress who is clever as well as beautiful.'

He dismounted in one lithe motion, and held out his hand to me but I ignored it and swung off the pony unaided. When we tried to lead the ponies towards the swell of the tomb, they dug their small hard hooves into the thin soil, and stretched their necks out with eyes rolling. My chestnut chewed on his snaffle bit in agitation, the iron grinding against his teeth and foam gathering on the bit rings. Before my eyes, both ponies broke into a sheen of sweat across their chests and necks, although the air was thin and cool. Failak laughed again, soothingly, and spoke to the ponies in his own tongue, yet still they refused to walk forward.

'I will wait here, and hold them lest they bolt away,' he said. 'My men have dug into a tunnel that leads into the centre of the tomb, and you can crawl along it and explore. There is a lamp set just inside the entrance. Here, a flint to light the oil.' He reached into one boot and pulled out a flint which he held out to me. I stared at him, the hairs standing up along my arms.

'A-alone?' I asked. 'I am to go a-alone?'

'I will sit and wait,' he said. 'And the ponies can graze. There is no rush, Kallisto. Once you have found the harness, if it exists, you can ride again for home and be in time to save your mare. You have until tomorrow night to bring the harness to Arash, you said?'

I nodded mutely. It was like the beginning of a dream as I watched myself, a tiny figure surrounded by the long sleep of the dead ones, stretch out my hand and take the flint from the warlord's ringed fingers. Then the small figure that was me stumbled around the shoulder of the barrow where the wind sprang up, rushing through the sparse tussocky grass. The figure tripped over a grey stone, and half fell towards the dark mouth of the catacomb tunnel that led into the tomb. Heaps of dry soil, threaded with cracks by wind and sun, marked where Failak's men had dug their way into the barrow, and the girl in my dream stooped and peered into the darkness. Then she reached into the shadows and felt around for the terracotta dryness of the lamp's belly, and used the flint to spark a tiny flame that quivered in the cold draught swelling from the tunnel. She looked around, her face rigid, and cast an anguished glance back through the rounded shoulders of the barrows and down the sweep of grassy track falling into the valley, but no one rode there. Nothing moved but the wind, and the shadows of small clouds, and the furry scamper of a marmot. No boy rode upwards on a black and white horse.

Then the girl fell to her knees and crawled forward into the tomb, and was lost from sight while the man on the hill gazed around peacefully, seated on a stone, beside the quivering ponies drenched in sweat.

The tunnel was narrow, lined with stones gathered from the mountain scree above. I inched my way along, holding the lamp with one hand. It was like going into the belly of a snake, that creature beloved of the evil Angra. I craned back once, painfully, over my shoulder, and saw a pinprick of daylight behind me at the entrance, and crawled on. The next time that I looked back, only darkness lay behind. I pressed my face into the darkness ahead, and crawled onwards shielded by the brave flicker of my lamp flame although occasional gusts of air made it leap and gutter. Now I felt the walls widening away on either side, and a yawning pit of darkness opened up. The tiny flame of the lamp threw leaping shadows over the burial chamber lying at the tomb's centre. I stood up cautiously, but the ceiling of tree trunks was higher than my head. Walls of rocks and soil curved away, and at my feet the soil was trampled and marred with drag marks from the robbers who had been here before me; those men who had found the golden harness. I lifted the lamp higher, spilling oil down my arm, biting back my whimper of fright.

I am alone here, I reminded myself. *There is nothing here to harm me.* But the ghosts of the nomads hunted across the emptiness, picking up their arrows with poisoned tips of bronze, mounting their excited horses, and narrowed their eyes as they spotted me, their prey, invading their sacred spaces, disturbing their long rest. Those ghosts could ride faster than I could run; there was no place on earth that I might hide from them, though I might travel as far away as my father and brothers had, to the far shining seas that lapped the shores of Greece and Arabia. Still those ghostly hunters would pursue me, seeking vengeance.

I could not move.

I could not breathe.

For an endless time, for a time when there was no time but only darkness and terror, I stood holding my lamp. Than I shuffled one foot forward. 'Swan.' I released her name into the darkness; a prayer, a cry, a whisper that licked and curled around the inside of the tomb, that made the ghostly hunters draw rein, and listen intently, like men listening to a change in the sound of the wind.

I shuffled my other foot forward. My toe nudged against an arrowhead, its three-lobed metal points crumbling with rust. My light fluttered over a broken clay jar, a pale oyster shell filled with the dried remains of body paint the colour of ochre, of ox blood.

My other foot moved forward. My lamp flame flattened low, as though a hand had passed over it. Then it wavered upwards again. I took a deep breath.

A deer antler, used to dig the central pit, clattered against a stone as I bumped it. Its points were worn to a jagged dullness. A blue bead rolled away into the darkness.

Something was behind me. I swung around, but saw nothing but leaping shadows. I turned back, and felt a cold breath on my neck. My hair crawled across my scalp.

In the centre of the tomb, the wooden coffin was aligned with the occupant's head facing east towards the rising sun, and was carved with stags' horns and with long, sinuous leopards twisting back on themselves, and snarling ferociously.

A clay altar stood beside the coffin, and a grimy bronze mirror lay on the floor nearby. I was in the tomb of a priestess, a woman with tattoos on her face and magic in her fingers, a woman who could toss the bones of sheep and divine the future, who could ride to battle with her tribe and lead them to certain victory. My fingers flew to the leather pouch of leopard hair that I wore at my neck, and I prayed for her forgiveness. Yet such a woman, I thought, would have power that reached beyond her death, and would bring great evil to those who desecrated her burial place.

My chest heaved as I sought for air. The tomb closed in around me, the walls shrinking, the air so thick with must and decay that I couldn't draw it into my lungs.

I stepped closer to the altar. The bones of many horses lay strewn and disordered in a semicircle at its base. Once they had lain side by side, wonderful horses that the warrior priestess would gallop across the grasslands of the afterworld. Now their bones were in disarray for the tomb raiders had thrown them around, stripping away the rich harnesses. The flame of my lamp ran over the bones' long pale shafts; forelegs and hind, the arc of ribs, the heaviness of skulls, the blank eye sockets. No harness remained, not a bit ring, not a strap of leather, not a single face mask with antlered horns, not a trace of gold inlay, not a stitch of embroidery, not a scrap of bright felt or wool, not the wink of one precious stone. Nothing. It had all been taken.

The lamp wobbled in my grasp.

I spun on my heels, and dashed to the tunnel. Faintly, behind my shoulders, I could hear the war cries of the tribes, echoing against the stones as they set their horses into a flat gallop, their long swords raised in their hands as they swept after me, hunting me now to the ends of the earth, and the end of my days.

I fell to my knees, sobbing, scrabbling at the tunnel. I was a badger when the hounds have sniffed it out, and have entered its lair.

'Failak!' I cried as I neared the entrance, the far-off gleam of shining daylight. It was only then that I realised the cave mouth was no longer the ragged oval that it had been when I entered it. Now only a sickle of light marked where I could escape. I dragged myself towards it on my elbows, the lamp spilling more oil down the sleeve of my old linen tunic. A flat stone had been shifted against the entrance, and was obscuring the light.

'Failak!' I cried again, and his face appeared in the slender gap, the sun shining in the fine hairs of his dark fur hat and in the gold inlay of one front tooth.

'No,' he said smoothly. 'Alas, no harness. I fear your mare must meet her fate. And you, Kallisto, need be in no hurry now to reach Ershi again. And it has come to my memory what a rich man your father is, a very rich man with a large city house filled with foreign treasures, with a farm in the valley where Persian horses run in the pastures. All year long, the camels and donkeys and ox wagons haul the trade goods into Ershi, goods from Arabia and India and the islands of the Mediterranean, from Greece, from the cold Baltic lands to the north, from the forests of the Caucasus, and the pastures around the mighty Don River. Such a man as your father, I think, has one thing that he treasures above all this and that no trading deal could bring to his door. Am I right?'

He stared at me, his eyes as intent and hungry as they had been on the previous evening when he looked at me across his plate of meat and rice. I was silent with shock.

'Yes, I am right,' he said. 'Above all the treasures in his warehouses and ledgers, your father prizes his only daughter. And if he wishes to see her again, he must pay. He must send me a great sum of wealth! He must atone for the swindle he pulled on me, cheating me when I traded with him, sending me less than the full weight of goods we had agreed upon!'

'My f-father does not cheat!' I had hoped to sound brave, even outraged, but my voice shot out in a high squeak. Failak's lips curled contemptuously.

'What do you know of trade?' he sneered. 'You run around playing at games, a spoiled child whining about the life of one mare. I will have a valley full of mares; your father shall send them in exchange for your life! He shall send camels here, laden with drinking horns of gold, with bales of brocade, with Arabian incense!'

He leaned down until his face was inches away from mine, silhouetted against the slice of light. 'You will stay here until your father pays your ransom,' he said. 'My men have already placed food and water, and extra oil, to the left of the main chamber. No harm shall befall you until the full ransom is paid.'

Then he was gone, before I could even protest, and after a pause the stone shifted with a grating roar, and I heard the voices of other men, Failak's servants who must have been hidden and waiting amongst the barrows before I even rode up the mountain towards the morning sun.

Then there was silence. No wind. No bird cry. No snort of horse, no voice. I lay in the tunnel, and felt the cold dirt beneath my cheek, while the lamp burned lower and the ghostly nomads crept towards me, their daggers drawn in their calloused fists and their tall, dry horses shining in the gloom like mirages in the desert.

I lay there while the sun's chariot rolled over the mountains, while Failak returned to his house and called for wine, while Batu hunted wild sheep with the warlord's men. I lay there while the army of the Middle Kingdom rolled their siege engines closer to Ershi's walls, while brave horses fell in cavalry attacks, while my mother fought for her life.

But I did not fight for mine. Not now. If my father returned home one day, and the war ended, and the ransom note was delivered to him and the terms fulfilled, still it wouldn't matter. None of it would matter because Swan would be dead. I had failed to save her, and she was trapped in Ershi still, grinding her grain with her teeth, slowly, peacefully, in the last days left to her.

I lay there on the cold floor, breathing the mouldy thickness, while the sun set in the west, and my lamp's flame sank into its puddle of oil and began to smoke. At last, I roused myself and dragged myself back into the main tomb, and found the jars of water and the extra oil that Failak's men had placed there, perhaps last night while I lay in a guestroom beneath the watchtower, tossing between the fine soft sheets.

Using a leather cup, I took water from a jar and drank it; it tasted as musty and cold as the air felt around me. For the first time, I noticed the funeral chariot standing behind the bones of the horses on its high wheels; its wooden sides were carved with flying swans. In my mother's tribe too, swans were a bird that could connect your spirit to heaven. I stared at the funeral chariot for a long time. Perhaps, if I died here in this place of despair, a white bird would come for me and lift me on its wide wings into the shining air. And perhaps the priestess lying in the coffin would forgive me for having disturbed her rest; perhaps she would understand that I had done this terrible thing for love of a white mare, a mare with wings on her feet.

Failak had said the tombs had belonged to the Scythians, a race lost and scattered now across the mountains and plains of the world. My father had a book scroll, written in ancient times by a man called Herodotus who had travelled through our lands. He had written about the Scythians, I remembered; and I had read his *Histories* aloud to my family as we sat on the rooftop in the oppressive heat of a summer evening, a lightning storm flickering over the foot-hills. There was one phrase of Herodotus' that my mother and I had liked very much. I repeated it now, softly, into the tomb's stillness, for it was a line about the Scythians: *'Their country is the back of a horse.'*

The words seemed to hang in the air; I felt the ghosts listening. I repeated the phrase more loudly, and my voice echoed back off the stones as though a ghostly chorus was speaking to me. I went rigid with fright, and remained too frightened to make another sound; I tiptoed to the wall of the tomb, as far as I could get from the coffin and the chariot, and slouched against the wall with the stones pressing their roughness into my back. I tried not to think about how far away my father was, or to wonder if my mother was still alive, or to try and guess where Batu had gone. He had been right, I acknowledged now, and I should not have come here. I let my anger at him slip away.

Even though by now it must have been dark with the moon climbing the sky, I was too afraid to close my eyes. Every time my lids began to drift shut, things moved stealthily in the corner of my vision and my ribs clenched around my heart. I pinched the back of my hand, hard, and straightened my spine against the stones. Staring into the shadows, I dared the ghosts to step into plain view before they seized my spirit. But perhaps I would die before that happened; I would die here alone, and no ransom could ever bring me back.

Chapter 15

Time stood still. Gradually the water in the jar sank lower. Occasionally I ate a handful of dried apricots or some walnuts but I had no appetite. My grief for Swan curdled my stomach, and slowed my heartbeat. Occasionally I refilled the oil in my lamp; its flames rose and fell, illuminating all that there was to see: the funeral chariot, the coffin, the horses' bones. I removed the golden torc that Berta had given me, and laid it on the altar as a gift, and begged the dead warrior priestess to wear it in her afterlife and to forgive me. Sometimes I squeezed my eyes shut and hoped that when I opened them again I would find I had been trapped in a dark dream and that around me I would see my own familiar room in our house in Ershi. But this never happened.

My mind plodded along, dull and slow, or roused itself into fits of fear and panic, scrabbling inside my skull like a marmot in a snare. When this happened, I would tell myself stories to calm my mind. I told myself about Bucephalus, the great Persian horse that had belonged to Alexander the Great, a conqueror who had ridden through our lands centuries ago. He and Bucephalus had campaigned and fought together through mountains and deserts, through howling blizzards and scorching summers, companions in conquest in many foreign lands. Alexander had a coin minted bearing the head of his horse, his forelock standing straight up and his mane hogged off short. My father had one of these ancient pieces in a chest at home. When Bucephalus had died at the great age of thirty, the grieving Alexander named a city in his honour.

But thinking about Bucephalus's death only made me cry for Swan.

So then I told myself the nomad tale about the winged horses that used to drink at an oasis pool, but were spied upon by a cunning king. One night he poured wine into the water, and the horses drank it and became giddy and weak. Thus the king's men were able to clip the horses' wings so they could no longer fly in the air, but instead had to fly over the land on their fleet feet, and serve mankind.

But thinking about this story only made me think about Swan too, a mare with wings on her heels when we ran together in the summer pastures.

And so, I tried to close my mind to stories, and I was dozing when the ground began to shake. The first vibration was so faint that I thought I had imagined it; it was like a tingle in my bones. I opened my eyes, and held myself very still. Perhaps now the ghosts were coming at last to rend my spirit from my aching body. The second vibration was stronger, running through the cold ground as though the horses in my stories had come alive and were galloping to me, shaking the earth with their pounding hooves. I sprang to my feet. Now the ground shifted beneath the soles of my boots, harder, faster. I whirled around, holding the lamp high. A cry of terror broke from my lips.

A dull murmur rose through the rocks and soil, and became a grinding roar: the mountain was speaking. Soil trickled between stones, and dust thickened the stale air. I pressed my sleeve across my mouth and struggled to remain standing as the tomb trembled. Now the floor shook like a rug hanging to dry in a strong wind. Roaring filled my head, dust blinded me. The ground pitched beneath me, and cracks zigzagged across the floor. Walls tilted and swayed.

Earthquake!

The mountain spirits were angry, fierce, shaking the world like a dog shaking its prey in its teeth.

I lurched as the ground rose under my feet, and pitched forward. My lamp flew from my hand and plunged me into momentary darkness. Then a burning thread of oil mingled its smoke with the swirling dust. I coughed and choked, dragging off my robe to throw over it and extinguish the flames.

All around me in the pitch darkness, I felt walls and roof beams, and the mountain itself, sliding and buckling and heaving. The mountain was a horse now, a bucking, twisting horse being ridden by the mountain spirits in their rage. I staggered in the dark, blind and terrified. A rock rolled across one foot. Something struck my head a glancing blow across the temple, and stars with ragged tails soared across my vision.

Slowly, the ground became still and the loud roar subsided into a growl. Crawling on my hands and knees, I felt around for my fallen lamp, and then took it to the oil jars. Spilled oil coated my palms, and I felt the rough shape of one of the jars, cracked open and rolling on its side. The other jar was still upright and I used its contents to fill my lamp. Then I pulled the flint from inside my boot, and struck a flame.

On one side of the tomb, the roof beams of round tree trunks were smashed into pale splinters, and had fallen across the altar and the coffin. My glance skittered away from the dusky bundle that lay inside, wrapped in crumbling felts and reed mats. Swinging around, I saw that the tunnel through which I had entered the tomb was blocked with fallen stones, and that I would never be able to crawl through it again even if my father came with a whole caravan of camels to pay my ransom. I stood up slowly and shuffled across piles of dirt and stone to the chamber's far side, where the wall had collapsed and the beams had fallen inwards. I stared at it for a long time, and felt a whisper of hope rise in me.

Fetching the antler bone, with its dull tips and its patina of age, I began to gouge at the tomb wall. Stones fell inwards, crushing my toes. Dirt showered into my hair and eyes; I felt it rolling down inside my tunic, gritty against my skin. I jabbed the antlers into the wall over and over, and scooped dirt out with my fingers. It felt as though I worked for hours, lying on my belly, sweat running down my sides, my fingernails breaking and tearing, my tongue pressed against my teeth as I struggled through the wall and the soil that the earthquake had loosened. From time to time, I stopped to rest. Once the ground vibrated again, and I flattened myself into the dirt fearfully, but then the tingle subsided. I continued digging and scooping, pulling the loosened rock and soil towards me and then pushing it downwards between my legs. My boot toes scrabbled for purchase as I climbed slowly up through the roof of the tomb. I strained up and up, like the pale shoot of some buried flower, trying to reach sunlight.

And then, there was the light, a thread of brightness. A blue woollen skein of morning sky. A patch of carpet woven with cloud patterns. A bird, flying southwards over the Pamirs. I pushed my hand out into that daylight and let it lick my dirty skin, my torn, cut, bleeding fingers. I opened my mouth wide and tasted the air filled with wind and flowering grasses and warm mountainside and the resinous oil of juniper. Weak tears of gratitude ran down my face. Someone's prayers had reached the ears of the mountain spirits; perhaps Berta had prayed for me, seated by the hearth fire of her yurt; or perhaps my mother, lying queenly and proud in her high Greek bed; or perhaps Batu had implored aid for me. Or maybe, even, the dead warrior, lying in her coffin surrounded by her wonderful fleet-footed horses, had accepted my gift of a golden torc, and had roused the spirits to set me free. The mountain had released me from its belly's dark embrace.

I wriggled forward until my stomach was pressed into the grass and only my legs still dangled down into the tiny cavity I had cleared between the loosened stones. And then I felt it a third time; that trembling in my bones. The mountain roared again, grating and grinding and shifting. A bird shrieked. Clouds rushed past, grass waved as though a great wind swept down upon it. I twisted and rolled on the heaving slope; behind and beneath me there was a louder roar as more of the tomb roof collapsed inwards. I cried out as the weight of a tree beam landed across one of my legs, pinning me in place. As the quake subsided, I gripped handfuls of grass and tried to drag myself out from under the beam's weight but the stems broke in my grip, or tore out by their pale roots. I stretched as far as I could and searched through the grass for a stone to grip but found nothing. I kicked and scrabbled with my free foot but couldn't dislodge the beam.

Anger rose in me and I clawed and beat at the ground. Still my leg remained trapped in the mountain's pinch. I lay my head on my arm and waited for my pounding heart to quieten.

Faintly, from the valley below, came cries and shouts of alarm, and women's high wails. The bellows of yaks mingled with the roars of camels and the shrill neighing of ponies. Hoof beats drummed in my ears. I lifted my head to squint through the grass and there, on the curve of track leading up the mountain's flank, galloped a band of shaggy horses, rushing upwards. And there, ahead of them, a flash of gold!

I whistled, the shrill call of a bird, the sound my stallion had been familiar with since he was a colt with legs as long and fine as the spokes in chariot wheels. The horses had passed from my line of vision now. I whistled, over and over, at intervals.

The grass swayed. A hard black hoof appeared, a slender fetlock. A woollen hobble rope trailed between his legs, severed by a knife blade. A muzzle appeared before my face, shining like golden brocade, soft as velvet from Samarkand. He wore his own halter, one that I had made myself with Berta's help, twirling the rawhide on a wooden stick. Two lustrous eyes shone. Gryphon's hot breath gusted upon my arm, then my face, as he stepped cautiously forward, spooked, curious, obeying my whistle. I reached out and ran my fingers down his forelegs, talking to him, making his ears with their fringe of golden and cream hairs swivel in the sunlight. He ran his nose curiously over my body, snuffling at the tomb's grimy soil that clung to me, smelling my hair and my torn hands, before moving off a few paces and beginning to graze.

We were so close, yet he was free and I was trapped. Soon someone in the village below would notice that the tomb had collapsed, that the ponies were running on the mountain, and soon wild men with fierce dogs would come to return me to Failak's custody. 'Gryphon!' I called softly, urgently, my voice thick and raw in my parched throat. 'Gryphon!' I whistled and he drifted closer, closer, snatching at the summer grass, its flowers puffing dusty clouds into the air. I stretched my body out long, longer, my sinews burning, my fingers reaching. Then it was within my grasp: a thick fistful of black horse tail. I tugged, and Gryphon snorted and stepped backwards. I seized another handful of tail, higher up, and wrapped it around my fist.

'Gryphon,' I said, more commandingly, and he stopped grinding grass and swivelled his ears back, listening to me. 'Run!' I yelled. 'Run, Gryphon, run!'

He lunged forward, eyes rolling with excitement at this familiar command, and his tail tightened in my hand, cutting into my skin. For a moment, he threw himself against my weight and then he stopped, puzzled and confused by this strange manoeuvre that we had never practised. I stared at the slender length of his hind legs, tight with sinew, hard with bones that could break my arm, smash my cheeks. The curves of his hind hooves were hard as stone, sharp as dagger blades. He could kill me, but he was my only hope.

I spoke softly to him, waited until his eyes stopped rolling, cajoled him with a song that I had hummed when he slipped out of his mother's body and on to the stable floor, and as I wiped him dry with a twist of barley straw. Now, as he listened to my song, his hind hooves stopped stamping and he became still. Then I spoke his name again, and again I shouted at him to run. This time, when he plunged forward, the force of his motion jerked my arms in my shoulder sockets so that I felt a great tear run through my back, and I thought my bones would splinter. 'Run!' I shouted desperately, the world going black with pain, and my hands so tangled in his tail that I would never be able to free them. This was how men were punished, I thought: they were tied between four horses and then torn to pieces when the horses were made to run in four directions. My hands, wrapped with tail, would rip from my arms; my leg would tear free, inside the mountain, and lie by itself beneath the fallen beam.

'Run!' I screamed, and he dug his front hooves into the mountainside and lunged against my weight, his back hooves striking against small stones.

I lurched. I slid free! I flew over the grass, my boots dragging and the stallion's hind hooves whistling past my ears. Grass and rocks and shrubs raked my stomach. 'Whoa, Gryphon, steady, whoa!' I called and he stood still and began once more to crop grass in anxious snatches, his eyes rolling. He was on the verge of spooking, of running away across the mountain with my fists still tangled in his tail. Desperately I worked to free them; my fingers were white and bloodless from the tight wrap of the hair. I freed one hand, then the other, ripping at tough black hair with my teeth. I tried to stand but staggered, and was forced to wait for blood to run into my numb legs. Fumbling with haste, I untied the hobble ropes from Gryphon's fetlocks and retied the pieces on to his halter to make short reins. Then I used a stone to vault on to his back.

From this vantage point, I glanced around. Several of the tomb barrows had been damaged in the earthquake, and a great slide of rock had licked, like a long tongue, down the face of the mountain. One edge of this tongue had swiped at the warlord's village; I saw how its force had crushed the walls of houses, broken the garden terraces, and knocked over trees. The tiny specks of the villagers surged to and fro through the alleys and spilled out into the valley, calling and crying. Their ponies still ran loose amongst the tombs, edgy and excited. I nudged Gryphon with my heel, turning him away towards the ridge. We would escape over it into the valley on the far side, I thought, and ride away before anyone noticed us.

A flicker of motion caught my attention and I reined Gryphon back in. Below, where the track leading to the tombs began, a man was running as though for his life. A knot of mounted men eddied along the edge of the village. The running man dashed amongst a cluster of camels and disappeared. I waited for a long moment, while Gryphon shifted restlessly under me.

Batu? I could not be sure at this distance. If I rode down to find out, I might be caught – yet how could I ride over the ridge and leave him behind, if indeed he was alone in the valley, and on foot? I waited in an agony of indecision. Then the running man reappeared briefly, dodging at a crouch amongst the camels. I kicked Gryphon hard, sending him into a gallop, arrowing down the track with stones flying and with ponies dashing away in alarm. We pounded out over the valley floor, yaks gazing at us in mild curiosity, camels grunting; the narrow glint of the river filling my eyes. The knot of mounted horsemen burst from the shadow of the village and began to head straight for me with savage cries. The sun shone in their fur hats.

I swung Gryphon alongside the herd of camels, and the fugitive man rose from where he'd been hiding behind a lying beast, and began to run towards me, his arms pumping at his side, his legs knifing the sunlight. Faster and faster he ran. The horsemen were almost upon him now with daggers raised, and their ponies fighting their bits.

'Batu!' I screamed, and checked Gryphon's gallop slightly, holding him level with Batu's line of flight. The shadows of the horsemen surged into the corners of my eyes and I saw their black beards blowing in the wind, and the cruel gleam of their ponies' teeth. Then I swerved Gryphon around Batu in a tight arc, and watched as Batu dashed forward with a final, incredible burst of speed that brought him running alongside Gryphon. I kicked Gryphon on as Batu's feet left the ground in a flying leap, as he dragged at my waist, as his strong legs gripped my stallion's golden ribs. We surged away, the mountains a blur, the air cutting our eyeballs, our breath snatched from our lungs.

'Run! Run!' I screamed at Gryphon, and he went up the path towards the high pass like a shooting star. He was fresh from his days of resting in Failak's pastures, and even with two of us mounted on his back, he was still the fastest horse anywhere in these mountains. Once we had to skirt another rockslide caused by the earthquake, and once we had to dismount to lead Gryphon through a fissure that had opened in the ground. The knot of men gradually fell behind us as we crossed the high pass, weaving between the cairns of ibex horns and sheep skulls, and began the long descent towards the foothills. We were pursued for several hours, but eventually the last rider fell from view behind a ridge, and we were alone with the silence and the wind and the deep, tearing breath whistling through Gryphon's nostrils. Batu dismounted and jogged alongside.

It was dark when we stumbled into the shelter of the farm where we had spent the night before, on our way to find the golden harness. The buildings still stood, although a crack had opened in the wall of the house. The family had gone to bed; Batu fed the dog a morsel of dried meat to quieten it, and laid his palm upon Gryphon's sweating forehead. Then he wiped his hand on both our faces.

'The sweat of the winner is for luck,' he said softly, and I kissed Gryphon's face and led him around to cool him off. When I led him into the barn, I gave a start of surprise for I saw Rain's face turn to us as he nickered a welcome. I gave Gryphon a little water, slid his bridle off, and threw a blanket over his back. Finally, Batu and I climbed the ladder to the barn's flat roof. My leg, that had been trapped, was so stiff now that I could barely bend it, and I knew that blue bruises were blossoming on it like flowers. I collapsed on to a heap of hay being stored on the roof.

'Am I really here?' I asked Batu with a groan. I was so tired that I was floating. Every inch of my body ached; I was covered in spilled lamp oil, smoke, dust, bruises, scratches. My plaited curls stuck to my head as stiff as the plaits of a marble statue.

'Of course you're here. You didn't think I'd leave you in that cursed village, did you?'

'But what has happened? How long was I in the tomb?'

'The tomb?' Batu asked in astonishment. 'That's where you've been?'

I nodded. 'Tell me what has been happening.'

'After you rode to the tombs, Failak's men took me sheep-hunting. When we returned, Failak wouldn't tell me where you were; he said that you were being well cared for and you were comfortable, but that he was holding you for a ransom payment. He gave me a birchbark scroll to take to your father, who he was sure would soon be reaching Samarkand on his return journey from the Levant. He said I was to wait in Samarkand until your father arrived, then intercept him and give him the birch scroll with the ransom terms written upon it. He seemed to be preparing for a trip into the mountains, heading southwards. I was escorted from the valley by a band of horsemen and sent on my way.'

'When?'

'The morning after you rode to the tombs. After the horsemen left me, I came back to this farm and explained my situation. The farmer let me stable Rain here, because he is such a conspicuous horse that I couldn't risk riding him back to Failak's village. Then I borrowed a knife, and a bow and two arrows, and returned overnight on foot to Failak's valley. I have spent five days in hiding, spying on the village, trying to catch a glimpse of you and find a way to set you free. But I saw nothing. So this morning, I decided to free Gryphon from his guard and his hobbles, and to ride him away to fetch help, perhaps from your father if he could be found on his return journey from Samarkand, or perhaps from my own tribe.'

'It was you who freed Gryphon?'

'I shot his guard in the back, and then slid over the grass on my belly, and cut his hobbles with a knife. I was going to try to mount him and gallop away when the earthquake struck. Gryphon spooked; he was unmanageable and broke away to join the ponies that were running loose everywhere; all the herds were panicked and wild. I hid amongst some rocks and waited for a second chance to catch Gryphon. When the final quake happened, he galloped up the mountain track. I was trying to escape from view when you appeared, hurtling over the grass like a centaur!'

Batu's face split into an excited grin. 'You were magnificent!' he exclaimed. 'Where had you been for all these days?'

I told him about the tomb, empty of all treasure, and about the coffin of the warrior priestess. 'Perhaps it was she who set you free in return for the golden torc.' Batu made the sign with his hand to ward off evil power, and touched the amulet bags hanging from his throat.

'But even though I'm free, Swan is dead.' I burst into tears and cried against Batu's rough tunic for a long time, lying in the sweet, prickly hay beneath the dazzling stars. The horses rustled and chewed in the stable below, and far off a lone wolf howled, a note sad and thin on the still air.

'Hush,' Batu said at last. 'We will ride on soon, when Gryphon has rested. You must rest too. We will reach Ershi in less than two days. But how are you planning to enter the city?'

'I don't know,' I said, knuckling my eyes, worn out with crying. 'I hadn't worked that out yet in my plan . . . maybe I could join the cavalry as it fights, and then get back into the gates that way?'

'You have no armour now, and no weapons,' Batu pointed out. 'Maybe you had better stay in the valley with me and my raiding companions.'

'Maybe. But my mother! And our mares!'

'Hush,' Batu said again. 'We'll work something out. Go to sleep for an hour.'

I lay on my back and let stars fill my eyes; after the tomb's blank darkness, they were as beautiful as the notes of a song. For a brief flicker in time, I felt comforted.

But later, riding towards the dawn, towards the moment in the city when I would have to face Swan's absence, I sank back into numb grief. The landscape blurred past. Heat beat on to me. My bruised leg ached and throbbed. Batu whistled far away, in some place of his own. Shadows licked me. Birds stitched the high sky together. Gryphon swung along, easy and relaxed, unaware that his favourite mare had passed from the world. My chin sank against my chest, and my shoulders sagged under the heaviness of that grief. It was hard to breathe against it.

We reached Batu's valley on the second morning, and he exclaimed with surprise when we rode beside the river and were not stopped for a password. We arrived at the cave unchallenged, and Batu slid from Rain to duck inside; through my cloud of grief, I heard the murmur of voices. When Batu reappeared, his face shone.

'The war is over!' he cried. 'Some of the nobles rebelled, and killed the king. His head was sent out to the great general of the Middle Kingdom's army on a plate, accompanied by a letter! Ershi has a new king, who will deal peacefully with the Chinese, and will send horses eastwards for his cavalry. In return, silk will come into the Golden Valley.'

'The traders will be happy,' I said listlessly.

'The siege has lifted; my raiding band has broken up and the men are returning home. You can go and find your mother, Kalli!'

I nodded again but Batu's voice seemed as distant as the howl of a wolf, and of no importance. I waited while he went to the pasture to find the spotted Mountain, and to bring him with us on a lead rope. It was dusk as we dropped out of the foothills, and picked our way over the trampled fields, marred with the black circles of a thousand campfires. Trees stood like skeletons, stripped of limbs. The alfalfa crop was ruined, rolled over by thousands of wheels, trampled by the feet of oxen and camels and yaks. The canals were clogged with debris: broken harness, shattered arrow shafts, torn clothing.

'Too bad you aren't nomads,' Batu teased. 'You could just move on to fresh pastures.'

The enemy army was pulling out from the valley; already, its encampments were specks clustered along the foot of the mountains to the east, where once I had seen the dust rising as it marched to besiege us. Farmers and peasants moved silently along the valley tracks, creeping back from the mountains, returning home to their ruined fields, searching for missing oxen, bewailing the loss of their sheep and chickens.

We scouted under the willow trees where I had left my gear; surprisingly, the saddle was still there although my other things had been taken. I cinched it on to Gryphon's back before continuing. It was dusk when we approached Ershi's high walls, and slipped in the south gate through which I had surged fifteen days previously with the cavalry sortie. Then, anything had seemed possible. Now, I had lost my jewel casket and all its contents; they lay hidden under a mattress in the warlord's house beneath the watchtower. And now I had failed to find the golden harness. And now Swan – I turned my thoughts away from the memory of Swan, and pressed them against a blank wall of grief.

This is the darkest moment of my life, I thought miserably. *This is a terrible homecoming. I have failed completely.*

'Listen, the water is running,' Batu said as we rode up through the streets, and I heard the gurgle of the drains, and saw the stars reflected in a pool. Already, our engineers had repaired the harm done by the invaders, and had restored the flow of the river that kept Ershi clean and watered, its gardens green, its horse troughs filled.

Batu hammered on the door, and our young watchman, returned from the war, swung open the portal and demanded to know who stood outside. When I followed Batu in, Fardad rushed from the kitchen, wailing and crying my name. My legs buckled at the knees when I slid from Gryphon. Sayeh slipped from the stable, pushing through the yearlings and foals to take Gryphon's reins. The young horses turned their faces, their long, shining, dark faces, towards their stallion, and nickered gustily. I went past them without patting them, although I was jostled by hip bones and shoulders, and nudged by whiskered muzzles.

Swan, oh Swan!

Blinded by tears, I went up the stairs by feel, and blundered down the hall past the brilliant tapestries, and into my mother's chamber. Her head turned on the striped pillows and colour flooded her hollowed cheeks. With a grunt of effort, she pushed herself upright and leaned against the painted wall; tulips and tigers flowed around her head, behind her crown of golden plaits. Her blue eyes were clear and sharp, running over me.

'Mother!' I threw myself upon her damask coverlet, and laid my head against her chest; her fingers cradled me in a fierce grip.

'You're better now, Mother?'

'The fever has passed, and the wounds are knitting together. But you, my daughter ... what has happened to you?'

'I tried to save Swan, but I failed! I failed her, Mother! She is dead now, sacrificed by the magus because Arash stole her away from our courtyard and used her to win favour with the king.'

'That king is dead now,' my mother said. 'But Swan is still alive.'

'*What?*' I sat up, pushing escaped curls from my filthy face. 'What?'

'When the king's head was sent out to the enemy, a letter of treaty accompanied it. Lila's mother has been here and told me the very words in that letter. One of her daughters is married to a nobleman who took part in the rebellion and plotted to slay the king. The letter said that the people of Ershi would trade elite horses for silk, and provide the Son of Heaven with celestial steeds, if the enemy would lift its siege.

In return, Ershi would retain its army, and the safety of the city. But if the enemy would not agree to these terms, then all the horses inside Ershi would be slaughtered, and we would fight on until the walls fell, and there was not a warrior left to lift a weapon.'

'But Mother –'

She held up a white hand, ringed and calloused still, in an imperious gesture, and I subsided immediately into silence like one of her well-trained fillies.

'The terms were accepted,' my mother continued in her cool, steady voice. 'The Chinese general and his best horsemen entered our city, and chose the horses they wanted to take away with them, including most of our mares.'

'I'm sorry . . .'

'Listen, Kallisto. One of those horses they took was Swan, for Arash had not yet presented her for a sacrifice, and instead he gave her to the enemy. He could have kept her hidden but he wanted to obtain favour with the new king.'

'But Mother, are you sure? How do you know all this?'

A tiny smile quirked the corners of my mother's wide, stern mouth. 'Lila has been running around in this city like a nomad spy planning a horse raid, and your new body servant has been just as bad. And then, of course, Lila's mother can find news like a horse finding water. And Fardad has been in a state of pure agitation, and out gathering gossip in the marketplace like a man of half his years.'

Swan! Swan, *alive*!

My heart rose in me, like a phoenix rising from the ashes. I climbed to my feet, and my shadow leaped high upon the walls of my mother's room.

'I am going to wash, and eat!' I said, and then I kissed her firmly on both cheeks, and hobbled down the stairs to the courtyard, calling for hot water to be brought from the kitchen.

Swan, still alive. I had been granted one last chance to save her. It was time to leave myself behind; that timid, stuttering girl with the shy downward glance. It was time to raise my head high; to step through that door on the other side of war, as Berta had once said that I would. For Swan, I would transform myself, becoming a woman with a voice clear as a bird call, with eyes that did not waver; a woman who would be listened to when she spoke.

Chapter 16

'You cannot come with me – your mother would have a fit and lose her mind if she found out,' I told Lila sternly. She did not respond like a well-trained filly; she simply ignored me and continued applying purple imported mascara to her sweeping lashes.

'You had better go home and dress yourself,' she said at last. 'You said we will ride at daybreak, within the hour.'

As I sighed and turned to the door, Lila laid down her bronze-handled mirror and came over to hug me. 'The more servants you have with you, the more respect you will command,' she murmured, pressing her face to my shoulder. 'And Kalli, this might be our last chance for an adventure together. Now that the war is over, my father has decided I will be married before winter. I need to come with you to the army camp, I need one last gallop.'

A chill prickled my neck; I strained to hear the caged finches singing in their willow withy cage, but Lila's house was cloaked in silence. 'Of course you can come with me,' I whispered. 'But do you think you would be as splendidly dressed as this if you were truly my servant?'

She laid her long hand flat over her mouth, holding in a giggle, and her antelope eyes shone in the lamplight. 'The glory of the servant reveals the greater glory of the mistress,' she said, and ran a hand over the shimmering drapery of a new riding tunic; it was pale yellow silk with embroidery of blue and orange. 'My sister's husband obtained this silk from the Chinese generals,' she said. 'And my sister's tailor made it only yesterday. Will you please make sure to wear something as fine? Your green Indian silk?'

I nodded, and left her combing her hair, straight and long as a horse's tail, and dragged my sore leg through the withered garden. Bean vines crunched beneath my feet for the water had not been restored to Ershi in time to save them. As I changed in my room, pulling on the green silks and my best riding boots, Sayeh came looking for me, her blue eyes filled with anxious excitement.

'We are all ready in the courtyard,' she whispered.

I nodded, my stomach lurching with tension, and tiptoed into my mother's room where she slept peacefully and deeply; she did not stir as I lifted her long sword from its place against the wall. In the hallway, I buckled the sword around my waist. Then I followed Sayeh outside and gazed down. Batu, mounted on Rain, was splendidly dressed in new leather leggings over trousers of brilliant saffron, and had covered his dark head with a hat of wolf hair. He was flanked by three other tribesmen who had not yet returned home to their pastures. Still clad in their armour, they carried bows and arrows, long swords, and lances, and sat on their fidgeting horses with haughty ease.

'My father and most of his men have already gone home,' Batu said. 'But these men can spare you one day.'

Beside the tribesman, Lila, in her pale silks, sat astride Mountain while Sayeh stood holding the reins of the mule and of Gryphon. All the horses in the courtyard were splendidly arrayed in their best harness; the gleam of the dawn sky reflected off polished bits, semi-precious stones decorating brow bands, and inlays of gold and silver. Blankets lay upon backs, smooth and unwrinkled, and brilliant with embroidery; bright tassels hung from cruppers and breast plates. The horses' coats had been groomed to a high shine, and their fine tails lifted in the gusting breeze.

As I looked down at the assembled company, a grin split my face, and Batu's eyes lit up in response.

'Do you have the parchment and ink?' I asked

Lila, and she nodded. I felt in my own pocket one last time, my fingers curling around the cool lump of my father's seal, the extra one he left at home when he travelled away, and that would impress his mark upon any business document and make its contents binding. Then I took Gryphon's reins and mounted into my saddle, the one with the extra loops of leather that my mother had trained me, bruised and aching, to use through many long hours beneath the clapping poplar trees.

The wind lifted against my face as I rode towards the east gate at the head of my party of seven, and over the Alay Mountains the clouds were massing, boiling upwards in citadels of dazzling whiteness with dark underbellies. The elm and walnut trees tossed in the fitful air, and dust dervishes whirled in the road. We set the horses into an easy trot on a loose rein, and followed the retreating Chinese through the valley's broad bowl, passing fields where peasants swept the debris of the army from their mud homes and tilled their trampled fields into fresh furrows again.

'The horses are in the centre of the retreat,' one of the tribesmen told me in Turkic, trotting alongside Gryphon on a red roan gelding. His eyes were dark slits beneath the black curls of his astrakhan hat, and the wind snatched at his trailing beard.

'You are the spy?' I asked.

'Yes, I rode out last night after Batu came with

your request. The Chinese general has put the horses in the care of the horsemen he brought with him from the east. A high-ranking man named Sheng has been placed in charge of the elite horses and their care. Because the elite horses have been short of food and water during the siege, it has been decided that they need fresh fodder, and several days' rest, before being marched through the mountains. Some of the army will begin moving into the pass towards Osh today, but the remainder of the army will stay while the horses rest and eat before being moved on.'

'We will ride through the infantry until we reach the horse pastures,' I said, and the man nodded and dropped back to ride beside the other nomads.

The sun was high in the sky before we encountered the last fringes of the great army that had besieged us. We rode on along the track, through the midst of the tents and picket lines, the wagons and supply lines, the strange foreign tongues and slanting stares. No one stopped us, for now that the war was over, our countries were trading partners and at peace. I glanced once or twice at Sayeh, but my body servant's face remained impassive and I could not tell what she was thinking as she rode, the daughter of a woman with the same foreign tongue and stares as these soldiers. Did she wish to ride away with them, high over the roof of the world, and find her way to her mother's childhood home? But perhaps going back was never possible;

perhaps my own mother had known this even though she mourned for her lost tribes, her childhood herds. Perhaps she had known that only Ershi could be home to her now . . . or if not Ershi, then her farm in the valley, where the horses had learned to understand when she spoke her own language. And soon now, Lila would be going to a new home, the house of a husband inside the city walls, a house with high ceilings and carved niches and sumptuous tapestries and thick, knotted carpets. A home where finches sang in willow cages. But perhaps Lila would not mind, for she liked shopping and embroidering, weaving and gossiping with servants, far more than I did.

The wind gusted against me and I closed my eyes and tilted my face into its warm flow. Home was something you took for granted when you were a child, I thought, the way that newly hatched birds took for granted the twigs and grasses of the nest that held them. But finding a home was not an easy matter, not a simple thing as you grew older. And where would I be when winter crept down over the mountains and crossed the foothills on its white feet, with its keening winds?

A picture filled my mind: Swan and Gryphon, their thick coats ruffled by wind, galloping through the snowy pastures of the valley with drifts spraying around their knees like water, and the bare poplars laying shadows across their backs. A slow smile softened my face, and my white knuckles slackened on the reins.

'Horses!'

My eyes flew open at Lila's hiss from my left elbow, and I peered ahead through the encampment to see a pasture lying ahead, surrounded by tents but containing a dozen horses grazing in the long, fresh grass. Their Persian coats shone and glimmered in the shifting light but though I scanned them eagerly for a gleam of white, I couldn't see Swan. I gulped down my anxiety, the agitated flutter that rose up my throat.

'There are more pastures further down the valley,' the nomad spy said at my shoulder, but I drew rein.

'I am the lady Kallisto, not an errand girl,' I said. 'Batu, please find Sheng, the man in charge of the horses' care. Sayeh, please go with Batu as his interpreter. Tell the man that I will await him here on a matter of business.'

I sat very tall and still on Gryphon, surrounded by my nomad bodyguards, as Batu and Sayeh rode towards the tents. Hopefully I looked as calm and regal as my mother despite the churning in my stomach. Armoured men exited and entered the tents, conferring, gesturing. Other men, in splendid robes, were fetched to join in the consultation. Faintly on the wind I heard their voices mingled with Batu's Turkic tongue, and then Sayeh's light voice as she interpreted. There was a long passage of time while we waited. Cloud shadows drifted across the camp so that the tents gleamed and then darkened, and the wind lifted the battle standards upon their posts and made them flap and stream westwards like brilliant fish. Wild grain gleamed fiery gold on the foothills, then plunged into shadow.

'Perhaps the rain will come at last,' Lila murmured, but I did not reply for at that moment, a tall, imposing man in a wide-sleeved robe of blue silk broke away from the cluster of men at the tent and came towards me. Precious stones winked on the hilt of the great sword hanging at his waist, and on the rings on his fingers. Batu and Sayeh followed him, as did a number of soldiers carrying lances, and wearing lacquered leather armour. I did not dismount at their approach, or lead Gryphon respectfully forward. Instead I sat tall in my saddle, and waited.

The blue-robed man stopped in front of Gryphon, and stared at me with his foreign eyes, his mouth a severe line beneath the sweep of his thick moustache. For a long moment I returned his level stare; I did not drop my eyes or duck my head. I pressed my bones down into my saddle, and felt strength rise up my spine; the strength of my homeland flowing up out of the grassy ground and through the sinews of Gryphon's long legs and into my own body. There were mountains and cold water and storms in that flow of strength, mares who could fight wolves, foals who could dig for fodder in drifts, women who could lead tribes.

My words came from that deep soil beneath Gryphon's feet, the soil that grew the alfalfa and fed the herds, the soil that I had galloped over in sun and rain and wind, that nourished the grape-vines and the melons; the soil of my home. When I spoke to the foreign man, my words were smooth and loud and clear; they flew from my mouth like eagles.

'I am the lady Kallisto of the great trading house, the House of Iona of Ershi,' I began. 'I am here on a matter of business regarding a white horse.'

The man inclined his head in a bow, and straightened to give me a brooding, unreadable look as Sayeh translated.

'Your people have taken a white mare that was stolen from me. She is not a trade good to be taken from my household, from my valley, without permission. She was stolen from me while my father was away and my mother indisposed. I have come to take her home again.'

There was silence after Sayeh translated this; the wind gusted against our silks, and made the tassels swing on the horse harnesses; the nomads' ponies stamped and chewed their bits.

I inclined my head as the foreign man began to speak and as Sayeh's light voice translated. 'I am Sheng Mu, Master of Horses for the Imperial Army of the Son of Heaven, and I have three elite white mares in my charge. You must describe yours.'

'She has no mark or blemish on her; she is fourteen years old; she has a five-pointed brand on her nearside quarter. She belongs, as do all the mares you have acquired with this brand, to the House of Ershi for the five-pointed brand is ours. You may check your records on this matter. And yet, your records will also show that this mare was acquired from a man named Arash, son of the late king's Falconer.'

'My scribes will bring the scrolls,' the man Sheng said, and he turned to give an order. We waited while the clouds continued massing, and the silk standards snapped. Finally a scribe brought a jade chest filled with scrolls and unfurled one for his master to read; Sheng ran his fingers down over the strange marks of that foreign script.

'You are correct,' he said at last. 'Yet the man Arash might have owned this mare, might have bought her from your house.'

'He did not buy her! She was stolen from me and I have come to take her home. Is this how you begin your peaceful trading with us, by taking a horse that you have no right to acquire?'

His face darkened as Sayeh translated this, and I heard Lila's tense breathing; her hands tightened on the reins and Mountain awoke from his doze and tossed his heavy head. My nomad bodyguards shifted their hands to their daggers, and I knew I had to be more careful.

'I believe you are a man of honour,' I said. 'If you can bring my mare, I will seek to win her back through a fair contest. I will challenge your best rider to compete against me and if I win, I will take my mare home. My scribe will draw up a document promising a trading agreement between you, Sheng Mu, and the House of Ershi; each year, we will send you two foals. Every fourth year, one of those foals shall be from this white mare, and this golden stallion that I am mounted on, providing their foal lives. If not, I will send three foals in total in that year, as recompense. But if I lose the riding contest, you can take my white mare away now, my stolen mare, over the roof of the world.'

The man listened intently as Sayeh translated, stroking his drooping moustache, and then a gleam filled his eyes and a smile twitched the corners of his mouth. 'Some entertainment while we wait to go home!' he said, and he turned and spoke to the soldiers standing behind him. Laughter flashed amongst them, and one man ran away, shouting. Another soldier led forward a horse and the first man rode off on it while we waited in the gathering storm. Sunlight slid over the mountains, burning white in the snowy peaks, and was extinguished. Grass bent before the wind, and Sheng Mu's blue robe blew around his knees; its hem was embroidered with golden dragons.

A gleam of light caught a battle standard. A horse gleamed between the tents. A white horse. The light ran down over her like water. She turned her dark eyes to me and I stepped over the threshold of home.

'Swan!'

At the sound of my voice, she flung up her sculpted head, her slender upright neck, and nickered a welcome even as Gryphon pricked his ears and whinnied a note of high excitement. The soldier on the horse led Swan forward until she was standing before me. I wanted to fling myself from Gryphon and wrap my arms around her neck, and bury my face in her silken shoulder, but instead I kept my gaze calm. I held myself still on Gryphon; only my eyes ran over Swan, checking her for harm. She looked slightly thin, her ribs like fine shadows under her skin, but perfectly fit. Gryphon stretched out his nose and blew into her flared dark nostrils.

'This is the mare,' I said clearly to Sheng Mu. 'Find your best rider to compete against me. Meanwhile, a table, please, for my scribe. She will copy out our trade agreement.'

Batu took Mountain's reins as Lila dismounted and seated herself on a carpet that was hastily brought forward and laid upon the grass; a small table was also carried from the tent, and she spread the parchment upon it and began to write as I dictated. Sheng Mu sent for an interpreter of his own, and we were joined by a small man with ink-stained fingers, who leaned over Lila's shoulder and read aloud in the Chinese tongue as she wrote in Persian.

I promised two foals a year, from elite parentage, and a foal from Swan and Gryphon every fourth year. Sheng Mu promised silk, bolts of differing colours but of finest weave, in return for the foals. I promised Sheng Mu trade goods from Parthia and the west – coral and pearls, perfume and ivory – brought by my father's caravans, and Sheng Mu promised to pay for these too with silk. The silk would be brought to us in Ershi every summer, and we would have the other trade items, and the young horses, ready to return to China with Sheng's caravans.

Lila copied the same agreement on to another scroll. Then Sheng Mu signed his name, that looked like a drawing with many fine lines, on to both copies, and I added my own name in the Persian script. A crucible containing wax that had been melted over a campfire was carried forward and a drop was tipped on to our parchment trade agreement. Before the puddle of wax cooled, I rolled the great seal of my father's house into it and left an impression of a grape leaf and a horse's head.

'So, all this is good – but I will tear it up if you do not beat my best rider in this contest you propose,' Sheng Mu said, and his dark eyes again glinted with amusement. 'Here is the man you will ride against – Chang.'

Chapter 17

When I looked up, there was a mounted man waiting beside me; a small, wiry man with a fierce sallow face and eyes that did not smile. Those eyes ran over me like a knife skinning a dead sheep. I held myself very still on Gryphon and stared into the sharpness of those eyes for a long moment, to prove to him that I was not afraid, before glancing at the man's horse. He was riding a Persian horse, a bright gelding of dappled dun with a narrow head and dark stripes, like grass shadows, upon his hind legs.

'In this contest, I would like to ride my mare,' I told Sheng Mu firmly.

'She is not your mare, not yet, and maybe not ever,' he replied. 'You must ride the mount you have come here on if you wish to win her back.'

Gryphon was very fast, but he was much harder

to control than Swan because he was younger, and a stallion, and excitable and impatient by nature. My chances of beating this wiry, glaring horseman would have been much greater on Swan, who listened to every tug of my fingers, every whisper of my words, every twitch of my leg muscles, and who could twist and turn under me like a river current. I laid my palm upon Gryphon's withers and silently begged him to listen to me today, and to calm his fiery spirit.

'Come, let us begin,' said Sheng Mu, and I saw that a large space had been cleared beyond the line of tents, and that the perimeter of this space was lined with ranks of foreign soldiers who watched as I rode forward beside the rider on the dun, and followed by my bodyguards and servants. I twisted in my saddle, longing for a last glimpse of Swan but already she had been led away, out of sight. Sheng Mu had a large chair with carved feet, and a dragon along the back, carried outside and placed in the centre of the watching men. He seated himself upon it, ceremoniously draping his robes around his riding boots.

'These men on either side of me are my best horsemen,' he said, gesturing to where they stood around his chair in their bright tunics and leather armour. 'Together, we will judge the winner of this contest of riding skills. Let us begin with shooting at targets.'

Chang took first turn, trotting, then cantering and finally galloping his dun past the straw targets that had been set up. He was a good shot with a true aim, but not as fast as I hoped to be. When it was my turn, I borrowed a quiver of arrows and bow from one of the nomads, and kicked Gryphon immediately into a gallop. Dropping my reins on to his neck, I guided him with my knees. One hand reached for the arrows in the quiver against my thigh, the other hand notched them to the bow. The gut was a familiar burn against my fingers. The targets blurred past; for an instant in time, I held each one in the centre of my eyes. The arrows flew from my hand, one, two, three, four, five! They pierced the targets' straw and held there, the shafts thrumming. I kneed Gryphon around in a tight circle and flew past the line of targets a second time. One, two, three, four, five! Again, my arrows flew hard and fast, hitting their marks. A cheer went up from the watching soldiers, and when I rode Gryphon over to Sheng Mu and bowed from the waist, Batu's bright grin flashed in the crowd.

'Swordplay, only to dismount or disarm your opponent but not to wound,' Sheng Mu said, and I pulled my mother's long sword from its scabbard and held it up against the light. It felt heavy and cold in my hand, and my arm muscles trembled as I wheeled Gryphon into the centre of the grassy space. I had not practised this skill as much, and my mouth was dry.

The man Chang came at me sideways and hard; I reeled from the force of his thrusting sword, and metal blades screamed against one another so that my ears rang. Gryphon snorted and bucked, spooked by the noise, and my sword thrust swung wide of its mark. Soldiers jeered and shouted, and I saw money changing hands. Then I narrowed my gaze back to my opponent, remembering my mother's words: 'Keep your eyes on one thing only; whatever you are fighting is all you should see.' I dodged and swung in my saddle, parrying blow after blow, thrusting and cutting, my sword blade whistling through the air. Gryphon had broken into an excited sweat and he danced under me, increasingly hard to control. Suddenly, as he swung his quarters around, a fierce swing came under my blade, tipped my sword against the racing sky, and broke my grip on it. I heard the thump as it fell from my hand and landed in the grass. Gryphon bucked and broke into a gallop around the perimeter of the space and I fought to control him and bring him back to Sheng Mu seated on his carved chair beneath the dark blue mountains.

The wind was gusting harder now, hot then cold, sending shivers running over my sweating skin. My mouth was parched, my eyes straining in my face. Pain shouted in my bruised leg. I sought for Batu and Lila in the crowd and their smiles steadied me. *I can do this, for Swan*, I thought. *I will do better at whatever comes next.*

'Lances,' Sheng Mu said, and men carried forward the long poles with their sharp iron heads. I tucked mine under my arm and held Gryphon between my knees while soldiers ran on to the field to pull the arrows from the targets. Then I wheeled him around and kicked him into a gallop again, crouching over his neck, balancing the lance along my arm. The heavy metal head seemed to bounce with every stride that Gryphon took. *Higher,* I thought. *Get it higher! Hold it still! Look at the target!*

I took one deep breath, waited for Gryphon's leading leg to swing forward, and launched the lance into the air. It whistled ahead of me and struck the target's outer edge; for a moment it wavered there with shaft rocking but then it fell into the grass as Gryphon galloped past. Behind me, the man Chang rode at a furious pace, the dun's hogged mane brushing his cheeks and his eyes narrowed to slits as he flung his lance. It struck the centre of the target and held there, quivering. We rode five more times each, and my lance hit the target each of those times but still, the man Chang had now won two contests and I had won only the archery.

A terrible clawing despair tore at my insides. I stared down at Gryphon's neck as I rode over to Sheng Mu, and willed myself not to cry. Then I remembered that I was leaving behind that timid girl, and I straightened myself in the saddle and met the foreign man's gaze steadily.

'Pole bending, a race,' he said, and men ran on to the field to impale the ground with two long lines of sticks with their ends whittled into points.

Chang and I held our horses still, side by side.

Wind blew a scrap of cloth across the grass and Gryphon bounded sideways in excitement. I steadied him, pulled him back alongside the dun. My ears strained for the command to start; I willed Gryphon to pay attention, to focus on that line of poles. But he just wanted to be running, skimming the yellow grass, a creature of cloud and storm and fire, wild and free. His head turned, scanning the crowd, the racing cloud shadows, the flapping tents. He snorted.

'Go!' shouted Sheng Mu, and Gryphon sprang out from under me so fast that I was almost unseated. I swung him between the first poles, tight in the turn. He soared wide on the second turn, then came in closer again for the third turn, my leg brushing against the pole but not knocking it over. At the far end of the line, I swung him around in a tight circle and headed him back between the poles. The dun raced in the corner of my eye and the troops yelled and roared. We were neck and neck now, thundering between the last poles, shooting far out across the grass and skidding to a halt against the wall of spectators who scattered and ran as the horses cut long grooves into the grass with their hard hooves.

'No winner!' Sheng Mu said as we stood once more before his carved chair.

'Now each rider must have time in the ring alone, to show us whatever skills they wish.'

Chang took first turn, and hitched the dun to a

chariot beside another horse. He drove in dizzying circles, the light rig tipping over so far that one wheel lifted from the ground, then he ran out along the central shaft while the horses were cantering, and balanced there in his leather-soled boots. The soldiers roared and cheered, and I saw more money changing hands as Chang ran beside his horse, unhitched now, and jumped on and off its back at a trot. He dived off its side, turning a somersault before he touched the ground.

I could taste the oncoming rain now; it tasted like iron and sand, like hot stones and riverbeds and chalk and salt. The clouds raced over the Alay Mountains, building higher and darker, their bellies swollen with moisture. Anahita's grey mares were up there, I thought, driving the demon's black stallion away from our pastures, our orchards and nut groves. Soon, soon, the rain would fall.

It was my turn again. I walked Gryphon to the far end of the grass and then sent him streaking down its length at a gallop. Part way, I dived backwards off him and hung by one foot, my toe looped into a leather thong, my arms loose, and my head rushing inches above the ground. It was the manoeuvre that I had used to escape from the cavalry fight on Mountain. At the end of the field, I pulled myself back into the saddle and turned Gryphon's head around. This time, I jumped off him and ran five strides beside his cantering shoulder before jumping back on. Then I stood in my foot loops, and trotted the length of the field standing up, praying he wouldn't break into a faster pace. *I must win this*, I thought.

I must win! I must do something now that will impress Sheng Mu greatly!

'I need to borrow your horse,' I called to Chang, and Sayeh translated, her words snatched away on the wind's whistle. Reluctantly, the man climbed from the dun gelding and led him over to me. I had watched the horse running; his stride was very close to being the same length as Gryphon's, and they were almost the same height. Nonetheless, what I was about to do was risky, for I needed to practise it much more, and because the two horses were strangers to one another. 'Roman riding' my father called it, and my mother forbade me to do it because it was too dangerous; it was for this reason that I had not been able to practise it very often.

I took the dun's reins and positioned him beside Gryphon, who rolled his eyes and snorted at the stranger. I tugged on his rein and he turned his head forward again, his ears swivelling to the sound of my voice as I told him to pay attention to me. I eased him into a walk and the dun kept stride, kept closely against Gryphon with a tight rein. Holding my breath, I eased them both into a trot. The crowd was silent. I stood in my toe loops, kicked my feet free and jumped into the saddle, standing upright on Gryphon. His back undulated below me, swaying, surging. Wind filled my ears. The crowd floated past, far below, their mouths open in a roar of appreciation. I tugged on Gryphon's reins, slowing his pace, and waiting for the moment when his stride matched the dun's. Then I shifted my weight quickly, and set one foot over on to the dun's blanketed back.

There I was for one heartbeat, two, three – tall and invincible, riding the flow of the world with sun and wind in my eyes and two horses running beneath me.

Gryphon opened his mouth and snaked his head out at the strange dun, teeth flashing. The dun swerved, tearing the reins from my hand. My feet shifted, my bruised leg stiffened, and the world spun. I hit the ground with a blow that darkened my sight and knocked the wind from my lungs. I rolled over and felt the ground vibrating as the horses galloped around, wild with the approaching storm.

Hands pulled at me, rolling me over. 'That was crazy,' Batu said, grinning in admiration. 'Are you dead?'

I groaned and pushed him away. 'Of course I'm dead. Let me stand up.'

The packed ranks of soldiers cheered when I staggered to my feet but I glimpsed Chang scowling as he caught the dun and Gryphon and led them over to Sheng Mu. I stumbled after him and stared into Sheng's dark eyes, willing myself not to show fear although my ribs were tight and my heart was thumping. I could not speak a word, not in that moment of decision, not while Swan's fate trembled in the balance. At that moment, I could not even have spoken her name to save her.

Sheng Mu smiled. 'Two skilled riders, both deserving of honour. Great feats of horsemanship have entertained us. Who should win? My rider, Cheng, had more lances hit the targets, and won the sword-play. His chariot driving was magnificent. At the pole bending, there was no winner for the horses raced neck and neck.'

He tapped the roll of parchment, that held our trade agreement, lightly against the palm of one hand as he regarded us.

'Honourable lady of the House of Iona,' he said at last, 'you won the archery, and your attempt to ride two horses was magnificent though foolish. Take your white mare and return home. My caravan will come to your doors next spring with silk. You did not win everything, but you rode splendidly although you are young and only a girl. Take your white mare home.'

I fell to my knees as though I had been hit from behind. Batu's hands were under my arms, pulling me up. Lila had her arms around my shoulders. I lifted my chin and stared straight into the eyes of the foreign horseman. 'I thank you for your trade agreement,' I said. 'I thank you for the honour of dealing with so noble a man.'

When Swan was led forward, I buried my face in her neck, I ran my hands over every part of her. Then

I had her blanketed, and I pulled my stiff, aching body on to her smooth white back, and turned her head westwards, holding Gryphon alongside on a lead rope. 'Do you wish still to be my servant, or to go east with these men over the roof of the world to your mother's people?' I asked Sayeh.

She pondered for a moment, her narrow face inscrutable and her eyes like shuttered windows. Then she turned the mule to follow me. 'I will stay with you and your horses,' she said, and left the camp without a backward glance. We rode until the army camp lay behind us, and then Batu drew rein where the track into the hills swung away from the valley road.

'The men and I are going back to our tribe now,' he said. 'Do you remember the eagles we saw nesting in the pass on the day that the army arrived? I am going to return there and catch an eaglet before they grow any older. If they have time to grow much bigger, they will carry me away to their nest and train me to hunt marmots for them!'

Our eyes locked for a long moment. 'I will come to your pastures soon, to bring back the two-year-old herd,' I replied. 'Make sure you are in your father's yurt when I come, and not chewing marmot in a nest.'

He laughed, throwing his head back, the wild wind whipping his mane of black hair beneath his hat of wolf fur. Then his gaze sobered. 'The days will be long until you come,' he said, and leaned from

Rain to kiss my flushed cheek. Then he turned Rain's head towards the foothills.

'What about Mountain?' I called, realising that Lila was still mounted on the appaloosa.

'You can bring Mountain with you when you come for your herd,' he called back. 'I will expect him fat and well-groomed!' He kicked Rain into a trot, the other nomads keeping pace beside him.

'Aiyee, he is going to try and be a man now!' one of the nomads teased, slapping Batu's shoulder. 'A real man needs a fast horse, a good hound, and an eagle. He is going to see if he can manage this!'

Their bantering and laughter carried back to us as we watched them dwindle into the distance. When they were almost out of earshot, I raised my voice and cried, 'The starry sky at night –'

'– is a black horse decorated with pearls!' Batu called back, our old childhood password.

I smiled to myself, squinting my eyes until the riders passed from sight down a dip in the land and into a grove of windblown willows.

The rain began to fall then, great cool drops that hit my face and hands, and wetted my dry tongue when I stuck it out. Drops shimmered like pearls in Swan's white mane. A thick curtain of rain draped across the valley like a swathe of silk, and the citadel of Ershi lay upon it like an embroidered pattern as we headed our horses for home.

Chapter 18

It was still raining three days later when my father's party rode through the western gate of the city and clattered up the streets to pour into our courtyard in a tumult of noise and commotion. I flew down the stairs and into my father's arms, pressing myself against the great barrel of his chest, the curve of his belly beneath a robe stained with mud and smelling of wet camels. His thick fingers stroked my curls and I felt safe for the first time in many weeks.

'My sweet peach,' he said fondly. 'What have you been doing?' And he ran a broad thumb across my cheeks, where scratches from thorny branches, falling stones, and baked ground were still visible. But there was no time to reply then, for my mother came down the stairs, pale and queenly, her blue eyes blazing with light, her wide mouth smiling. She held herself so erect and straight that not even my father noticed how her left arm hung stiff as a dead branch from the tight knitting of her wounds. He took her into his arms and held her for a long time in silence, while I turned to my brothers: dark Petros with his sweet solemn smile, and tall golden Jaison with his boisterous embrace. Fardad ran around flapping his arms, and Marjan stood in the kitchen door watching while camels were commanded to kneel; while Sayeh slipped between the horses and donkeys, removing tack; while bundles of trade goods and bales of fabric and casks of wine were unloaded and dragged into the storage room. My father began striding around, giving orders as the beasts were unloaded. 'Bring that one, no, not that one – that casket there! And that package! Bring them inside.'

Finally we were all sprawled on divans upstairs, drinking tea and eating sugared almonds while Marjan lit a brazier in the centre of the room to take the dampness from the air. My father was already retelling his many stories, the gossip of the trade routes, the news of the world's great cities and ports, their foreign peoples, their strange customs, and all the amusing and entertaining things that had happened to him. Rivers rolled off my father's tongue, and mountains were scaled in the space of minutes, and exotic foods that were hard to imagine wove their fragrances into the air as he talked. Then there were the gifts to open, to unwrap from their oiled coverings, to take from their caskets: soaps perfumed with jasmine and sandalwood, perfume in a glass bottle, a red plate decorated with black chariot horses, ivory hair combs, a saddle blanket for Swan with stripes of blue and white. And for my mother, there were tapestries, and plates of chased silver, and a bridle with rubies on the brow band and a gold-plated bit. After all this, my father and brothers went off to the bath house for a long soak for my father said that the dust of the continent was ground into his skin like spices being ground into raw meat.

It was not until evening that the rain slackened into silence, and I prepared to dine with my parents upon the roof while my brothers went off into the town to visit their friends. I dressed carefully in a robe of pale blue velvet with embroidered hems of silver stars and lilies, and wound a strand of pearls – one my father had just brought for me – around my neck. Brushing my hair for a long time, and curling it around my fingers, I rehearsed what I was going to say when I stood before my parents. *I will not stutter or stammer,* I thought. *I will not blush or drop my head. The girl who used to behave like that is gone; she is left behind on the other side of the war and now I have closed the door on her timidity.*

Sayeh brought me a green ceramic bowl, made by the potters in our valley, and containing water in which I washed all my rings. Then I held my face very still while she lined my eyes with kohl, and brushed powder upon my cheeks.

'Do I look older?' I asked anxiously but Sayeh only shrugged her bony shoulders and replied, 'Here are your sandals,' as she laid them at my feet. The plaited straps felt flimsy and strange when I slipped my toes between them, for I had worn only riding boots for many weeks. The soft drapery of my robe felt equally strange against my legs as I climbed the steps to the rooftop.

My parents both turned their heads as I paced across the flat surface towards where they sat on stools placed upon a knotted carpet. Beyond them, the valley was cloaked in a mist of new green growth, like a gauzy veil, and it burned fiery bright as the sun finally broke through the clouds and stroked the fields with long fingers. A bird began to sing in the apricot trees beyond our wall.

My father beamed at me. His face was soft and tired above the oiled curls of his long beard, threaded with the first few strands of grey, but his eyes were bright beneath their heavy lids.

'Be seated, daughter,' he said. 'Your mother has just been telling me of all you have done in my absence. It is a tale more remarkable than any I have heard in months of travelling. Who would have thought my plump dove was such a fierce spirit after all?'

I flushed in spite of myself, and ducked my head shyly at his praise.

'I am not as plump as I used to be, Father,' I said, and my mother gave an uncharacteristic snort of laughter. My father's hands, clasped loosely across his belly, rose and fell as he chuckled.

I lifted my head and stared him in the eye. 'Father, I will not marry Arash,' I said calmly. 'He is a boy without honour. He is skilled in deceit, and though he can draw a bow, and ride a horse, he is a boy who lives by lies.'

My father inclined his head thoughtfully; he could not argue with my reasoning. The boys in our city, whether Greek or Persian, were taught these three things first and above all else: to ride, to shoot, to tell the truth. Only the evil Angra could approve of a man who was dishonest.

The fleeting sun spilled over my father's striped robe of Syrian damask, and cast the shadow of his heavy nose across the generous curves of his mouth. At his side, my mother was as still and tautly upright as a leopard hunting in the long grass.

'Father,' I entreated softly, 'I cannot marry him.'

Still my father reflected, lifting his onyx drinking horn carved in the form of an antelope, and taking a long sip of his wine. He considered it as it ran over his tongue. The evening sun sucked mist from the wet fields and the canals so that it rose over the valley soft as thistledown. Above my left shoulder, the palace's sprawling ramparts flared red, and the peaks of the snowy Alay Mountains gleamed brightly white as teeth.

My father gave a long sigh and set his drinking horn down.

'If you will not marry him, what is to become of you?' he asked.

I shrugged, feeling myself tugged and stretched the way I had been once before, gripping Gryphon's tail as he struggled to pull me from the dark jaws of the tomb. For what was to become of me? The distant mountains called to me on the still air; their voices were like wind sighing in grass, like rivers murmuring over cold stones, like the singing of wolves and the drumbeat of horse hooves. But here, here in the valley, was where I had caught foals wet from their mothers' bellies, had quenched my thirst with the sweetness of summer grapes, had trained Swan and Gryphon in the pastures around my mother's stables while red poppies lit the grass on fire.

'What is to become of you?' my father asked again.

'There is Batu,' my mother said. 'He is the son of a white bone chief, and heir to good pasture and fine herds. He is honourable and loyal, and will hunt with eagles when he is a man.'

'Nomads,' my father grumbled. 'Does this girl seated before us look as though she has been raised to live in a tent, cooking food inside sheep bellies? No! Whether she likes it or not, she has been raised in luxury. She might be a warrior when life requires it, but at night she sleeps in an imported bed and not on the ground with her feet in the fire! I am not letting her marry a nomad!'

'Perhaps she is too young to be married anyway,' my mother said soothingly, and my father subsided with a grunt.

'I have an idea,' I said, and my parents' eyes flickered away from each other and stared at me with such intensity that I squirmed. Then I straightened my shoulders and drew myself up as tall as I could.

'I would like my bride-wealth now,' I said clearly. 'I would like Swan, and her yearling filly, Pearl. I would like some of the two-year-old mares that are in Berta's care, and I would like some of the other yearlings. I would like a stable to keep them in, on Mother's farm, and I would like some pasture to run them in. I would like my own brand for their quarters, a full star.'

There was a long silence. A camel bellowed; the sun slipped from the palace, and long purple shadows puddled at the feet of the mountains and stretched across the plain.

'A horse trainer,' my mother said softly, and a glow of pride kindled in her eyes.

'Could she do this?' my father asked.

'She has arranged a trade deal for the House of Iona with the silk caravans that will begin coming to our city now from the east. She has brought wealth and fortune to us, and made a shrewd bargain with this foreign man, Sheng Mu. Already, they are saying there will be a silk road over the mountains, that the caravans will journey along it bringing us bolts of fabric in exchange for our Persian horses. Your daughter has made sure that bolts of silk will come to your warehouse, that the trade goods of east and west will meet here in Ershi, and bring you riches. Of course she is capable of raising and training horses!'

My mother's eyes locked on to my face and I felt it at last: the praise I had sought from her all my life, since I was a chubby child with legs so tired they could barely grip a horse. A glow of pleasure warmed me inside my soft robe.

My father nodded and took another long sip of wine. 'Yes, so be it,' he said at last. 'Kallisto, I will not give you your mother's pastures or stables, but you shall have your own. There is land for sale in the valley, adjacent to your mother's farm, and I shall have the deeds of purchase drawn up in your name. You shall raise horses with your mother's help, and when Sheng Mu's caravans arrive next summer, you shall receive some of the silk that he sends. Perhaps it will not be called the silk road, that path over the mountains, but the horse road! And you, my sweet peach, you will be part of its history.'

He raised his drinking horn to me in a silent toast, and drained its contents as the servants arrived bearing trays of steaming rice, beans with coriander, and meat braised in garlic and sesame seeds. My father fell to eating with gusto but every so often, I felt his eyes leave his plate to linger quizzically upon me.

'And how did you know,' he asked at last, wiping his mouth on a flat bread, 'how did you know how to write up this trade agreement with Sheng Mu?'

I laughed. 'Oh, Father, that was easy! Remember how you taught me my numbers? One camel-load is the basic unit of measurement. A donkey-load is worth only half a camel-load. But a wagon-load is worth four camel-loads. This was how you taught me to do sums!'

My father laughed, his chest vibrating, and ran his hand tenderly down my mother's stiff arm, caressing the lines of her wounds with the tips of his fingers. 'Such a daughter you have given me,' he said.

'What about Failak, the warlord?' I asked.

My father's face darkened into a deep scowl. 'He will never trade in this city again – I shall see to it! And your mother is going to speak to Berta's people about riding against him, and driving him from his stolen valley!'

I gulped and took a deep breath. 'I left all my jewels under a mattress in his house,' I said but my father waved a hand dismissively.

'When you begin selling your horses with their star brands, you will not need your old father to buy your jewels. You can buy your own then!'

'Thank you, Father!'

I rose and kissed my mother's cheek; it was still too thin, but warm and firm beneath my lips, and her grip on my wrist was as strong as it had ever been while she kissed me in return. My father pressed my head to his chest and stroked my hair and patted my cheeks. 'Too many scratches. Put some salve on them or I will never find you a husband!' he joked.

'Yes, Father,' I said with a giggle, and then I ran down the stairs two at a time. Camels were dozing in the courtyard, and donkeys drank from the full water trough. I ducked into the stable's fragrance of straw and grain, and called her name. Swan's pale sculpted face turned to me in the dusk while her nostrils fluttered in a loving nicker.

'Your foals will journey far, over the horse road,' I whispered, stroking my hands over her muzzle. 'But you, you will stay with me for always!'

Then I laid my face against her shoulder, and peace ran through me like a shining river.

Heavenly
Akhal-Tekes

S everal thousand years ago, a magnificent creature appeared in the deserts and grassy steppes
of Persia (now Iran) and Central Asia. The
horse was tall, around sixteen hands high, and
elegant with a golden bloom upon its silky coat.
Bred for war by the Persian and Scythian nomads,
this Turkmen horse allowed for the development of
superb cavalry units and was greatly prized for its
endurance, speed, power and beauty. Although the
nomads left no written documentation of this horse,
warriors were sometimes buried with their favourite mounts. In the ice tombs of Pazyryk, archaeologists
have found the skeletons of tall noble horses dating
back to the fifth century BC. Showing no scars from
whip or spur, these horses were intelligent and bold,
ridden on a loose rein, or even just by leg pressure
alone. On them, the Persians developed their famous

'Parthian shot', shooting arrows backwards while racing away from their enemies.

Over the years, the golden horses maintained their size and speed, for the nomads bred them selectively, and fed them on a nutritious leguminous crop called lucerne (alfalfa) as well as grain, fat, and even eggs. When Alexander the Great (356–323 BC) waged war against Persia, he imported 5,000 of the Persian horses into Greece, and they were used to improve the shorter-legged Greek horses, eventually becoming the foundation for the Roman cavalry horses. It has been suggested that Alexander's famous mount Bucephalus, whom he rode for decades over thousands of miles of military campaigns, was of Persian stock – as was the mount of the conquering warrior, Genghis Khan, whose light cavalries swept the grasslands.

Meanwhile, far to the east, the Chinese Emperor Wu-Ti was having difficulty defending the borders of his country, despite the building of the Great Wall to keep the nomadic Huns from attacking on stocky Mongolian horses. In 138 BC, Emperor Wu-Ti sent a spy, a political adventurer named Chang Ch'ien, to sneak through the Hunnish territories and find allies to help the Chinese fight their enemies. What Chang found instead were horses – the golden horses of Ferghana, Samarkand, Kokand, and Bukhara in Central Asia. When Chang returned to China thirteen years later, he described these horses as having tails that swept the ground, a double spine like a tiger, and hooves like a thick wrist. Emperor Wu-Ti remembered the legend of celestial (heavenly) horses written of in the *Zhouyi* (Book of Changes) – horses that would come from the north-west, and which possessed the qualities of heaven: feelings, consciousness and omnipotence. The legend promised that such horses would make the emperor wise and immortal. Also, Wu-Ti realised that these tall, powerful, fast horses would give his cavalry an advantage over his old enemies, the Huns.

Chang also told Wu-Ti how these horses from Ferghana sweated blood – this was a mystery at the time, but nowadays, it is believed to be caused by a parasite that lives in the rivers. When the horses drink, the parasite burrows just beneath the surface of the skin and causes slight bleeding when the horses sweat.

Determined to possess these heavenly horses, Wu-Ti sent envoys over two thousand miles of mountain and desert to trade for them with gold. The exchange was refused and the ambassador was murdered. A military expedition also ended in failure. In 102 BC Wu-Ti sent a second campaign against Ferghana, consisting of 60,000 men and 30,000 horses; he sent engineers to cut off the city's water supply, and arranged for supplies of rice to keep his large army fed.

At first it seemed that this attack might also fail

for the people of Ferghana shut themselves and their horses inside their walled capital city and threatened to kill all the horses. However, the citizens eventually killed their king and replaced him with one more favourably disposed towards the Chinese. He ended the siege by agreeing to allow the Chinese to take some celestial Persian horses back to the emperor. Trade agreements were forged, allowing the flow of horses to the east in exchange for silk; thus the eastern portions of the famous trade route, the Silk Road, were opened up. The spy, Chang, is credited as being the father of the Silk Road, and trade in horses continued long after the secret of making silk had been discovered by the west.

Today, no one knows the true origin of the Persian horse (also known as the Turkoman) or the location and name of the besieged city in Ferghana written about by Chinese chroniclers – this information has been lost to history. However, the modern Akhal-Teke horse is believed to be the closest and most direct descendant of the Persian horse from Ferghana. The nomads relied on oral tradition to record the genealogy of their horses, but the modern Akhal-Teke stud book was first printed by the Russians in 1941. Akhal-Tekes are a hot blood, dry type of horse with a genetic difference in the structure of their hair; their coats have a distinctive and beautiful golden, metallic shine. With high-set neck, long slender legs clearly showing the tendons, large expressive eyes and a narrow body, the Akhal-Teke has been called the greyhound of the horse world. Its endurance is still considered phenomenal. In 1935, a group of Akhal-Tekes participated in a ride from Ashkhabad to Moscow, a distance of 2,600 miles completed in 84 days, including 3 days crossing 225 miles of desert with almost no water.

DNA studies from the University of Kentucky suggest that the Akhal-Teke is the oldest domesticated breed of horse. Throughout its history, the breed's development has been shaped by the nomads' practices. They let the mares run in semi-wild herds which must protect themselves; they begin training horses for racing at age one, and use layers of felt blankets to induce sweating and keep the horses lean. The horses are given high-protein feeds every few hours both day and night, and are bred selectively for speed and stamina. Celebrated in Chinese paintings and Tang dynasty ceramic statues, the Persian horse also contributed directly to the foundation of the modern Thoroughbred through the stallion the Byerley Turk.

Although now found on stud farms in various countries, especially in Russia, Germany and the USA, the Persian Akhal-Teke remains a rare breed with fewer than 3,000 horses worldwide. It continues to be a highly athletic horse, excelling at dressage and jumping, with its lean elastic body and floating stride. The Teke named Absinthe was one of the top

Olympic horses of the twentieth century, winning medals in 1960, 1964 and 1968. Tekes are easily aroused and need sensitive training from a person with whom they've bonded; they can be difficult for strangers to handle. They still prefer a loose rein, and a rider with soft hands and strong legs who will fully appreciate their bold intelligence, just as their nomad masters did so many centuries ago on the great grasslands of Asia.

Acknowledgements

With thanks to my wonderful agent, Dr Eckhart Prahl in Munich, for taking a chance and enthusiastically backing a dark horse. And with thanks also to my wonderful editor, Dorit Engelhardt, for being a pure pleasure to work with. The encouragement and support you both have given to me is much appreciated!